Silver Springs
Mystery Series
Book 2

# Murder at Goldenleaf Apple Farm

## The Maplewood Crafters Club Investigates In This Cozy Mystery

### Jodie Morgan

- Audiobook: 978-1-923587-09-0

- eBook: 978-1-923587-08-3

- Hardcovers

  - Dyslexic Print: 978-1-923587-11-3

  - Large Print: 978-1-923587-12-0

  - Regular Print: 978-1-923587-10-6

- Paperbacks

  - Dyslexic Print: 978-1-923587-14-4

  - Large Print: 978-1-923587-15-1

  - Regular Print: 978-1-923587-13-7

Published by Cozy Cozies

https://cozycozies.com



All inquiries can be directed to: permissions@cozycozies.com

# DEDICATION

*To Zach and Cam. Thank you for everything!*

Thanks for your purchase! Get your surprise reader bonuses here: **cozycozies.com/pages/ss2thanks**

# About the Book

**In the second page-turning novel in the Silver Springs Mysteries, within Fall's beauty lurks deadly deception...**

Laura Evans thought managing the General Store café in Silver Springs, Vermont would be a peaceful change from her high-pressure Boston restaurant career. But when apple farmer Vernon Reed is found dead, suspicion falls on Laura's friend Izzy—the outgoing theater enthusiast whose fingerprints are all over the murder weapon.

As damning evidence mounts and the town turns against Izzy, Laura refuses to believe the kind-hearted young man could be a killer. Teaming up with her wise landlady Evelyn and fellow café worker Jasmine, she digs into Vernon's secretive final months.

But the murderer is watching Laura's investigation—and they'll do anything to keep their lies from unraveling. In a community where everyone knows everyone, the deadliest secrets hide behind the most trusted faces.

*This engaging book serves up the perfect blend of mystery and comfort. Every clue unfolds at just the right place, and justice is as satisfying as a refreshing glass of sweet cider.*

**Thanks for your purchase! Get your surprise reader bonuses here: <u>cozycozies.com/pages/ss2thanks</u>**

# ABOUT THE SERIES

**In Silver Springs, everyone knows your name. And your secrets.**

In this Green Mountain State town, Laura Evans isn't just the General Store's café manager...she's the town's unofficial detective. Alongside her observant landlady Evelyn Chan, Laura discovers dangerous secrets hiding beneath the picturesque veneer.

But Laura and Evelyn don't have to do it alone. They're members of the Maplewood Crafters Club.

This seemingly innocent club are also the town's secret helpers. Over craft projects and potluck dinners, they arrange random acts of kindness...and help solve mysteries.

What makes this series irresistible:

- A stunning setting

- Delectable culinary details

- Richly developed characters

- Ingeniously crafted mysteries with satisfying endings

If you love culinary cozies, craft and hobby cozies, Ellie Alexander, Agatha Frost, Laura Childs, Maddie Day,

Diane Mott Davidson, or Jenn McKinlay...or you enjoy books with new starts, close-knit communities, amateur sleuths, found family, personal growth, secret helpers, and food as comfort and connection...

You'll love Silver Springs. Because in Vermont's most charming town, the only thing more complex than the local craft projects are the secrets hiding just out of sight...

**Thanks for your purchase! Get your surprise reader bonuses here: cozycozies.com/pages/ss2thanks**

**And there are more books coming soon, so if you'd like to read the next before anyone else...sign up at cozycozies.com/pages/newsletter!**

# Table of Contents

# CHAPTER ONE

I f happiness had a scent, it'd be apple trees during harvest. Exiting her car at Goldenleaf Apple Farm, goosebumps rose on Laura Evans' fair skin as her boots crunched on the leaf-strewn gravel. The countless tree canopies overhead cast dappled shadows across the orchard.

Jasmine Williams, her friend and co-worker, got out of the passenger seat, and they smiled at each other. No one else had arrived yet. The vehicles in the lot must've belonged to the staff. The only one she recognized was a burnt orange pickup truck, at least four decades older than all the others. A smile crossed her face.

Weathered wooden buildings sprawled across the farm, each bearing the marks of a different decade. At the center stood the cider house, its cupola crowned with smoke curling from the chimney. Nearby was the visitors center, while the office occupied a converted farmhouse with green shutters and a wrap-around porch.

Near the storage shed, a tall man with cropped hair stood beside a shorter figure. Though their voices didn't carry, the taller one was rigid, jabbing his finger toward the main building while the shorter figure shook his head. Even from this distance, the tall man's shoulders hunched forward, while his companion kept glancing around. The shorter one grabbed the other's arm, his mouth moving in an urgent whisper. The tall man jerked away, and they both stalked toward the tree line, disappearing into the apple rows. Perhaps...just a disagreement about harvest schedules? Something about the furtive way they'd acted...didn't sit right. Laura shook her head, refocusing. She'd come to enjoy herself.

"Looks like we've made good time! We're here early," Laura said.

As the roar of a distant engine grew louder, Jasmine tucked a red-tipped box braid beneath her patterned bandana, her sharp cheekbones prominent under her dark-brown skin. "It sounds like someone's just around the corner."

An older forest-green SUV pulled into the parking lot, stenciled with the Silver Springs General Store logo. It stopped beside Laura's dark-blue sedan, and a woman got out. She had dark brown hair streaked with silver cropped into a pixie cut which peeked from beneath a wide-brimmed sun hat. Her cream-colored skin, dotted with freckles from years of working outdoors, contrasted with the black maxi skirt and a light sweater that'd seen its share of early mornings. Maggie Brook, one of Laura's bosses, and a co-owner, smiled at them both.

From the passenger side emerged a taller, younger woman with olive-toned skin and auburn hair threaded with silver, tied into a plait, and tossed over her shoulder. Her ever-present tool belt was slung around her hips—Kathleen 'Kathy' Quinn, Maggie's wife and business partner.

"Good morning!" Maggie said. "How are you both?"

Laura grinned. "Great, thank you. I've been looking forward to this!"

Jasmine made a muffled noise of agreement as she sipped from her water bottle.

"Morning," Kathy said. "The weather's working in our favor."

Laura couldn't help smiling. "Is this anyone's first time at the farm, or have some of you been here?"

Maggie's expression showed feigned offense. "What sort of General Store co-owner would I be if I didn't have that covered?"

"Good point," Laura said, and she smiled. "Isn't it beautiful here?"

"Real magic's inside," Kathy replied, hands stuffed into her cargo pant pockets, hair ruffling in the morning breeze.

Laura couldn't stop a shake of her head, a grin spreading across her face. "I must say, it's special. I still find it hard to believe I'm in a role where we get to enjoy team-building exercises."

After fifteen years at a prestigious restaurant job in Boston, she'd worked fourteen-hour shifts, seven days a week, only to be passed over for her promised promotion. Silver Springs had been a welcome change of pace. It made sense to everyone she'd explained the situation to...except her mother. A month in, and still, her mother's most recent phone call made her disappointment clear. Laura had tried to explain, for the hundredth time, about burnout, needing a change, and the opportunity to be part of something meaningful in a small community.

But to Bridget Evans, her eldest daughter slipped backward, while her sons moved forward. Danny thrived as the program director at one of New York's most renowned cultural institutions, and Connor built a flourishing tech career and picture-perfect family in California. Her mother's words still stung: "I just don't understand why you're wasting all your professional experience, Laura. Danny may be divorced, but at least he's building something meaningful with his career. And Connor's providing for his family. What are you doing up there in that little town?" What was she doing indeed?

Maggie smiled. "You'll enjoy this, I promise."

Laura nodded. "I know I will. Could you tell me who's leading our tour this morning?"

"Roy," Kathy said. "Vernon's off Mondays. Always has been."

Jasmine nodded. "He hikes with the Woodland Watch, but he hasn't joined us these last few weeks."

Maggie squared her shoulders. "Come along then, let's head inside. The others should be here soon."

⸺⸻◆⸻⸺

The visitors center was bright and inviting, its tall windows revealing the picturesque farm beyond. Rustic wooden tables and chairs dotted the space, and an illustrated display of various apple varieties decorated one wall. A small counter sat with a sampler bowl offering candies wrapped in red foil. Behind it was a reception desk, and a pair of double doors leading deeper into Goldenleaf Apple Farm's facilities.

The thundering echo was close now. An old cruiser motorcycle, hand-painted with green-and-blue swirls across the otherwise black chassis, rumbled into the parking lot, followed by a compact red hatchback, and a station wagon in a sensible white. The rider of the first arrival, clad in leathers, cut the engine and removed their helmet. Two men got out of their respective cars and followed the first to the visitors center.

"Looks like the cavalry's arrived," Maggie said with a chuckle.

Several minutes later, the front door opened to admit three more colleagues. Jesse O'Connor entered first, still pulling off a motorcycle jacket, followed by the two men. The shorter and younger one was Eli Carter. The other, Anton Reynolds, the chef at the General Store's café, outstripped Eli's pace with his broad frame and long gait. He smiled at the group, squinting at them from beneath bushy eyebrows.

"Did I miss anything important?" Jesse asked with a grin.

"No, for once," Jasmine replied, her gaze drifting to Jesse's cruiser outside. "You must be freezing, riding that thing! Aren't early fall mornings too cold for motorcycles?"

"You can keep asking, but you'll get the same answer every time," Jesse said. "Why settle for warmth when I can make an entrance? Cars are for people with no imagination."

"Keep making excuses, sure, but you're just jealous we're comfortable," Jasmine said, grinning.

"Comfortable and boring," Jesse said, letting out a huff of laughter. They looked around at Eli and Anton. "Wow, I arrived before these two again? Shocking."

Kathy scoffed, though there wasn't any malice in the sound. "Don't get smug, kid. Showing up a few seconds earlier doesn't buy you the right to tarnish their good names. Those two are punctual to a fault!"

Jesse grinned. "Get used to it. I run on time, unlike some people."

Eli rolled his eyes. "We'll never hear the end of it now."

"You guessed it," Jesse said, grinning.

"Morning, all," Anton said. The man spoke little and was the only one of the staff who wouldn't lower themselves to engage in silly squabbling. Laura had to admit, sometimes, she was grateful for that.

Jesse's gaze settled on Laura. "So. Be honest. Are you here for the educational value or the promised breakfast?"

Laura laughed. "You've discovered my weakness! I've been excited to try those apple cider donuts."

The double doors at the back swung open, and a familiar face burst through. Isaac 'Izzy' Lennox, a farm employee, theater enthusiast, and friend. Long curls braided back into a bun, golden-brown skin, and a patchwork jacket hanging off his wiry frame: there was no other way to describe the man than a whirlwind. He bounded toward them, reaching Laura first. "Laura! Always a delight to see you!" As if remembering there were others present, he added, "And everyone else! Welcome!" He rattled off their names, greeting each with his characteristic grin and spirited handshake for all who accepted it. Something about Izzy's animated gestures and theatrical enthusiasm always made her smile—so much like her brother Danny. The same inability to stand still, the same need to fill silence with warmth. Izzy spun around to the other man who'd followed him in. "And this, if you're not already familiar, is the man himself, Roy Beckett!"

Roy, a tall man just shy of sixty, with weathered ruddy skin and a buzzcut, nodded at them. He was far less enthusiastic than Izzy, but that was easy to do. "Welcome to Goldenleaf Apple Farm! I'm the co-owner. Since he didn't say so before, this is Izzy Lennox, an employee here."

Izzy swept into a bow. "He undersells himself! Folks, you're looking at the fellow who's been nothing but dedicated to this fine establishment. Keeps us, and the orchards, running smoothly."

Roy shook his head with a smile. "Thank you, Izzy, but I don't think we need that level of theatricality. It's only a tour, after all." He turned to the group. "We might as well get started. Please, follow us." He held the double doors open for them, which led into a short hallway with an exit to the farm beyond.

⸺◆⸺

As Roy led them toward the production facility, he explained the farm's history. It took all Izzy's strength to not jump in every few seconds to add anecdotes of his own.

From where Jesse stood next to Laura, they leaned over. "Five bucks Izzy knows every apple tree by name."

"Ten bucks he invented the naming system, and he's the only one who remembers any of it," Jasmine said.

Jesse grinned, and Laura couldn't resist smiling.

"This place has been making apple cider for decades. Vernon, the other co-owner, is the latest in a long line of people just like him," Roy said. "He was the first to work with someone outside the family." He allowed himself a smile. "Now it's the biggest operation in town." He gestured toward the press and grinder. "This is where it starts."

A series of shiny filters and buckets lined a bottling station, and a refractometer sat ready to measure the cider's quality. The sweet scents and rich colors created a different world, an escape from the ordinary outside.

"This is incredible," Laura said.

"Isn't it?" Izzy grinned, sweeping his arms wide. "We even have a new cold-pressing system now to make things faster." He pointed to a machine in the corner. "Vernon is a hard man to convince, but even he couldn't deny how well it works!"

Photos along the wall chronicled the farm's progress over the decades—images of old hand-operated presses, then newer systems, leading to the traditional-meets-modern setup they stood around now. Roy and Vernon had their feet in one era, and Izzy was pulling them into the next.

"Vernon and I have done things a certain way," Roy said, offering Izzy a smile that was more polite than inviting. "But it's worked well so far."

Laura studied the photos more closely—a progression of grainy black-and-white images of the first Reed generations to color ones of a youthful Vernon and Roy. In one, they wore Halloween costumes; in another, they stuck out their tongues, pulling goofy faces. As the years went on, their smiles grew more subdued, more serious.

Izzy caught her attention by gesturing to a wall of labeled bottles. "My role around here is to make sure we're ready for anything—new systems, new ideas! This is where we test different cider grades and styles." His voice was bright. "Roy and Vernon maintain standards, and I handle innovation."

Roy smiled a little at that. "Vernon and I have always been hands-on. We know every inch of this place." He paused as a senior employee approached him with an apologetic expression. "Excuse me for just a moment."

Jasmine came to stand beside Laura. "Pretty amazing, isn't it?"

"Yes, it truly is," Laura replied.

Izzy's voice rose above the mechanical hum as he explained further. "Besides being the steady hand at the helm, Roy's a shrewd business manager who deals with our numbers."

Roy reappeared in time to catch the last of Izzy's declaration, waving off the compliment with an abashed smile before continuing the tour.

# CHAPTER TWO

With all Laura was learning, the cider house already felt like a distant memory. As the group wove its way through Goldenleaf Apple Farm's winding trails, she fell into step beside Jasmine. They exchanged smiles. Around her, the farm hummed with sounds—footsteps rustling through mulch, Izzy's animated voice, a faint mechanical whir, and birdsong.

Izzy spoke again. "I'd say these trees are our bread and butter, for lack of a more appropriate metaphor. Everything revolves around them!"

Jasmine gave an affectionate sigh. "He never changes, does he?"

Laura smiled. They crested a low rise. Rows upon rows of apple trees stretched across the landscape, their branches sagging with ripening fruit. They drew the eye in orderly lines. Along the farm perimeter, trees of various species stood in reds, greens, and yellows, hinting at the approaching peak of Vermont's fall splendor.

"Dare I be as bold to say Silver Springs wouldn't be Silver Springs without our farm, or any apple orchard! We have over two thousand trees," Izzy said.

The group let out an appreciative murmur.

Roy nodded. "We plant new trees every year so that the farm keeps growing. We'll pass three thousand in another decade. This venture isn't for the impatient."

"Or the undedicated!" Izzy said. "We've got big plans."

Roy gave a half-hearted sigh. "Someone has to keep this one in check, or he'll have us outgrowing the state."

"Only Vermont?" Izzy shot back with a grin. "Why not the East Coast?"

Roy shook his head. "I'm not giving you any more ideas."

Jesse arched an eyebrow at Izzy, a smile playing at their lips. "Do you ever run out of energy?"

Izzy mirrored their expression. "Apple fritters will slow me down. Briefly." A short distance later, Izzy stopped beside a tree and patted the trunk. "This one's even older than Roy and Vernon combined, if you can believe it."

Roy rolled his eyes, but couldn't stop the half-hearted smile tugging at his lips. "These are over two centuries old. The old guard. They're not used for harvesting anymore, but they're still critical for the ecosystem."

Gnarled branches like long, twisting memories stretched toward the sky, with just a few small apples clinging to their ancient limbs. The farm's legacy was there, in the bark that had seen more than any of them ever would.

⸺◦⸺

Roy ushered them from the visitors center into an adjoining room, the unassuming entrance leading to a dining hall. Sunlight spilled through a wide window, bathing a broad-leafed plant in its warmth. A long table ran down the center, flanked by benches and chairs, each unique in wood grain and color.

"All reclaimed wood from this farm," Roy said, catching Laura's glance.

Eli paused beside the plant, brushing a finger along one leaf. "That Monstera looks happier than mine ever has. How are you pulling that off?"

Roy glanced over, bemused. "I...don't know. One of our staff must've taken care of it."

Eli nodded. "You should tell them they've perfected their method. I've never gotten mine to be this happy."

Jesse grinned and cupped their hands around their mouth like an imaginary megaphone. "Breaking news! The General Store's resident green thumb admits defeat for the first time ever! Personal growth, everyone."

Eli groaned, rolling his eyes, but a smile tugged at his lips.

Izzy, already pulling out a chair, tilted his head. "Are you the fellow everyone talks about at the community garden?"

Eli scrunched his nose, giving a sheepish smile. "Yeah, that'd be me."

Izzy made a thoughtful 'hmm' sound.

"And now, for a sweet apple cider tasting," Roy said, clapping his hands once.

Jesse interrupted, grinning. "Is that breakfast waiting over there?"

Laura's gaze followed Jesse's outstretched finger. A large four-section countertop bain-marie awaited them on a nearby side table. French toast casserole, crisp-edged and glazed with melted butter and boiled cider—the syrupy reduction of sweet apple cider. Next came bacon, apple cider donuts, then baked oatmeal studded with raisins and apple chunks. A chafing dish promised apple fritters. Laura's stomach growled.

Roy allowed himself a small smile. "All in good time. The different apple varieties we use for our sweet ciders create unique flavor profiles that develop throughout the harvest season." He gestured to the sampler trays. "We'll progress from our Early Season to our Late Harvest varieties."

Chairs and bench seats scraped against the hardwood floor as the group settled.

"Let's begin," Roy said, holding a cup of pale golden liquid, "with our Early Season blend. Made from Gala, McIntosh, and Honeycrisp apples harvested in early September."

"Bright with delicate floral notes! Like drinking fresh autumn air!" Izzy burst out.

Roy had to smile. "Yes, you'll notice a lighter sweetness and more pronounced apple character."

Laura took a sip. The sweet cider was crisp, with hints of honey.

Jesse sampled it. "You might be onto something here."

"Perfect for breakfast or an afternoon drink," Izzy said.

Anton nodded. "Might be good in a new recipe."

"Now, let's move to our Mid-Season blend," Roy continued. "This one features Jonagold, Empire, and Cortland apples harvested in late September."

Raising the cup, Laura noted its deeper golden color and richer aroma.

"You'll notice a fuller body and more developed sweetness," Roy explained. "The natural sugars have had more time to develop in the fruit."

"This is really layered," Eli said after taking a sip. "I'm getting a hint of honey in there."

Roy nodded before moving to the third sample. "Our Harvest Blend combines mid and late-season varieties—Golden Delicious, Northern Spy, and Ida Red. This creates a more robust profile."

The amber cider offered a rich aroma of baked apples and caramel, its complex flavor revealing lingering layers of fruit.

"You can really pick out the different apples," Eli said.

Roy nodded, then pointed to his last glass, a deep amber liquid. "Our Late Harvest Reserve. From apples picked after the first frost, when the sugars are most concentrated."

The aroma was reminiscent of apple pie.

"A slow extraction process preserves the rich flavors of these late-season apples, creating our most complex offering," Roy said. "It's thicker and more intensely flavored than our other ciders."

Laura sipped, its rich, full-bodied flavor a perfect balance of sweetness and tartness, never cloying.

Jasmine leaned in. "What's going through your mind?"

"It's amazing how little I knew about apple cider until now," Laura said, before grinning.

Roy concluded the tasting with a brief explanation of their small-batch process versus commercial production. "Thank you for coming. I hope you enjoyed the tour. I have a conference call in ten minutes, but Izzy will join you for breakfast to answer any questions."

"That was fascinating," Jasmine said, her eyes bright.

Laura nodded. "Yes, thank you, Roy."

Kathy made a noise of agreement. "Solid work. Well-executed tour. Takes craft. Appreciate you both putting this together."

"There's more to cider than just sugar and apples!" Jesse said.

Eli nodded. "It highlights how much goes into each bottle."

"Thanks for letting us see this," Maggie said. "Selling your cider is great, but it's even better to know how the magic happens."

Anton offered a nod. "Exceptional quality. Consistent across all varieties."

Roy gave a modest smile. "Thank you all, that's what we strive for. Enjoy the breakfast." With that, he left through the side door.

Izzy grinned at the group. "Hungry? I know the sweet cider tasting was a big deal, but you haven't lived until you've tried our apple fritters!"

The group descended on the side table, grabbing plates and cutlery. For the fritters, the Goldenleaf Apple Farm staff had laid out several choices of toppings: cinnamon, berries, jam, and of course, boiled cider. Laura smiled. Even though she'd worked in the food industry her whole life, the excitement of trying new things never ceased. Laura selected a plate, choosing a little of everything, a fritter, and an apple cider donut, because, of course. She settled on a bench seat at the long table, and smiled when Jasmine claimed the spot to her right, and Izzy took one to her left. Jesse sat opposite, a small stack of fritters and fruit already disappearing from their plate. Eli and Kathy joined them, while Maggie and Anton lingered near the coffee urn, pouring steaming mugs for everyone.

"Not for me, thank you," Izzy said between mouthfuls of baked oatmeal as Anton offered him a cup of coffee. Despite how he'd talked up the fritters, he hadn't selected them yet. Perhaps he was pacing himself.

Jesse grinned. "Who needs caffeine when they've got your energy?"

Izzy smiled, though it wasn't as bright as his usual one. "True."

"Who makes the food?" Anton asked.

Jasmine couldn't resist the opportunity. "What's the verdict? Good enough?"

Anton nodded, to everyone's surprise. "Nice to do the eating for once."

The group laughed.

"Our staff includes prep cooks who manage breakfast for large groups," Izzy said, using years of practicing stage whispers to his advantage. "I chip in when they let me. I like to think I can cook, but...they might say otherwise."

The food was delicious. So that was why the farm had built such a reputation among both tourists and locals. Conversation flowed around the table, and even Anton, who let silence speak for him, seemed content. At last, a moment of rest. It wasn't often she got to just sit and enjoy.

After breakfast, Maggie turned to Izzy. "Lovely breakfast, truly. Thanks for having us."

Izzy beamed. "A pleasure." He jumped up. "I wish you all the liveliest of days! Alas, the harvest season waits for no one." Ever the strange yet considerate gentlemen, he swept open the door and waved them through, fending off Maggie's protests about helping with cleanup.

Maggie had one final announcement to make before the group dispersed. "We couldn't ask for a better team. Kathy and I mean it. The General Store wouldn't be what it is today without you."

"Even if a few of you are burdened with too many opinions," Kathy said, eyeing Jesse with a crooked grin.

Jesse shrugged as they all laughed.

# CHAPTER THREE

"**S**ee you Tuesday," Kathy said to the group. She was just reaching for the visitors center door when a blur barreled into her. "Easy, kid." She jumped back and held up her hands. "What's wrong?"

The young man, wearing a zippered vest open over a Goldenleaf Apple Farm shirt, would've been about Izzy's age, but he seemed more like a teenager now, eyes wide, hands trembling, face pale. He didn't speak for several seconds.

"Is everything okay?" Laura asked.

Jasmine stepped forward. "Take it easy. Whatever it is, we're here to help."

The youth's speech came out in staccato bursts. "I need—I need—"

Izzy put a gentle hand on the younger man's shoulder. "Noah, look at me. What's going on?"

He tried to formulate a sentence, but he could only splutter.

Izzy gripped Noah by the shoulders with both hands, shaking him gently. "Noah. Come on. What is it?"

The young man forced the words out. "Vernon. In the garage. I think he's—dead."

The light drained from Izzy's eyes. He stepped back, reeling, hands dropping from Noah's shoulders. Izzy stared into nothing for a split second, then turned on his heel, and sprinted out the visitors center entrance doors.

Kathy snapped to attention. "Eli, call nine-one-one. Jesse, Anton—find Roy. His office is out back. Once you've told him, meet Maggie here and stay put. Noah, Maggie—stay calm and hold the line. Laura, Jasmine, you're with me. We can't let Izzy do something he'll regret. Vernon's place is next door—left of the lot. The garage runs along the boundary fence." The older woman took off through the open door, Laura and Jasmine at her heels.

Keeping up with Izzy was a tall order, nigh impossible. He'd disappeared in seconds. It was just as well Kathy knew where he was headed and had the good sense to run at a pace Laura could match. Chest heaving, Laura skidded to a halt outside what must've been Vernon's garage, and dashed in through the open roller door after Kathy. Jasmine arrived behind her mere seconds later. The garage was dim, and a strange unease crept over her. She found Izzy kneeling next to a crumpled form on the concrete fl oor.

Laura's stomach lurched. Vernon Reed lay motionless. This wasn't supposed to happen in Silver Springs. Not again. She'd seen something like this before—when she'd found Jeremy in the General Store Stables—but she'd hoped that was an isolated incident. The unreality of it happening again made her head spin.

"Oh no," Jasmine said, her hand moving to cover her mouth.

"I checked. He's..." Izzy swallowed. "He's gone." Tears pooled at the corners of his eyes.

Kathy ushered the three of them back.

Izzy did as she'd asked, moving to a stool before sitting with his head in his hands. "I should have checked on him. I should have..." His voice cracked, and he didn't finish.

Laura placed a comforting hand on his shoulder. "Please don't blame yourself. It's not your fault."

Izzy didn't look up. "He—" His throat caught again.

Laura kept her hand there, steady, hoping to provide some calm for his trembling form.

Kathy crouched in front of him. "We're with you, Izzy. You couldn't have seen it coming—none of us could've."

He sucked in a deep breath and nodded.

Kathy stood. "The police and ambulance should be here soon."

Laura forced herself to take in the scene.

Vernon lay beside an overturned stool, motionless. He'd fallen. A window above the workbench stood open, letting in a faint breeze that carried a trace of machine oil and fallen leaves. Tools hung in tidy rows on the wall, their stillness unnerving. His hands bore streaks of yellowish oil. Laura's gaze drifted to the cluttered workbench—half-repaired antique clocks, delicate gears exposed, a forgotten cup of tea long gone cold. Clock pieces lay broken near his feet. Another flash of metal caught her eye beneath the bench, just at the edge of the sh adow.

Laura's mind raced—not with conclusions, but with questions. It could be an accident, but something gnawed at her—a sensation she couldn't shake off.

Sirens broke the stillness, wailing in the distance and growing louder.

Laura exchanged a worried glance with Jasmine. Her friend rubbed the side of her neck behind her ear, where her singular tattoo, a crescent moon, was inked into her skin. A nervous, self-soothing gesture. Laura's breath hung in the cool air, like everything else: unexpected, suspended, unclear.

Roy appeared in the doorway. "What the—" His expression shifted from confusion to horror. His hands twitched at his sides, fingers curling and uncurling, as if grasping for something that wasn't there. "This can't—who'd—" His voice cracked.

◆◦◆

A woman with an athletic build, hair in a no-nonsense bun, and warm olive skin entered the garage. Dark jeans, a leather jacket, and chunky lace-up boots completed the look of someone ready for action. Detective Sergeant Ramirez. Behind her came Officer Littlefield, and a younger officer with a buzzcut Laura didn't recognize.

"That's Officer Patterson," Kathy murmured to Laura. "Came back after the academy—been a few years now."

From outside came the crunch of additional footsteps on gravel. Through the garage door, several other patrol officers from the Silver Springs Police Department approached, and what must've been the medical examiner.

Ramirez took in the scene. "I'm going to ask you all to clear the area and wait outside while we do our work."

Kathy nodded at her and directed the other three out of the building. Littlefield secured the perimeter while Patterson began photographing the scene. The group stood outside in silence, their breath forming light clouds in the early fall air. Izzy was silent and shivering. Laura placed a hand on his shoulder.

Roy wrung his hands. "What happened? How—" His mouth opened and closed. "What was he doing in there? Today was supposed to be his day off. He should be hiking!"

No one spoke. They waited.

Ramirez reappeared, her expression focused and professional. Had she always been this calm? Or was it something she'd learned along the way? "Thank you for waiting. We'll need to ask you a few questions." She addressed Roy. "What space can we use?"

"The dining hall in the visitors center," Roy said, his voice quiet. "Next to the parking lot. It's just for tour groups, not accessible to the public. There should be enough room."

Ramirez nodded. "Lead us there, please." She turned to the others. "Follow me."

Izzy struggled as he tried to get off his stool.

"Let me help you, Izzy," Laura said.

Izzy gave her a grateful smile. Once he was steady, they joined the others. The group trooped after Roy and Ramirez, and Littlefield and Patterson brought up the rear, leaving the others to their tasks. Laura glanced skyward, where clouds gathered. A chill crept into her bones. It'd be a brisk September afternoon.

# Chapter Four

The room was too warm. Laura entered the visitors center with Jasmine and Izzy, followed by Kathy and the two other police officers.

Laura's mind reeled. Vernon Reed. Dead. The words were surreal, disconnected from any meaning. She'd rarely spoken to him, except when he visited the store for deliveries or stock level discussions. Now he was gone. She shivered, despite the cloying warmth. The overhead lights were too harsh for what'd just occurred. Jasmine kept chewing her bottom lip, and Izzy stood still beside her. The only movement he made was his hands drumming at h is sides.

"Where's the dining hall?" Ramirez asked Roy as she spun around to face them. The group came to a halt.

"Just through that door," Roy said, indicating it with a half-hearted gesture.

Maggie, Eli, Jesse, Anton, and Noah, who'd all been sitting in the chairs around a coffee table in the corner, got to their feet. Maggie's face was ashen, her fingers twisting the silver bracelet on her wrist. Noah remained separate from the others, shoulders hunched. Laura wanted to say something to him, but what could help? Anton stared at the police folk, his jaw tight. Eli's eyes had widened half-an-hour ago and had stayed that way, still caught in the instant it all went wrong. Jesse didn't seem to know where to look.

Ramirez's gaze flicked over the group. "Who's willing to tell me what's just happened in the last half-an-hour?" She opened her mouth to continue speaking, but closed it as Kathy took a step forward. "Go on."

"Noah found Vernon in the garage," Kathy said. Her hands trembled slightly, but she shoved them behind her back. "I had him stay here with Maggie. Izzy, Laura, Jasmine, and I went to the garage and stayed there until you showed up. Roy arrived before you did." She pointed to each person as she named them.

Everything had happened so fast. Laura swallowed hard, forcing back the image that threatened to surface in her mind. Beside her, Jasmine shifted her weight from one foot to the other.

Ramirez nodded and turned to the others Kathy hadn't singled out. "Officer Patterson will collect your contact information, just in case we need to reach you later, then you're free to leave."

Eli and Jesse acquiesced, approaching the second police person to give their details, but not without a nervous glance in the others' direction. Laura caught Jesse's eye, just long enough to see them make a 'call me' gesture, mouthing, "I'm here for you."

"I can stick around," Anton said. He stood still.

Kathy gave him a knowing but kind look. "On home, Anton. I'll text you."

The three of them left, not without Anton giving a backwards glance.

Roy stood apart from the others, back to the wall, shoulders tense, expression oscillating between bewilderment and horror, like it had been for the last half-an-hour.

"I'll need to question each of you," Ramirez said. "I'll start with—"

A commotion from the entrance interrupted her—raised voices growing louder with each passing second. The double doors burst open, and a woman with dark brown curls hastily gathered into a ponytail rushed in. Another followed close behind, reaching out as if to stop her. It was Ruby Callahan, part-time employee at the Village Skein, the local yarn shop—which meant the woman ahead could only be her best friend, Dulcie Sanderson. Vernon's partner. Ruby had mentioned her often, and how excited Dulcie had been for their long weekend in Alpine Glen. What a terrible thing to return to.

"You've cordoned off the garage! Your officers said to come straight here," Dulcie said, her light-brown complexion appearing ashen. Her gaze swept across the room. "What's going on?"

Ramirez straightened. "And you are?"

Roy stepped forward. "This is...Vernon's partner, Dulcie Sanderson. And Ruby Callahan, who works part-time at the farm."

Ramirez approached the women. "I'm Detective Sergeant Ramirez. I have some difficult news. Vernon Reed was found dead this morning in his garage."

Dulcie stared at Ramirez, her face blank. Several seconds passed before any reaction registered—first in her eyes, which widened, then in the confused tilt of her head, as if she hadn't processed the words.

Ruby didn't wait for Dulcie to respond. She stepped forward, slipping a protective arm around Dulcie's shoulders. "What happened?" Her voice was steady, but only just, her porcelain-pale skin and rosy cheeks now drained of color as she surveyed the scene. "We were out of town. We just got back."

Roy looked toward Dulcie, trying to replace his worry with a look of empathy. "I'm so sorry. It's...unbelievable."

Dulcie met his gaze for half a second, then lowered her eyes.

"I forgot," Roy continued, shaking his head. "We'd scheduled a meeting with Warren today. The negotiation about—"

Before he could finish, yet another figure appeared in the doorway—a stocky man in his sixties, with dark hair flecked with gray and a plaid flannel shirt beneath a worn canvas jacket. "Someone wanna explain why half the police force is parked outside?" the man asked, looking around at the assembled faces, tanned skin creasing into deeper lines as he frowned.

Ramirez turned toward him. "This is a current investigation area. Who are you?"

"Warren Fisk," the man replied, straightening. "Fisk Apple Works. I had a meeting scheduled with Roy and Vernon this morning." His gaze darted around the room again. "Where's Vernon?"

"Vernon Reed was found dead earlier this morning," Ramirez said.

Warren's mouth fell open. "Dead? Vernon? What happened? Was it...an accident?" The silence stretched.

His shock gave way to something else—an unsettling flicker behind his eyes.

Roy shifted against the wall, his jaw tightening. "Cut the act, Warren."

Warren's head snapped toward Roy. "What's that supposed to mean?"

"You know what it means." Roy's voice was low, controlled, but it trembled underneath. "We all heard what you said about wishing Vernon would just disappear."

Warren's face flushed, but he kept his voice steady. "That was business frustration, nothing more."

Dulcie, who had been silent until now, made a small sound—half gasp, half sob. Everyone looked at her. Ruby's arm tightened around her shoulders.

Warren's gaze settled on Dulcie, his expression softening. "Dulcie, I'm sorry for your loss. Truly."

"Don't." Ruby shook her head. "Everyone knows how you felt about Vernon."

Warren glared at her. "And what about you? Hovering around, whispering in Dulcie's ear. We've all seen it."

"That's enough." Ramirez said. "Everyone will remain calm and cooperative."

Littlefield and Patterson gestured for everyone to give each other some space. Izzy shifted beside Laura, looking anywhere but the scene unfolding in front of him. Kathy remained impassive, though her fingers had curled into tight fists at her sides.

Ramirez surveyed the room with a nod before turning to Noah, her expression softening. "Noah, wasn't it? Please come with me to the dining hall. Kathy, you're next."

Noah straightened, his Adam's apple bobbing as he swallowed hard.

Warren took a step toward the exit. "If you're starting with those who were at the scene, I'll come back later. I have no information to—"

"You'll stay right where you are," Ramirez cut in. "Everyone present remains until questioned." She turned to Ruby and Dulcie. "That includes you two."

"We weren't even here!" Ruby said. "We just got back from—"

"I didn't ask for comment," Ramirez said.

Warren opened his mouth as if to argue further, then moved to an unoccupied chair and sat with a huff. The patrol officers positioned themselves—one by the door, the other near the middle of the room—as Ramirez led Noah away. In the uncomfortable silence that followed, Laura caught Jasmine's concerned glance. Her friend's eyes held a question Laura wasn't sure how to answer. Across the room, Kathy leaned against the wall, eyes focused on the scene in front of her. Izzy had taken a chair, his shoulders slumped. Maggie remained where she was, twisting her bracelet, her gaze darting between the various people in the room.

⸻◦⸻

The room was silent, save for the ticking of the wall clock. How did it keep such a steady rhythm when everything else was falling apart?

Eleven minutes after Ramirez had taken Noah away, he emerged from the dining hall looking wan and dazed.

He sat next to Maggie, staring at the ground. Kathy was gone the longest. When she finally returned, she sank into her seat with an exhale and offered Laura a nod meant to reassure. It didn't. Izzy followed later. He looked more shaken and didn't say a word.

Then Ramirez turned to Laura. "Your turn."

Her heart thudded. She rose, legs stiff, and trailed Ramirez into the dining hall. The door clicked shut behind them.

"Please sit," Ramirez said.

Laura sat, hands open in her lap.

Ramirez studied Laura with an intensity that made her shift in her seat. "You've found yourself in this situation before, haven't you?"

Laura swallowed.

Ramirez sighed. "I feel the death...like last time...wasn't natural." She straightened. "Tell me what you saw."

Laura inhaled deeply. "The moment Noah told us, Izzy just took off. Kathy got Jasmine and I to accompany her to Vernon's garage. We were concerned Izzy might do something impulsive in his distress."

Ramirez nodded, motioning for her to go on.

"We arrived at the garage and Izzy was already inside, standing near Vernon, who appeared to have fallen from a stool. Something seemed off. He had a strange yellowish oil on his hands, and..." Laura paused, trying to arrange the images in her head into a coherent order. "The window was open. A half-drunk cup of tea was on the workbench, and there was something metallic on the floor. I thought it might've been an accident, but...it didn't look like one."

Ramirez exhaled. "What makes you say that?"

"It could be just a feeling I have," Laura said. "I don't know for certain, but it really seemed...not as it should be."

Ramirez nodded and leaned forward. "You seemed concerned about Izzy's reaction. Why was that?"

"I know from Izzy he and Vernon had a strong friendship," Laura said. "So for Izzy to see him...to see Vernon like that...it was undoubtedly an immense shock."

"And you're close with Izzy?"

Laura tried to sound confident. "We're friends, yes, but—"

Ramirez gave her a long look. "But?"

Laura hesitated. "I suppose I don't know him all that well. We were introduced soon after I moved to Silver Springs, when he kindly—"

"When he got wind of your arrival and showed up at your door declaring himself the 'one-man welcoming committee'?" Ramirez raised an eyebrow. "I'm aware of his...community spirit and...excitable behavior."

"If you're concerned he could've been involved in something like that...there's simply no way." Laura protested.

Ramirez watched her. "What makes you so sure?"

"Because," Laura said, "it's Izzy we're discussing. He used his only day off to show me, a complete stranger, around town and even helped me move into my apartment. I've only known him for two months, but in that time, he's been kind to everyone I've seen him with."

Ramirez sighed. "That's the thing about people. You never know, do you?" She continued before Laura could protest further. "We searched the area and found what looks like the murder weapon."

Laura's eyes widened. "Did you say murder? So what happened was actually...?"

"We won't know until the autopsy's complete, but we suspect foul play." Ramirez paused. "What we found was a hardwood bung hammer, used to insert or remove stoppers from the cider barrels, but in this instance..."

Laura blinked as the implication sank in. "So, are you suggesting it might be someone connected to Goldenleaf Apple Farm? Or perhaps from one of the other apple farms?"

Ramirez frowned. "We'll need to investigate every possibility. For now, we know he suffered a head wound. And we suspect he was killed last night."

Laura jerked back. Foul play. It had to be. Everyone they'd seen at the farm that morning—Dulcie and Roy's shock, Warren's bluster, Ruby's defensiveness, and Izzy's sudden stillness. What had their relationships with Vernon been like? Did any of them have a motive? And the other staff members—let alone the ones at Warren Fisk's establishment. Might one of them have wanted Vernon dead?

"We found something else at the scene." Ramirez shifted in her chair and pulled out an evidence bag from her pocket. Inside was a thin bracelet, knotted from multicolored string. She placed it on the table. "Do you recognize this?"

Laura's gaze dropped to her left wrist, where a near identical bracelet sat. It had been a welcome gift, one Izzy had presented with flair and enthusiasm, the kind of gesture that defined him.

Ramirez watched her. "Did Izzy make both of them?"

The question lingered in the air. Laura hesitated, then nodded. "That seems likely."

Ramirez slid the bagged bracelet back into her pocket. "And you're sure you know him as well as you think?"

Laura flinched. "Wait a moment. He makes a point of not wearing them for work."

Ramirez tilted her head.

"And also, he wasn't supposed to be working then. It was late on a Sunday!"

The room swirled. Could it have been Izzy? Her mind flashed back to the garage. Surely not! There was no way he could've...

Ramirez watched her. "Anything else I should know about?"

"No, that's the extent of what I saw."

Ramirez leaned back. "That's everything I need from you for now."

Laura stood and moved toward the door.

"Laura," Ramirez called before she reached it. "This is where I'd tell you last time it was a fluke. That you shouldn't get involved again. But...you haven't done anything that would require intervention. I still caution you against investigating. Your safety is important. And you're too close to this. You care about Izzy, which means you're biased."

"I—" Laura said.

"Please," Ramirez interrupted, "consider what I've said. Come straight to me if you notice anything."

"Yes, of course," Laura said.

Ramirez didn't look convinced, but she accepted the response and opened the door to the larger room.

"Jasmine," Ramirez said, "you're up next."

Jasmine rose, her face drawn, and followed Ramirez. Laura settled beside Izzy, a question in his wide eyes.

"Was it...okay?" he asked, his voice low.

She nodded, trying to smile but failing. Izzy appeared on the verge of speaking further, but remained silent.

When it was Dulcie's turn, she'd had to all but wrestle herself from Ruby's grip. Ruby's shoulders sagged the moment she was out of sight. She pressed her fingers against her temples, closing her eyes for a long moment.

"Are you alright?" Laura asked.

Ruby's eyes snapped open, and she frowned. "I'm...fine." She studied Laura's face, before her gaze drifted over to the closed door. "You don't understand what it's like to watch someone you care about suffer, and blame themselves for things that aren't their fault. Dulcie doesn't deserve this. She's been through enough."

⬥

After an age, Ramirez left the dining hall with Jasmine. With hands clasped behind her back, she addressed the group. "Thank you for your patience. You're all free to go, but please don't leave town. We may need to ask you more questions. Officer Littlefield will collect your contact details on your way out."

Everyone's postures loosened...a little.

Ramirez didn't look at anyone in particular when she said her next piece, but Laura was pretty sure it was directed at her. "As this is an active investigation, I remind you to be careful. If you remember anything at all, come straight to us."

Warren eyed Dulcie and Ruby. "Certainly, Detective Sergeant. I'll pass on any information."

Ramirez pressed her lips into a thin line. "I only want to hear objective facts, not baseless accusations."

The apple farmer had enough sense not to say anything more, at least. He glared at Roy, scowled at Ruby and Dulcie, grimaced at the patrol officers, and marched out. Though not before sending an imperceptible nod to...Izzy?

Ruby drew herself up to her full height, looking disdainfully at the police people. "Since you've turned Dulcie's property into an active crime scene, if you must speak with us further, you'll find us at my address." She linked her arm with Dulcie's and dragged her out of the building.

Roy stood from the wicker chair in the corner, his expression still vacant. "I need to return to work, it's the only thing that makes sense right now." He glanced at his employees. "Maybe you should too."

Izzy spluttered. "You expect us to continue working? Like nothing's happened? Are you—"

Roy's expression tightened. "I don't like the tone you're using, Izzy. I understand this has been a stressful situation—"

"Only 'stressful'? Vernon's dead! There are no words to describe how I'm feeling!" Izzy's body shook, shoulders up to his ears. "We can't go back to work. Not like this."

Roy's shoulders slumped, fingers twisting the ring on his right hand. "You think I don't feel the same? But if I stop moving, I won't know what to do with myself."

Ramirez stepped between them, firm but calm. "Mr. Beckett, I suggest you notify your staff and suspend operations for today. No one is in a state to continue."

Roy let out a breath. "You're right. You both have the day off. I'll...tell the others."

Izzy's shoulders dropped. "Thank you."

Roy tilted his head in acknowledgement and turned to Noah, who was still pale. "If I can help you, please let me know."

Izzy nodded. "Seriously, Noah. Anything."

Noah's gaze bounced between both men, the floor, and the visitor center's entrance, legs frozen yet raring to leave. He stuttered through something incomprehensible before spitting out: "No! I mean—no, thank you, I'm fine, I—," he heaved in a much needed breath. "I'll go home and call my partner." He darted out of the building with an unsteady gait.

Roy nodded at what was left of the group before turning on his heel to exit through the back. As he passed Izzy, he said something just low enough for the younger man to hear. Laura caught the words, too.

"Just don't...turn to the drink."

Izzy went rigid, hands clenching. He strode out without another word.

⸻◈⸻

Laura walked alongside Jasmine, trailing their bosses as they headed to the parking lot.

Kathy stopped in front of their respective cars. Her voice was firm, but her eyes were weary. "I'm sorry this happened. If you need anything, call us."

"You only have to ask," Maggie said, taking Kathy's hand.

"Thank you, I really appreciate it," Laura said.

Jasmine nodded. The two older women gave their employees a final glance before getting into Maggie's SUV. The doors shut with a hollow thud, and Maggie pulled away.

Laura turned to Jasmine. "How are you holding up? Are you okay?"

Jasmine let out a humorless laugh. "No, not at all."

"Me neither," Laura said, shaking her head. She paused. "This might not change things, but would you feel a little better with a hug?"

That got a smile from her friend, the first in a while, however small. "Yes please, Laura."

When they pulled apart, Jasmine seemed more settled. "That mind of yours is already working overtime, isn't it?"

Laura tried to smile. "You've got me there. To be honest, I don't know. There's so much to take in." She glanced around the parking lot. Izzy's vintage pickup still sat in amongst the other staff cars. "Izzy must still be here."

Jasmine followed her gaze and gave Laura a quizzical look. "Did you want to make sure he's okay before we leave?"

Laura nodded, then leaned in. "I was wondering, did Detective Sergeant Ramirez mention anything specific in your conversation with her?"

Jasmine shook her head.

Laura let out her breath in a long exhale. "The police believe Vernon died from a blow to the head. And they've apparently found what they suspect is the murder weapon. A bung hammer."

Her friend's eyes widened, and she shivered.

"They also found a bracelet at the scene like the ones Izzy makes," Laura said. "Detective Sergeant Ramirez saw the one he gave me and put two and two together."

"And made seven," Jasmine said with a grumble. "Surely she doesn't believe he..."

"I don't believe for a moment it was him," Laura said. "I'm determined to understand what's happening here."

Jasmine's expression softened. "You've already decided you're helping him, haven't you?"

Laura hesitated, then nodded. "Regarding our lunch today...how would you feel about including Izzy? It just seems to me he could use some company right now."

Jasmine smiled. "Of course. And if Evelyn can come, all the better. She brings the calm with her."

Laura thought for a moment. "That sounds like an excellent idea."

Footsteps approached, so she turned. Izzy stalked toward his truck, hands deep in his pockets, hood pulled over his head.

"Excuse me, Izzy!" she called, speed-walking over to him. Jasmine followed close behind.

Perhaps that hadn't been the best idea, because he jumped near a foot in the air. He sucked in a breath as she reached him, flashing a wan smile. "Laura, for the love of everything, I've had enough jump scares today."

Laura gave him what she hoped was a sympathetic look. "Sorry about that. I was wondering...did you have any plans for what you're going to do now?"

He gave her that same half-hearted grin. "If I did, I don't think I do anymore."

"Why don't you come and have lunch with us?" Laura asked. "At my place. And I'd invite Evelyn too, if that sounds good to you."

His expression softened. "Thanks, Laura. I'll always accept an invitation you send my way." Still, Izzy paused, rocking back and forth on his heels. "If this was brought on by hearing what Roy said...look, I get it. You don't have to worry."

Jasmine tried to hide the confused look she gave Laura, but Izzy noticed it.

"Roy was just...'concerned' I'd return to an...old coping mechanism." He let out a bitter laugh. "Never mind, it was a brief thing, and I'm five years sober."

Neither Jasmine nor Laura knew how to respond to that, so he filled the awkward gap, as he always did.

"Look, I know things aren't looking good for me. Detective Sergeant Ramirez told me they found the bracelet." He took a quick glance at Laura's wrist. "Darned if I know how it got there. And the bung hammer." Izzy let out a hollow laugh. "I wouldn't be surprised if the forensics on that thing comes back with my fingerprints."

Laura stared at him. "May I ask why?"

He sighed. "I'm the one responsible for checking and sealing the barrels. Use them all the time. Once the Maplewood Memo hears about this, and the forensics results come back, my fate's sealed." Somehow, he had the strength to smile, no matter how weak it was. "Still. I know

I look like a ticking time bomb. But I'll be fine. I have to be. It's...not like anyone else can make it better for me. I...have to look after myself."

Laura tried to say something, anything at all, but words failed her. They didn't fail him.

"If lunch is still on...I'd love to come. And I appreciate you inviting me. I'll follow you into town."

# CHAPTER FIVE

After such a tumultuous morning, Laura was desperate for a comforting presence. She found one the moment she knocked on Evelyn Chan's door. It appeared the older woman had expected her arrival as the door opened mere seconds after. As ever, Evelyn's warm golden-brown complexion radiated calm.

"Laura! It's so wonderful to see you," Evelyn said. "Come in and make yourself at home."

"Hi, Evelyn. I was just calling to see if you might be free to join us for lunch?" Laura asked. She gestured to Jasmine and Izzy behind her.

Evelyn's eyes moved past Laura, registering Jasmine first with a friendly nod, then widening at the sight of Izzy. Though her expression flickered with surprise, she recovered quickly as she grabbed her cardigan.

"I'd be delighted. Thank you for inviting me."

Laura fished her keys from her pocket as they reached the third-floor landing. She unlocked the door and stepped aside to let everyone enter her small but welcoming kitchen and dining area.

"Why don't I get lunch underway?" Laura asked, moving toward the refrigerator. "I have everything we need for some toasted sandwiches. Ham, cheese, and some of my homemade tomato relish."

Jasmine moved to help, opening cabinets. "The plates are in here, aren't they?"

"Yes, that's right, and you'll find the glasses in the cupboard just next to that one," Laura said.

Evelyn went straight to the sink and washed her hands. "Slicing the ham shall be my contribution."

"Why don't you sit and relax, Izzy?" Laura asked, pulling bread from her breadbox. "You've had a rough—"

"Please don't stop me from assisting," Izzy said, pulling open drawers until he found two baking sheets. "I'd...appreciate the distraction." He preheated the oven and took the bread from Laura's hands, placing it on a chopping board. Selecting a bread knife, he began slicing the loaf into generous widths.

"Yes, of course. I'll take care of getting the cheese ready," Laura said.

Soon they were all focused on their tasks—Evelyn slicing the ham, Jasmine setting the table, Izzy prepping the bread with generous smears of Laura's tangy tomato relish, and Laura cutting the cheese and assembling sandwiches.

⎯⎯◆⎯⎯

The open toasted sandwiches were as she'd wanted them: a golden tint to the bread, cheese melted to the right consistency, sending a delicious smell wafting through her apartment. They gathered around Laura's small dining table, the clink of glasses and crunch of toasted bread the only sounds. Laura slid into the seat beside Jasmine, facing Evelyn and Izzy across the table. Laura caught Jasmine's eye, asking who should start the conversation. Jasmine gave a small shrug. A silence hung between them.

Evelyn set down her sandwich. "Tell me, what's troubling you? I can see something's on all your minds."

Izzy took a bite of his sandwich, chewed, then swallowed, looking up from his plate. "I appreciate you for having me over, given everything. This is great, though I'd expect nothing less from folks in hospitality and the mother of the best chef this side of the coast." He drew in a deep breath. "Still…I can't pretend this morning didn't happen."

"Are you sure you feel up to talking about it?" Laura asked. "Please know there's no pressure at all. We don't have to discuss it if you'd rather not."

Izzy's laugh, for once, held no humor. "Of course I don't. But best to get it done."

Laura and Jasmine exchanged glances. A worried frown creased Jasmine's face.

Izzy stared at his sandwich for a long moment, then set it down with trembling hands. "This morning—" his voice cracked, eyes wide. "Vernon Reed, my boss, was found dead in his garage at Goldenleaf Apple Farm. Murdered." He talked with his hands, as usual, but his gestures were now jerky and uncoordinated. "I still can't—I keep thinking I'll wake up and none of this will be real." He attempted a bite of his sandwich but forgot what he was doing mid-motion. "They found one of my friendship bracelets at the scene, and the murder weapon was a bung hammer from our farm. One I've probably u sed."

Evelyn's eyes widened, expression shifting from shock to sadness to a quiet determination. The woman leaned forward. "My dear boy. I'm so sorry for both your loss and this ordeal. After all my years in Silver Springs, I've come to realize things are rarely as they seem. I know your character, and you have our help—this will be resolved."

Laura smiled at Izzy. "Please remember, we believe you completely. Detective Sergeant Ramirez has a duty to ask thorough questions, considering the findings. I was just hoping you could tell us what you're comfortable sharing about your history with Vernon."

Izzy considered for a moment. "I don't mind. It might help to talk about it with people who believe me."

Laura leaned forward. "Only if you're sure. We can always wait if you'd prefer."

"I think I'm okay," Izzy said. "What did you want to know?"

Evelyn's phone vibrated in her bag. She glanced at it and frowned. "I'm sorry, but I need to take this call. Would you mind if I stepped out for just a minute?"

"Sure thing," Laura said. "Take your time."

Evelyn moved into the living room.

Laura turned back to Izzy with a gentle expression. "So..."

After she'd finished asking a few questions, and Evelyn had returned, they finished their lunch in peaceful quiet, with only occasional comments about the food.

Izzy pushed out his chair and stood. "Thank you all for lunch. I should probably head off. There are a few things I have to take care of at home." He picked up his plate.

Evelyn looked up at him. "Are you sure you'll be all right?"

"Yeah, thank you," Izzy said, attempting a smile. "Just going to tidy up a bit and continue with all the projects I've been neglecting." He carried his plate to the sink. "I hope...tomorrow will be better. For everyone."

"And please, call if there's anything you need," Laura said as she got up to follow him to the door, opening it for him once he'd put on his shoes.

Jasmine nodded. "Anytime, Izzy."

Izzy nodded, said goodbye to the three women, and slipped out of the apartment. Laura returned to the table and collected their plates, the ceramic clinking as she stacked them, but Evelyn raised a hand.

"Leave the dishes for now. I want to hear about this morning, and anything you learned from Izzy," Evelyn said. "Start from the beginning and tell me all you can recall."

Laura settled into her chair again. "We were at Goldenleaf Apple Farm for a team-building event. They'd arranged a tour and breakfast for us. Everything seemed normal and pleasant until—" her voice caught.

"Noah, an employee at the farm, came running in, looking terrified," Jasmine continued. "He was so shaken up, Izzy had to jolt the words out of him. Then he told us what he'd found."

Evelyn shook her head. "Is Noah alright?"

Jasmine hesitated, her shoulders lifting in an uncertain shrug. "He said he was fine, but...he didn't look it. How could he be?"

Evelyn frowned, motioning for her to continue.

"Once he found out...Izzy ran straight to the garage. Kathy took charge. She got Jesse on the phone to nine-one-one, Eli and Anton went off to find Roy, and

Maggie stuck by Noah. Kathy took me and Laura, and we followed Izzy. When we reached the garage, he'd already gone inside." Jasmine wrung her hands. "That's when we saw Vernon..."

Evelyn nodded.

"I remember his garage was packed with clocks," Laura said, wanting to avoid picturing the scene but finding no way around it. "Close to him was an overturned stool, which made it look like he'd fallen, and his hands had this strange yellow oil on them."

"That may be the only ordinary thing in this whole mess," Evelyn said. "Vernon loved tinkering with clocks. If he'd been working on one, it would make sense the substance was clock oil."

Jasmine shrugged. "That sounds right to me."

Laura continued. "I also remember seeing a metallic object beneath one workbench. But before we could get a better look, Detective Sergeant Ramirez appeared with Officer Littlefield and Officer Patterson. She directed everyone to the visitors center, where she interviewed us one at a time."

"Who did she question first?" Evelyn asked.

"Noah, then Kathy, then Izzy, then Laura," Jasmine said. "That's when Laura found out the bung hammer was the murder weapon and they found Izzy's bracelet at the scene. I think the hammer was what Laura saw under the bench in the garage."

A flash of surprise crossed Evelyn's features. "The Detective Sergeant gave you that information? My, that says something..."

Laura rubbed her temples. "I just keep thinking there must be more to this story." She counted off her observations on her fingers. "For example, Warren Fisk came for his scheduled appointment with Vernon and Roy. Roy accused him outright of being pleased about what happened to Vernon. Warren responded by saying both Dulcie and Ruby had been acting out of character. Ruby fired back a similar comment about Warren. And perhaps most curiously, when Warren left, he gave Izzy a nod that seemed to imply a shared secret."

"That seems rather out of place," Evelyn said.

Laura frowned. "Roy's comment was unusual. Just before he left, he warned Izzy about not 'turning to the drink.'"

Evelyn sighed. "That was far from tactful. I'm sure he meant well, but..."

Laura looked at her. "Is this something you were aware of?"

The older woman didn't reply for several moments. "It was never mine to divulge, but yes...he struggled with that."

Jasmine nodded. "He's been sober for five years." When Evelyn shot her a look of surprise, she continued. "He told us in the parking lot, right before we asked him to join us for lunch."

"We just thought it best if he had some company," Laura said.

Evelyn nodded. "As we're talking about lifting spirits...my earlier call was from Yanni. He's preparing a batch of his chicken and wild rice for Dulcie. That poor woman will need some comfort food after losing Vernon. He'll slip in a portion over to Ruby, since Dulcie's staying with her."

Before Laura could reply, all three of their phones buzzed with notifications. Laura pulled out her phone to see the Maplewood Crafters Club group chat lighting up her screen.

"What's this about a murder at Goldenleaf?" Martha had written in her characteristic all-caps style. A shocked-face animated emoji from Judith followed that message.

Laura's stomach tightened. Of course, everyone would find out eventually—this was Silver Springs after all—but she wasn't ready to be explaining it so soon.

She inhaled deeply and typed: "Yes, it's true. Vernon Reed's body was discovered this morning. I'm still processing everything." She hesitated, then added, "Everyone's safe, but we're all pretty shaken." She put her phone down and looked at the other two. "We need to come up with a plan. I feel like I could make one if my mind was clearer right now."

Evelyn stood up, a glint in her eye. "We have a few hours before the Maplewood Crafters Club meeting." She looked at Jasmine. "Do you have plans for the rest of the day?"

Jasmine shook her head. "Nothing is more important than this."

"Right then," Evelyn said. "A new murder board is in order."

# CHAPTER SIX

As Laura rinsed the rest of the lunch plates, Evelyn sat at Laura's kitchen table, arranging index cards, colored markers, and adhesive notes in neat rows. The older woman had a system for everything, now including...murder investigations. Jasmine dried the cutlery and put it away.

"Laura," Evelyn said, absorbed in her organizing, "what's your impression of Izzy? Not just from today, but overall."

Laura handed a clean plate to Jasmine and wiped her hands on a dishcloth. "He has a real passion for everything he does, occasionally to an extreme. All his community efforts." She leaned against the counter. "He feels things strongly. I've seen minor issues cause him a good deal of distress."

"And he's loyal, too," Jasmine said. "Always kind and willing to pitch in. I don't know him super well, but now and then you catch this flicker of sadness, like he's working extra hard to seem happy."

Evelyn nodded, uncapping a red marker. "Izzy hasn't had it easy. He moved here as a teenager to live with his aunt to start over, but after his aunt passed away, it's been one hardship after another. He finds comfort in the arts, and in steady work at Goldenleaf."

"I wasn't aware of that at all," Laura said. "He always seems so...lively."

"He's worked hard to rebuild his life," Evelyn said, shaking her head. "And after all he's been through, now this."

Laura and Jasmine finished the last of the cleanup and joined Evelyn at the table.

Jasmine picked up a blue marker and pulled a card toward her. "Alright, which names are we circling as suspects?"

"Warren Fisk," Laura said. "Considering those accusations he made, and that strange nod he gave to Izzy...my instinct tells me something isn't right with that situation."

Jasmine nodded. "And have we thought about Ruby? Her reaction to the news was...off."

Laura let out a groan. "The real challenge is all the information we're missing. For example, how did Izzy's bracelet get to the scene in the first place?"

"And a bung hammer, of all things," Jasmine said. "You can't convince me the choice of weapon was accidental."

They sat in silence for a moment, surrounded by blank cards waiting to be filled with information.

Laura straightened. "Of course, we should be considerate of how everyone is feeling, but perhaps we could consider mentioning this at the Club meeting tonight. And tomorrow, during my lunch break, I was thinking of stopping by The Village Skein. I need to pick up some tapestry needles. It'll be a good chance to talk to

Ruby." She turned to Jasmine. "Would you be willing to accompany me?"

It had been hours, but Jasmine at last managed a smile. "Of course. Especially with my last skein running low."

"Perfect pretext," Evelyn said. "Ruby might let something slip in a casual conversation."

"Alright, that sounds like a good plan," Laura said, taking out an index card. "Let's try to organize what we've learned so far."

Later, Laura stood in Evelyn's living room. They'd spent the past hour arranging chairs in a circle, setting out snacks, and preparing for the evening's Crafters Club meeting. The building's intercom system buzzed, its electronic tone cutting through the quiet apartment.

Evelyn glanced at her watch. "Perfect timing. The first of us has arrived." She walked to the entryway and pressed the speaker button. "Hello? Please, come on up."

Moments later, there was a knock at the door. Evelyn opened it with a sunny smile. "Jasmine, welcome."

Jasmine stepped into the apartment, her box braids styled in a bun. She carried a canvas tote bag over one shoulder and had changed clothes since Laura had last seen her, wearing a royal blue grandpa-collar shirt.

"Hi, Evelyn. Hi, Laura." She plopped her bag down, sighing. "Word travels fast. I got grilled by my landlady for ten solid minutes when I got home. She wanted a minute-by-minute recap."

"That happened faster than I expected," Laura said, shaking her head.

As Jasmine settled into an armchair, Monty, Evelyn's dignified cat, approached her with measured steps, his tail held high. After a moment's consideration, he jumped onto Jasmine's lap and settled in, purring.

Evelyn chuckled. "Monty is so particular, but you've won him over."

Jasmine couldn't resist a wink. "I feel like the luckiest person in the room."

As if summoned by his brother's purring, Oscar bounded into the room. He circled Jasmine's chair twice, meowing, before spotting Laura and making a beeline for her. He rubbed against her ankles, his purr loud compared to Monty's dignified rumble. Laura reached down to scratch behind his ears, and Oscar flopped onto his side, exposing his belly.

Laura laughed and gave him a pat on his head. "Sometimes I wonder if he believes he's a dog."

Evelyn smiled. "That wouldn't surprise me in the least."

———◆O◆———

With a soft creak of the floorboards, the last of the Maplewood Crafters Club sank into a seat, and the room exhaled in welcome.

Christopher O'Reilly grabbed his reading glasses and placed them on his pale, freckled nose, opening his sketchpad. The retired carpenter's fingers, still nimble from years of crafting wood, held his pencil above the page with a thoughtful expression—fitting for the editor of The Whittled Word, a local hobbyist newsletter.

Across the room, Yanni Petros and Marcela Torres shared a quiet laugh. Yanni, the Australian transplant who owned Wanderer Pantry, worked his crochet hook with a surprising delicacy for such large hands, adding features to a smiling amigurumi chipmunk. Beside him, Marcela had shed her Town Clerk formality along with her blazer, her roller-derby-toned forearms now free in short sleeves that complemented her amber-brown skin. A coloring book lay open beside her, a kaleidoscope of pencils fanned out next to it.

Near the window, Francesca 'Fran' Palermo's needle flashed in the light as she added vibrant orange thread to her Baltimore Oriole embroidery. Her complexion, once ghost-pale before years under the Arizona sun, now carried the weathered confidence of someone at home in the outdoors—a perfect fit for her work at the state park since moving to Vermont.

Martha Henderson, the vice president of the Historical Society, and president of the Good Neighbor Guild, sat, as always, next to Judith Yoon. The second woman was a retired editor from a New York publishing house, and contributed puzzles to The Maplewood Memo. Never mind their tendency to bicker like sisters. Or their inclination for teasing each other about everything from Martha's incessant busyness to Judith's rather...wild theories on social dynamics. Martha smoothed the fabric of her navy skirt as she got comfortable in her chair.

Evelyn drew the room's attention. "Thank you, everyone, for coming this evening. Let's take a moment to see how we're all progressing on the 'Warmth Where Needed' project."

Laura smiled, remembering how excited Evelyn had been when proposing the idea—creating handmade wool scarves with hidden pockets containing apple cider caramels and attached tags saying, 'Please take this for the upcoming winter if you need it.' They'd leave them at local bus stops for people.

"How are the scarves coming along, everyone? If anyone needs more yarn, just let me know," Evelyn said.

Martha, ever eager, spoke first. "I've finished three already. I started a fourth yesterday." She pulled out three knitted scarves in varying shades of blue. She had such speed and precision.

Judith peered at her work, the warm-beige skin on her forehead crinkling. "I'm still working on the pockets for mine. Getting them sewn right is trickier than I expected—almost as tricky as the cryptogram I'm designing for the Memo. Has to be done for next week." She showed her technique.

Yanni held up his single crochet scarf and grinned. "Went better than I expected. Look at me, branching out from something small to something...less small!"

Marcela reached into her bag and retrieved a stack of small cards. "I finished the tags. I used my calligraphy pens on the cardstock. Thought the blue ink would look nice against the cream paper."

Laura leaned forward to examine the beautiful handwritten notes. Each tag contained the message in flowing script, the curves and flourishes dancing across the paper. "These are gorgeous, Marcela."

Fran dug into her bag and pulled out a container. "I picked up the apple cider caramels from the farmers' market." She passed it around. "Try one."

Laura popped a caramel in her mouth. It melted on her tongue, releasing layers of sweetness.

Judith looked up from her knitting, her eyes sharp behind her glasses. "Shouldn't we talk about what happened this morning?"

The room went silent.

"Judith!" Martha scolded. "That's the last thing Laura and Jasmine want to talk about right now."

Judith lifted her chin. "Maybe Laura wants to ask what we know. She always does. It's not like we can pretend it didn't happen."

"This is supposed to be comforting for them," Martha said, her voice rising. "Not making them relive seeing a dead body!"

Those two words caught everyone's attention. Christopher looked up from his drawing, hand going still. Yanni stopped mid-stitch.

Marcela set her yarn down, her eyes darting between Laura and Jasmine. "I also heard about what happened. And if Laura is going to investigate again, we should discuss it."

Laura's cheeks flushed.

"As the town clerk, I feel a certain responsibility for what happens here," Marcela said, her voice soft. "And from what I've been hearing, this wasn't an accident. The police department is already treating it as suspicious." Her shoulders tensed. "It's unsettling to think someone in our community might've harmed Vernon. Isn't the

Maplewood Crafters Club's mission to do good for this place? How is this different?"

"Marcela's right," Christopher said. "If we can help, we should."

Fran nodded. "What happened isn't right."

Yanni gave an agreeing hum. "Can't let them get away with it."

Laura sighed. "I hesitated to mention it earlier because I didn't want to spoil the pleasant atmosphere." She turned to Jasmine, whose fingers were still stroking Monty's fur. "Would you be okay if we discussed this now?"

Jasmine nodded, her expression resolute. "I want to be involved. It feels right, since we both witnessed everything."

"Alright," Laura said, straightening her shoulders. "Perhaps it's best if we discuss what we know, and then put it aside for now. I promise this won't consume our entire evening." She explained what had happened that morning.

"Wait," Martha said. "A bung hammer?"

Laura nodded, then hesitated. "I should also mention...they found one of Izzy's handmade bracelets there."

Gasps circled the room.

"I was hoping you might share anything you know about Vernon, or his relationships with others. Even anything unusual you noticed recently could be helpful," Laura said.

Martha and Judith exchanged glances.

"Vernon and Roy have been partners for thirty years on that apple farm," Martha began, lowering her voice. "They started small after Vernon inherited that land from his father."

Judith nodded. "They were always competitive. Especially with Warren Fisk. Those two farms have been rivals for as long as I can remember."

Christopher leaned forward. "Speaking of Warren, I saw him and Vernon arguing outside the post office last week. It got heated before they noticed me. Warren was red-faced and pointing his finger at Vernon's chest."

Martha leaned in. "And I overheard Ruby at the Village Skein yesterday telling a customer 'some men deserve what's coming to them.' It feels...significant."

"There's something I forgot to mention," Jasmine said, her fingers still stroking Monty's fur. "Vernon stopped coming to the hiking group, and he's been pulling away from Woodland Watch, too. He said he was caught up with the farm, but it never sat right with me."

After everyone had shared, they resumed their usual chatter, while Laura recorded what she'd learned. The topic returned to the Maplewood Crafters Club's latest project.

"Once we get these scarves distributed, I have the loveliest idea for our winter project," Martha said. "We could create indoor comfort kits with homemade tea blends and mug cozies. Perfect for people to stay warm and comfortable during these cold months."

"I love the tea idea," Judith said, "but what about people who don't drink tea?"

"We could include recipes for hot chocolate or mulled cider too," Christopher said.

Yanni nodded. "I've got several winter comfort drink recipes from Wanderer Pantry I could share!"

"What if we painted mugs with bright winter designs?" Jasmine asked. "It might be a fun project."

"I could write up cards with affirmations and self-care tips for the winter blues," Fran said. "Make them accessible for anyone struggling with the dark season."

Marcela tapped her chin. "The library has been wanting to host a winter wellness event. We could leave our kits there for them to distribute. Anonymously, of course."

Evelyn smiled, her eyes crinkling at the corners. "So it's settled! Comfort kits to spread warmth this winter."

Laura looked around the room at the people who had become her friends. Despite the darkness that'd touched their community today, here in this group, she found comfort. Whatever challenges lay ahead, she wouldn't face them alone.

# Chapter Seven

Three days ago, Laura couldn't have imagined her Tuesday morning shift would be so chaotic, but the Laura of now understood—Vernon Reed's murder had transformed the café into a hotbed of small-town speculation. Whenever something terrible, scandalous, or unexpected happened, the locals convened here to discuss it. Everywhere she turned, hushed conversations about the town's deceased apple farmer filled the air.

"Order for Greta! One double shot latte with oat milk," Laura called, setting the reusable cup on the counter.

A woman with salt-and-pepper hair collected it with a distracted "Thanks." She recognized a group huddled at a corner table and walked over to join them.

Their voices carried just enough for Laura to catch snippets.

"...found him in his garage. Police questioning everyone who..."

"...can't believe it happened right here in Silver Springs..."

Laura wiped down the counter, trying not to look too interested. She needed every piece of information she could get.

"Laura, can you handle the register for a minute? I need to check something in the back," Eli said.

"Of course," she replied with a smile, moving over to the cash register where a line of three customers waited, all clutching their wallets and all, she was certain, bursting with theories about what had happened to Vernon.

Maggie emerged from the back as Eli entered the area she'd just come from, creases etched across her forehead. She scanned the busy café, waiting for the line of customers to be served before making her way to Laura. "Morning. Has anyone from Goldenleaf dropped by yet?"

"I can't say I've seen anyone. Is there a particular reason you ask?" Laura questioned.

"I'm worried about our cider supply," Maggie said. "Goldenleaf's our primary source, and with what's been happening lately..." She trailed off, glancing toward the retail section where Kathy restocked shelves. "We've got enough for the moment, but...we might have to look at other options."

"I'm confident we'll come up with a solution," Laura said, trying to sound encouraging. "In the meantime, if I can be of any help, let me know."

Maggie shot her a grateful smile and exited through the back rooms.

A customer approached the counter, and Laura took their order—a chamomile tea and blueberry muffin—while a man in a flannel shirt approached Kathy.

"Terrible business with Vernon," the man said, gesturing with his shopping basket. "You two knew him, didn't you?"

Kathy's shoulders stiffened as she shelved jars of local honey. "We did."

"Any idea who might've—"

"That's my phone ringing upstairs." Kathy straightened, head tilted. "Sorry, I've been waiting for a call from a supplier. Excuse me." She set down her pricing gun and hurried toward the stairs.

The café hummed with a blend of chatter and the relentless hiss of the espresso machine. Amidst it all, no phone rang. Warmth spread through Laura, bringing a smile she didn't stop. The excuse was paper-thin, yes, but would she blame Kathy for needing it? Not at all. Not after what they'd been through at Goldenleaf.

Balancing a tray with a plate piled with eggs and toast, another with pancakes, and a teapot, Laura navigated her way toward table five. Two women sat together, huddled in conversation, and looked up as she approached. She set down their food. "Here we are! Enjoy."

One, wearing a fuzzy green cardigan, fixed Laura with a knowing expression. "You know that Izzy fellow, right? The one from the apple farm?"

Laura paused. "I know him, yes."

The woman glanced at her companion, then focused her attention on Laura. "All that drama and emotion...I've always thought he seemed...unstable. You probably hadn't moved to town yet, but one time, he kicked up such a fuss because the Selectboard Members didn't approve funding for the theater group."

Her friend shifted. "Still, murder seems like a stretch, Iris."

"My cousin's husband works at the farm," Iris continued, lowering her voice. "Says Izzy and Vernon had been arguing lately. Getting heated about something."

Laura's hands trembled as she finished pouring their tea. "Anything else I can get you?"

Iris gave Laura another pointed expression. "No, thank you. We're right."

She nodded and moved away to collect empty mugs from a nearby vacated table. Her cheeks flushed. She screwed up her lip, just stopping herself from glaring at the women. Yes, Izzy was passionate, but unstable? That didn't align with her impression at all. She scrubbed harder than necessary as she wiped down tables near the window.

As Laura approached to clear another customer's table, occupied by a bearded man in his sixties and a younger woman, the man gestured for her attention.

"Excuse me. Do you have a minute?"

Laura paused in loading plates onto her tray. "What can I help you with?"

"You'd know this better than I do. Vernon Reed's farm is a supplier here, right? Did he ever mention working on any new products? My daughter here is curious about the cider business."

Laura set down her cleaning cloth, her brow furrowing. "I...don't believe so. Did you mean something specific?"

"A spiced cider mix," the younger woman said. "Someone at the farmers' market mentioned Vernon was developing something revolutionary."

The man nodded. "Apparently, Warren Fisk was working on something similar. Some folks are saying Vernon might've borrowed the idea, if you catch my meaning."

"Dad," the woman said, face going red. "You can't just accuse people of stealing recipes."

"I'm not," he said, then looked at Laura. "But it makes you think, doesn't it? All this secrecy over a cider recipe?"

Laura tried to steer the conversation back to her task at hand. She finished clearing their table, offering refills of their drinks, which they declined. A potential theft of ideas...was it connected? Laura's gut tightened, urging her to find out more.

As she moved to wipe down another vacated table, an inaudible murmur caught her attention. A woman with a bright pink beret leaned toward her companion, a cup of tea held halfway to her lips.

"And Agnes told me," the woman said, eyes wide, "her cousin who does some temp work down at the county courthouse heard Detective Sergeant Ramirez wasn't messing about. She's requested full background checks on all of them! Vernon himself, Roy Beckett, that flamboyant young man Izzy, Ruby Callahan, Warren Fisk, and Vernon's partner. Every single one! Ramirez is determined to shake every tree until something interesting falls out."

Her companion gasped.

"Look over there," the first woman continued. "I think that's her."

As Laura worked, through the large front windows, Ramirez sat on a park bench tucked in a corner of the Village Green...accompanied by...was that Warren? Laura pretended to wipe an already clean table as she watched. Warren's animated gestures suggested he was being pressed for details, his hands moving as he spoke. After several minutes, Ramirez handed him something—a business card, perhaps—and stood. Warren remained on the bench, staring down at whatever she'd given him.

Ramirez was indeed leaving no stone unturned.

———◦———

Though Laura had only worked in the General Store café for over a month now, already she was noticing patterns. Regulars would come in at the same time each week, or order the same drink each morning. They found comfort in their familiar routines, and she could almost set her clocks by their cadences.

So when Martha entered, wearing a name-tag and carrying her tall stainless steel drink container...it was late Tuesday morning. In the rough fifteen-minute window between eleven-thirty and eleven-forty-five on the second day of the week, Martha would approach the counter and ask for her customary 'history fuel.' This, so she said, got her through her volunteer shift on Tuesday afternoons, supervising the Silver Springs Historical Society's archives in the Public Library. Martha handed the metal thermos over to Eli. Laura watched from where she was cleaning up after a large group of coffee-drinking older folks who'd just left, smiling. The order was the same each time, Jesse had told Laura—a peach and ginger smoothie, with a dash of plain yogurt, almond milk, and chia seeds for a little protein. Martha loved it even more in the fall, when they used ripe pears.

She waited for her drink, eyes roving the café, until her gaze fell on Laura. She hurried over. "Good morning, dear." Without waiting for a reply, she continued.

"Something I just heard. Supposedly, Vernon fired Cheryl, the accounts manager, from the farm last month. There were discrepancies in the quarterly reports."

Laura raised her eyebrows as she wiped down the table. "That sounds...unusual."

"That's the thing," Martha said, lowering her voice and glancing over her shoulder. "Apparently, she'd found something concerning and had scheduled a meeting with Vernon to discuss it. Never got the chance. They found out she'd done something...questionable at her previous job."

"What caught her attention?" Laura asked. "And if you know, where was she working before that?"

Martha sighed. "I couldn't get any specifics. Which is strange, considering Goldenleaf has been doing so well. Let me think..." She pressed her fingers to her temple, remaining silent for several moments. "Of course! Hearthstone Street Legal Services."

"Smoothie for Martha!" Eli called.

Martha straightened and gave Laura a smile. "Must be going. If I find anything else, I'll let you know."

Laura could only give a nod of thanks before Martha was off, bustling toward the counter, and then out the door.

---

The Village Skein was a world apart from the frenzied atmosphere of the General Store café. Laura and Jasmine, on their lunch break, stepped inside. The sound of wind chimes announced their arrival, and the scent of wool enveloped them. Balls of yarn in every imaginable hue lined the walls in neat cubbies and every other surface available.

"I need tapestry needles," Laura said to Jasmine as they browsed.

Jasmine nodded, feeling a skein of deep teal yarn. "And I need more of this for my hat."

Ruby emerged from behind a display of pattern books, her usual energy dimmed. Dark circles shadowed her eyes, and her braid had loose strands escaping at odd angles, but she managed a tired smile. "Afternoon. Can I help you find anything?"

"Right now, we're just looking, but thank you," Laura said, then added, "How are things with you, Ruby? Are you alright?"

Ruby's hands paused on the book she'd been re-shelving. She glanced up, studying their faces. "I'm...managing. It's been a difficult few days." She straightened several items, her movements deliberate. "I heard about you helping solve that case at the Summer Cheese Festival, Laura. Now with Vernon..." Her voice caught. "I imagine people are talking."

Laura blinked.

"We really just came for some supplies," Jasmine said.

Ruby gave a huff. "Yeah right." Her shoulders sagged. "I'm sorry. That came out wrong. It's just...I know how these things work in small towns." Her voice grew firmer. "I care about Dulcie. She's been through enough already. If you have questions—and I suspect you might—I'd rather you ask me instead."

Laura hesitated. "We're just trying to understand what happened—"

"Promise me," Ruby said, her voice breaking. "Promise you'll leave her be." Before either of them got the chance to reply, she continued, her words tumbling over each other. "You don't understand. Dulcie's been hurt before. By people who claimed to want to help. I...can't let that happen again."

"We won't come to your house to question her or bother her," Jasmine said before Laura could speak. "You have our word."

Laura shot Jasmine a look. That hadn't been part of the plan!

Ruby's shoulders relaxed. "Thank you. What do you want to know?"

Laura started with something neutral. "To begin, I was curious. How did you and Dulcie become friends?"

"College roommates," Ruby replied, straightening a display of knitting needles. "We were randomly assigned freshman year and just...clicked. Stayed close after graduation. I introduced her to Vernon three years ago, and they started dating not long after. I was thrilled for her." A shadow crossed her face. "At first."

"If I remember correctly, you and Dulcie were in Alpine Glen over this past weekend?" Laura asked.

Ruby nodded. "A mini vacation. We'd planned it months ago. Left Friday afternoon, came back Monday morning." She pressed her lips together. "So neither of us could've...you know."

"How had Vernon and Dulcie's relationship been?" Jasmine asked, selecting a ball of yarn and turning it in her hands.

Ruby's expression darkened. "Different. He'd become secretive in the last few months. Distant. Dulcie tried to talk to him about it, but he kept saying it was just 'work stress.'"

"In what way did he seem secretive to you?" Laura asked.

"Checking his phone at odd hours. Hiding it when Dulcie entered the room." Ruby's fingers tightened around a skein of magenta yarn. "He'd started spending time at the library, claiming he was 'reading,' but Dulcie had never seen him pick up a book the entire time they'd been together. Something wasn't right."

A sensation settled in Laura's stomach. "Do you think Vernon might've been..."

"Having an affair?" Ruby's gaze dropped to the floor. "I suspected it. I've been trying to find evidence. Dulcie deserves to know the truth—deserved to know," she corrected herself, voice catching.

"Did you confront Vernon about your suspicions?" Jasmine asked.

"Once," Ruby admitted. "About three weeks ago. We had a...heated discussion. I told him Dulcie deserved better, that if he was cheating, he should at least have the decency to end things." She twisted a loose thread on her sleeve. "He denied everything, of course. Got angry, said I was interfering in things that weren't my business."

Laura studied Ruby's face and the flush creeping up her neck. "That sounds like it must've been a difficult situation for you."

"It was," Ruby said, then caught herself. She straightened her shoulders. "I know how this sounds, but confronting your friend's partner about being difficult doesn't make you a murderer."

Laura nodded. "And you work part-time at Goldenleaf Apple Farm, don't you? During the harvest season?"

"For years now," Ruby said. "I run tours, manage the visitors center, and help with production."

"Did you observe any tension between Vernon and other people at the farm?" Laura asked.

Ruby hesitated. "Warren and Vernon have been rivals forever. Competing farms, competing products. Recently..."

Katie Fowler emerged from the back room, carrying a box of new merchandise. She gave them a curious look before setting it down behind the counter. "Laura! Jasmine! Hi! Find anything special today?"

"Hi, Katie," Laura said, hiding her disappointment with a smile. There went their chance of asking more questions. "I was just hoping to pick up a packet of tapestry needles."

"And I need some more of this lovely yarn!" Jasmine said, holding up two skeins of teal merino.

Ruby glanced at them both. "Is that all?"

Jasmine nodded, and Ruby gestured for her and Laura to follow her to the register, taking their purchases and ringing them up.

As Ruby handed over their items, she hesitated, then leaned forward. "Look, I know I can't stop you from asking questions. But please..." Her grip tightened on the register's edge. "If you want to help her, maybe consider whether stirring all this up is worth the pain it might c ause."

<hr>

Laura and Jasmine left the Village Skein with their purchases tucked into their respective bags.

Laura waited until they were well down the street before turning to Jasmine with a sigh. "I was wondering why you felt it necessary to make that promise to Ruby?" She kept her voice low as they passed a group of tourists admiring the historic downtown. "We've lost our chance to speak with Dulcie directly."

They paused at the corner to let a small delivery truck rumble past, then turned right, heading back toward the General Store.

To Laura's surprise, Jasmine grinned. "I promised we wouldn't go to Ruby's house to question her. Not that we wouldn't question her at all."

Laura couldn't stop herself from smiling. "That's...brilliant."

"I know," Jasmine said with a wink as they continued down the sidewalk. "We just need to find a neutral location where we might run into her. What did you make of Ruby's protectiveness?"

Laura considered this. "Either she's just being a supportive friend to someone who's grieving, or..."

"Or she knows something she's not telling us," Jasmine said. "Something that might make Dulcie look suspicious."

Laura frowned, thinking back to Ruby's revelations. "Or maybe she's protecting Dulcie from finding out something painful."

She nodded to the mail carrier as they passed. Up ahead, the Village Green sprawled in its usual picturesque glory, the General Store's familiar shopfront just a few buildings away.

"What do you think about Vernon's secretive behavior?" Jasmine's question pulled Laura back to their investigation. "The phone checking, the mysterious library visits?"

An affair? It seemed the obvious explanation, but Laura's instincts nagged at her. "Ruby could be right, but..." Her mind raced through other possibilities. Secret business deals? Financial problems?

"We need to find out more," Jasmine said.

⸺◦⸺

The afternoon rush had given way to the quiet lull that preceded closing time. The café held only a few lingering customers—a woman typing on her laptop, an older couple sharing a slice of pie, a teenager with headphones flipping through a textbook. Eli exited the back room carrying a small misting bottle, working through each potted succulent on the café's tables, stopping to pluck a yellowing leaf.

Just as Laura tucked her cleaning cloth away, her phone vibrated in her pocket. Laura pulled it out, expecting a text from her Gran or perhaps a...'concerned' question from her mother. Instead, Izzy's name appeared on her screen.

"Short notice, I know, but are you free tonight? Seven pm? Just made stew."

Laura stared at the message, considering, and typed a reply. "Hope you're doing ok. Thank you, that'd be lovely. See you then." She slipped her phone back into her pocket and resumed her closing duties.

Later, a few minutes after her shift had ended, and as she was doing the last checks, Jesse entered through the back room. They'd removed their apron and replaced it with their motorcycle jacket. "Any thrilling events on your calendar tonight, or just the usual?"

Laura nodded. "Izzy invited me over for dinner."

Jesse raised an eyebrow. "He's at it with the stew again?" When Laura nodded, they smirked. "It's tasty. That almost compensates for his tendency to break into show tunes at random intervals."

Laura laughed. "I'll consider myself warned."

# CHAPTER EIGHT

The road narrowed as Laura left downtown, buildings giving way to trees. She'd driven this route before—rolling fields dotted with farmhouses, patches of forest adorned with early fall colors, and the distant silhouettes of the Green Mountains catching the last rays of sunset.

"You'll reach your destination in three miles," her phone announced from its perch on the dashboard.

Laura tapped her fingers on the steering wheel. What did she know about Izzy Lennox? Passionate about theater. Worked at Goldenleaf Apple Farm. Prone to grand gestures and emotional outbursts, according to town gossip, but during their interactions, Laura had only witnessed enthusiasm and kindness.

The road curved, and a sign appeared: 'Silver Springs Mobile Home Park.' Laura slowed her car and turned onto a gravel drive. What she could see of the park spread before her—neat rows of lots arranged in a horseshoe pattern around a central green space. Some were traditional mobile homes, others were more permanent structures. As she pulled into the visitor parking area near the entrance, the last rays of dusk disappeared behind the mountains, leaving the sky a deep indigo streaked with pink and orange. In the distance, lights through windows came on in homes across the park—warm squares of yellow against the gathering darkness.

Laura grabbed her bag, stepped out of her car, and locked it. According to the park rules, all visitors needed to check in at the management office, so she walked towards it. It was a plain building with wooden siding and a covered porch. A neon 'Open' sign glowed in the window, and rakes and baskets stacked near the door—ready for the approaching fall.

A bell jingled as Laura pushed open the door. The office was warm, with painted walls covered in community notices, park maps, and framed photographs of summer picnics and holiday gatherings. A woman in her sixties looked up from behind a desk cluttered with paperwork, a mug of tea steaming beside an ancient desktop computer. Meredith Perkins and her husband, Stewart, had owned the park since its inception.

"Evening, Laura," Meredith said. "Terrible business, isn't it? About Vernon?"

Laura blinked. "Yes, I know. It's just awful."

Meredith slid a clipboard across the counter. "Here to visit Izzy?"

Laura nodded, taking the pen and signing the visitors' register.

Meredith took the clipboard back and keyed something into the computer. "Police were here yesterday, asking about Izzy's whereabouts the night it happened."

Laura's heart rate quickened. "Really?"

Meredith nodded. "Truth is, I don't know where he was. My husband and I were watching television, and didn't notice if Izzy came or went. He's a good tenant.

Always pays on time, takes part in community events. Makes the best lemonade for our summer picnic." Her fingers hovered over the keyboard. "Though he's been acting strange."

Laura kept her voice calm. "In what way did it seem strange to you?"

"He started a construction project out the front of his place! Using the most bizarre collection of materials you've ever seen." Meredith gave a fond sigh. "My husband told him he's ridiculous, building with pieces of old theater sets and random lumber. Half of what he's got so far looks like it belongs in A Midsummer Night's Dream, and the other half like some abstract art installation."

"What's he building, do you know?" Laura asked.

"An extension, he said. Izzy brought a load of painted backdrop pieces from the theater and scrap wood he's collected from half the town. He's been out there whenever he wasn't at work or at rehearsals, sawing and hammering." She shrugged. "At least he doesn't make any noise during quiet hours."

Laura nodded. "Maybe a project like this is a helpful distraction for him."

Meredith softened. "Could be. Poor thing. You should get going. Don't want to keep him waiting."

Laura offered a faint smile. "Bye, Meredith. Always lovely to see you."

"You too, dear," Meredith said as she waved goodbye.

Back outside, the park's street lights shone, and Laura pulled her coat tighter. Walking toward Izzy's place, she passed homes with their evening routines on display through illuminated windows—families at dinner tables, silhouettes moving in kitchens, the blue flicker of televisions. As she walked, the rhythmic thunk of an axe splitting wood grew louder.

Izzy's vintage caravan came into view, its painted exterior lit up by a series of solar-powered lanterns arranged around the yard. On the side of his caravan, a painted nature scene blended with the surrounding landscape. During her last visit, she'd complimented him on it. Turned out Jesse had done it for him. It'd been wonderful to see her younger colleague was putting the art school degree to good use.

Izzy's place wasn't like the tidy lots of his neighbors. His space had a creative messiness—raised garden beds full of late-summer veggies, a fire pit surrounded by random wooden chairs, and his pickup parked out back. What really caught Laura's eye was the extension on the caravan's right side—a wooden frame with a slanted roof. He hadn't finished it yet, but it was becoming something. The extension was a riot of colors and textures—repurposed castle battlements from a previous theater production painted stone-gray with purple accents covering one wall. Another section featured ornate balustrades that might've once belonged to a Shakespearean balcony scene.

Under this partial roof, Izzy stood with his back to her, positioning a piece of wood on a chopping block. He wore emerald-green overalls with patches over a t-shirt. He raised an axe and brought it down, the log splitting. The sound echoed as he set up another log. Laura paused, watching. This wasn't the theatrical, exuberant Izzy. This Izzy moved with a contained intensity, his movements economical and focused. He wiped his brow, shoulders set tightly.

"Izzy?" she called.

He turned, the serious expression on his face transforming into a tired grin. "Laura. A pleasure to see you." He embedded the axe in the chopping block and pulled off his work gloves. "Apologies for the right state of this place."

Laura approached, taking in his setup—mismatched lumber piles sorted by size, a table with a circular saw, and containers of nails and screws. "Don't worry, it's impressive. What are you building?"

Izzy gestured to the frame above. "Kitchen and living extension. The caravan is a noble thing, but she's...a little cramped. You'd think I knew how to live with it now, being here for eight years. Sometimes you have to admit defeat. Plus, all the better for hosting folks." He glanced toward the park entrance. "Did Meredith chat away at check-in?"

"She's always friendly," Laura said.

Izzy gave a faint smile. "Probably told you I've gone construction-crazy. Folks next door aren't happy with the noise, but...it's just me and an axe most of the time. I'm not using a jackhammer." He blinked. "What am I doing? You came here for food, not detailed reports of neighborly disputes. Let me just clean up a bit." He moved around the workspace, covering the circular saw with a tarp, stacking the last few split logs on the woodpile, and hanging tools on hooks attached to the frame.

"I came here for more than just the food!" Laura said. "I'm your friend, and I want to support you. Have you always been into woodworking?"

Izzy gave a half-smile. "My grandfather taught me. Aside from my aunt, he's the only one in the family worth knowing. He built furniture. Said working with your hands clears the mind. I sure needed some mind-clearing."

He finished the task and led her toward the caravan, switching on another solar lantern. As they approached the door, a savory smell wafted out—herbs and tomato. Izzy stepped aside, holding the door open for her. "After yo u."

With an appreciative nod, Laura climbed the small metal steps. Inside, vintage wooden cabinets lined one wall. A compact dining nook with a table that could seat four occupied one end, while a living area with a built-in bed took up the other. Colorful textiles—handwoven blankets, embroidered pillows, and macramé wall hangings—softened the metal curves.

Laura's eyes were drawn to a small collection of potted plants near the window. "Those weren't here before, were they?"

Izzy followed Laura's gaze with a sheepish smile. "My neighbor moved in with her partner a few weeks ago, and she had to downsize her collection, so I took them off her hands. They look nice, but I wouldn't know the first thing about indoor plants! They're just sitting there, judging me."

Laura chuckled.

"I swear I can hear them plotting a revolt," Izzy said, giving a huff of laughter. "I've been wanting to ask Eli for advice. That Aloe is barely hanging on."

He moved to a narrow kitchenette where a large pot bubbled on a portable induction element. The savory aroma of his stew permeated the space—herbs, tomato, and slow-cooked vegetables. Izzy stirred the pot with a hand-carved wooden spoon, then replaced the lid.

"It smells amazing," Laura said.

Izzy grinned.

As Laura sat, her gaze caught on a cork pinboard affixed to the back of the door. Ticket stubs, notes, and photos covered most of its surface—Izzy with theater cast members, at community events, hiking in the Green Mountains. Several small squares of the cork appeared lighter, as though photos that'd once been pinned there had been removed. If she remembered correctly, those spaces had held photos of Izzy with Vernon and others at Goldenleaf Apple Farm events. Their absence was...conspicuous. Nearby was a sketch of the extension he was building, with notes showing which parts came from which theater productions and which townspeople had contributed materials.

"Make yourself comfortable," Izzy said, opening a cabinet. "The stew needs a few more minutes. How about some cheese and crackers?"

"Sounds lovely," Laura replied.

Izzy pulled out a wooden board and a knife from the top cupboard, along with a block of cheese from his fridge. He'd explained on her previous visit he'd had to take out a few cupboards just to make room for a refrigerator that wasn't tiny. "Vermont sharp cheddar. Diana's from Mountain Valley Dairy, because, of course." He reached for a glass jar on a shelf above his head. "And I've got some dried apricots and apple slices." He set the plate on the t able.

"Looks delicious!" Laura said.

Izzy smiled, gesturing to a food dehydrator tucked in the kitchenette's corner. "Made them myself. Amazing what you can do with a little patience and electricity."

As he sliced the cheese, his hands trembled, the knife unsteady in his grip. He plated up some slices, pieces of dried fruit, and crackers for her before fixing himself a plate, bringing them both over. He returned to the kitchenette, this time fetching a jug, filling it with water from the sink, and bringing it to the table with two glasses. Once finished, he sat opposite her, reaching into his overalls pocket, pulling out a half-finished macramé plant holder.

"The theatre folks call it my 'fidget project,'" he said, attaching it to his belt loop with a small carabiner he also produced from one of his many pockets. His fingers worked the cord, tying knots. "Better than my leg bouncing during rehearsals."

Laura selected a cracker and cheese, eating one, before leaning forward. "That looks great so far."

Izzy smiled. They fell into a silence until Izzy sighed. "The police questioned me again today."

Laura tried to look surprised. "Not again, surely?"

"They had more questions...about what I did that night..." He groaned, his fingers never stopped working the cords as he spoke. "I was at the theater building sets until nine-thirty...but they wanted to know about the twenty-five minute window when I left. Everyone saw me leave and heard my truck start up, and they all saw me return." Izzy's jaw tightened as he continued. "The police checked my phone records. I received a call at eight that lasted fourteen minutes. Longest of my life. I didn't want to tell Detective Sergeant Ramirez...but...I had to."

"If you don't mind my asking, who was on the phone?" Laura asked.

"My father called." Izzy's fingers stilled before resuming their knot-tying. "We've been estranged for years, but he keeps reconnecting whenever he needs something. This time, I told him I never wanted to hear from him again." His voice cracked. "Blocked his number afterward. I was so rattled I just drove around for a while to clear my mind." He shook his head. "Can't believe it took me this long."

Laura leaned forward, her expression softening. "That must've been difficult. Standing up to family takes courage."

Didn't she know it? And he had more bravery than she did.

Izzy's eyes met hers, surprise flickering across his features. For a moment, his composure wavered, making him look younger. He gave a small nod, his throat working as he swallowed. "Thank you. Few folks understand how hard it is to just...walk away, even when you know you should." He let out a long sigh. "And I can't blame Detective Sergeant Ramirez for being skeptical. Even called his number to verify. My father wasn't helpful." For the first time since she'd known him, he allowed anger to cross his features. "Drunk. Of course. So that's...a lot of time unaccounted for and a shaky alibi. And now they know about my family's history with...damaging coping mechanisms."

"Family history doesn't define you, Izzy," Laura said. "Anyone who's spent five minutes with you can see that." She poured him a fresh glass of water, sliding it toward him. "You've built a life for yourself here, with friends who care about you. That's what matters."

A flicker of gratitude passed over Izzy's face as he accepted the water. "Strangely though...Detective Sergeant Ramirez asked me about who might've wanted to hurt Vernon." He shook his head in disbelief. "I mean, sure, he and Dulcie were having problems. Ruby was angry with him about how he treated her. He and Roy disagreed about business decisions. And Warren..." He trailed off.

Laura's gaze drifted to a stack of papers on the counter—a script for the Silver Springs Players' upcoming performance of The Wind in the Willows. The margins were filled with angry scribbles in red ink.

The lid of the stew pot rattled, and Izzy stood. "Wonderful! Dinner's ready." He moved to the kitchenette, ladling the rich stew into ceramic bowls. The simple action calmed him, his hands steadier as he placed a bowl in front of Laura and set down another across from her. "Sourdough bread?" he offered, unwrapping a loaf. "You know how good Layla's baking at Red Trillium is."

As they began eating, Izzy appeared more relaxed. The stew was delicious—chunks of potato soft enough to cut with a spoon, root vegetables, and a savory sauce.

"This is wonderful," Laura said after several spoonfuls. "You're an excellent cook."

Izzy smiled, but there was something hollow behind it. "Thanks. My aunt taught me. Said a person should know how to feed themselves." He took another piece of bread.

"It seems like you had some good family members in your life, despite the difficulties with your father," Laura said.

"I'm lucky," Izzy said. "When my grandfather and aunt passed on, I found a family here in Silver Springs. That's what made Vernon's death so..." he trailed off, stirring his stew. "Aunty Kayla and Grand-père did everything they could to raise me right. I guess...Vernon continued what they started. Everyone keeps asking what I might've done to him, but Vernon was the only person who helped me feel I belonged somewhere."

"I'm so sorry, Izzy," Laura said. "I know I keep saying that...but I don't know what else to say. Losing someone who meant so much, and then having people question your relationship with him...it's not kind. It's not fair."

Izzy made a strangled sound he tried to cover by shoveling in a mouthful of food.

"But Evelyn, Jasmine and I...we're here for you. You have friends, the Silver Springs Players...people who care about you, who know you for who you are. We're going to set this right."

He managed a smile then, no matter how watery.

"So...if it's alright, may I ask...did you notice anything different about him in the months before his...passing? Anything that might help make sense of what happened?"

Izzy's spoon hovered midway to his mouth. He set it down, his expression guarded. "He was dealing with some personal matters," he said, the words sounding rehearsed. "I...anyway. How's the General Store treating you? Keeping you on your toes?"

Laura smiled, allowing Izzy's deflection, and shared some funny stories from the past few weeks. As she spoke, her gaze landed on a pamphlet sitting on the counter behind Izzy—the logo for Hearthstone Street Legal Services. What was that doing there?

Izzy followed her gaze, then nodded. "Oh, that. Roxanne Beckett gave it to me."

"Beckett? Roy's..."

"His wife," Izzy said. "Hearthstone is her solo practice. Roxanne's always been kind to me." Izzy broke off a piece of bread, dragging it through his stew. "She approached me after rehearsal yesterday, offered some pro bono legal advice...just in case." He sighed. "I hope it doesn't come to that."

The statement hung between them.

⸺◆⸺

The crisp fall air nipped at Laura's cheeks by the time she reached her car. A light breeze swirled fallen leaves in her headlights as she drove out of the park, her mind replaying the evening with Izzy—the trembling hands, the missing photos, the carefully worded responses to her questions about Vernon. Each detail seemed insignificant on its own, but together, they formed a pattern she couldn't ignore.

Izzy's explanation for Vernon's behavior echoed in her mind—so careful, so measured compared to his usually expressive way of speaking. He'd been hiding something, that much was clear. The angry notes on the margins of his script troubled her. Laura had assumed they were from a director, but what if they weren't? What if they were Izzy's frustrated scribbles? The handwriting had been angular, aggressive—red ink slashing across the page. She should've looked more closely. And then there was the peculiar extension—the mismatched pieces from various theatrical productions cobbled together with donations from friends around town. Why start on it now?

Laura slowed as she approached a curve in the road, her fingers tightening on the steering wheel. The lights of the town appeared in the distance, a soft glow against the darkening sky. She passed the 'Welcome To Silver Springs' sign and drove through the quiet streets.

Laura pulled into her designated parking space in the alley behind the Morrison Building and turned off the engine. For a moment, she sat in the quiet, listening to the soft tick of the cooling engine. The questions swirled in her mind like the fall breeze outside her window.

Was Izzy capable of murder? Was someone framing him? Who else had secrets worth killing to protect?

With a sigh, Laura gathered her tote bag and stepped out into the cool night, locking her car behind her. Tomorrow, she'd share what she'd learned with Jasmine and Evelyn.

---

Laura's apartment welcomed her with familiar silence. She flicked on the lights, hung her coat on the rack by the door and slipped off her boots, wiggling her toes against the light warmth of the heated floors—one of the unexpected luxuries of her third-floor apartment in the renovated Morrison Building.

Laura filled her kettle and set it to boil, selecting a tea from her collection. Her mind buzzed with thoughts of Izzy and Vernon and the tangled web of relationships that connected everyone in Silver Springs. The kettle clicked off, and Laura prepared her tea, carrying the steaming mug to her comfortable reading chair. She sipped her drink and let her mind wander through the facts.

Later, she'd changed into pajamas and was turning down her bed when a buzz disturbed the quiet. Her phone, rattling against the wood of the nightstand. She picked it up. It was a text from Jasmine.

"Meet me at the General Store at six-thirty tomorrow morning, before our shift? I have an idea about what we could try next for the investigation."

Laura smiled, typing back: "I'll be there. I have news too."

While she scanned her unread messages, she saw some from her brothers.

From Connor: "Heard about the murder. You okay? I'm here if you need me."

Another from Danny lit up her screen: "Sis! Are you safe? Sending hugs and good vibes your way."

She replied to both. Bedtime, at last. Only for her phone to ring. The caller ID made her stomach clench. Mom. She considered letting it go to voicemail, but Bridget Evans wouldn't take no for an answer.

"Hi, Mom. How are you doing?"

"Laura, thank goodness you answered. I just saw the news online. Another murder? In that little town of yours?" Bridget's voice carried her classic blend of concern and accusation.

"Please don't worry, Mom, the situation is being handled. The police are involved and—"

"First that business at the cheese festival, now this. It's not safe, Laura. You need to come back to Boston."

Laura closed her eyes. "Silver Springs is where I live now, Mom. It's my home."

"Living in some rented flat isn't a home. It's...like you're playing house." The familiar edge crept into Bridget's voice. "And you're...what? Making coffee and chasing murderers?"

"I have a wonderful job managing a café. Plus, I like to help in the community when there's a need—"

Laura could almost hear her mother shaking her head. "By getting involved with dangerous situations? I looked up this Izzy person online. They're saying he's unstable."

The unfairness of it hit Laura like a physical blow. "Izzy is one of the kindest people I've ever met. He's innocent, and he's been treated terribly by people who don't even know him."

Bridget tsked. "See? This is exactly what worries me. You get too attached to these...projects. People who aren't even family. I care about your happiness, sweetheart. I just want you to have a real life. Security. A future."

"I have those things in my life. Perhaps they just look a little different from the version you'd envisioned for me."

After they hung up—with the usual unsatisfying exchange of "I love you" that was more like obligation than affection—Laura stared out her window at the Village Green. She set an alarm and plugged in her phone to charge. Laura slipped between the sheets and comforter, and as she drifted toward sleep, one thing remained clear: someone in Silver Springs was hiding the truth about Vernon Reed's death. And she was determined to uncover it, no matter what Bridget Evans had to say about it.

# CHAPTER NINE

The early morning light was just dawning over the Village Green as Laura unlocked the side door of the General Store. She'd arrived twenty minutes before her arranged time with Jasmine, partly from habit—early rising from years in restaurant management—and partly from anticipation. Laura flicked on the lights, illuminating the familiar space. She moved through her opening routine: bringing in and organizing the pastry deliveries Layla had left in the supply entrance, starting up the espresso machine, humming a favorite song as she worked. The side door opened at six-thirty-two am, and Jasmine hurried in.

"Running a little behind for your meeting, are we?" Laura teased. "Would you like a coffee?"

"Yes please," Jasmine said. "And I'm only two minutes late!" She smiled, setting her bag down, then washing her hands and putting on her apron. "What did you get up to last night?"

"Izzy invited me for dinner," Laura said. She recounted her visit while they continued the morning preparations—filling sugar dispensers, setting out clean mugs, checking the coffee supplies.

Jasmine frowned, arranging pastries in the display case. "It's been so hard for him."

Laura nodded. "That's why we need to sort this out."

Jasmine made a thoughtful noise. "Which brings me to the idea I had last night." She moved to the espresso machine, checking that it was warming up. "The Woodland Watch monthly meeting is tonight at the Good Neighbor Guild's community center. Vernon was a member too. A pretty active one. My friend Leo Nash, who works security at the Medical Center, has been on the board for years. He knew Vernon better than I did, since he's lived here longer."

Laura paused in the middle of arranging napkin dispensers. "So, this would give us an opportunity to connect with people who knew Vernon outside his work?"

"Exactly. It might give us some insight into what kind of person he was, even what he was involved with before his death." Jasmine straightened a stack of saucers. "The meeting's at seven tonight. We should both go, if you're free."

"That's a great idea!" Laura said. "My only question is...am I able to join you if I haven't become a member?"

Jasmine waved away her concern. "As long as I give warning, it should be fine. Especially if you're interested in volunteering sometime."

"I'd be happy to join you," Laura said. "It'd be lovely to become more involved in our community."

"Great! I'll text Leo later and let him know I'm bringing you," Jasmine said. "So, who are our prime suspects at this point?"

Laura leaned in. "Don't you think Ruby seemed almost suspiciously protective of Dulcie? And then there's Warren Fisk—"

"Warren?" Kathy's voice came from behind them.

Laura and Jasmine jumped, turning to see Kathy standing in the doorway that connected the café and retail space to the back rooms, keys in hand.

"Good morning, Kathy," Laura said, trying to sound casual.

Kathy heaved a deep sigh, reattaching her keys to her toolbelt. "Of course you're getting involved in another homicide investigation."

Laura began to deny it. "We're just...trying to make sense of it all."

"Right, you're only curious." Kathy said, arching an eyebrow. "Warren made your list?" There was a glint in her eye as she spoke. "You're in luck. I'm doing a supply run tomorrow—need to restock his cider and review the updated contracts."

Laura blinked. "Are you saying you'd be willing to help us?"

"I'm inviting you along because I could use the extra support," Kathy said, a grin tugging at the corner of her mouth. "Besides, it still falls within your scope of work."

"That would be perfect," Laura said. "Thank you."

Kathy gave a terse nod. "Not fond of how this is shaping up. If there's something I can do, I will." She checked her watch. "I'll be in the stockroom. Give me a holler if you want anything."

As Kathy left, Jasmine raised an eyebrow at Laura. "Looks like you've got two leads to follow now."

Laura followed Jasmine up the gravel path toward the Good Neighbor Guild Community Center, a pale half-moon providing just enough light to illuminate the grassy grounds. Through the windows, around thirty figures moved about, setting up chairs in a large circle.

"Ready to meet the Woodland Watch members?" Jasmine asked, pulling open the door.

Warmth and the murmur of voices greeted them as they stepped inside. The entrance's bulletin board overflowed with announcements for upcoming events from different organisations, with volunteer opportunities and workshops.

"The meeting room is this way," Jasmine said, leading Laura down a corridor. "Leo texted and said he's saved us seats."

The meeting room was a large, open space with exposed beams and walls painted a soft sage green.

"Everyone's taking Vernon's death hard," Jasmine murmured. "He was pretty central to the group."

Laura nodded, scanning the room. She recognized several faces—a postal worker, a teacher from the Silver Springs High School, and a librarian.

In one corner, a small group had formed around a gray-haired woman who gesticulated as she spoke. "He'd promised to lead the habitat restoration project this fall. We'll need to find someone with similar expertise."

"Warren could do it," a man suggested, then grimaced. "Though I doubt he'd want to take over Vernon's pet project."

"Too soon to discuss replacements," another woman said. "Let's give proper respect to Vernon's memory before divvying up his responsibilities."

Jasmine nudged Laura and nodded toward a tall, broad-shouldered man in his late-thirties with close-cropped red hair. "That's Leo."

They walked over, accepting the chairs he'd saved for them.

"Great to meet you, Laura," Leo said, his handshake firm. "Jasmine says you're interested in what we do here."

"That's right," Laura said. "I've been looking for opportunities to get more involved in the community."

"You've picked an unusual meeting to attend," he said, his expression sobering. "We're all still processing Vernon's passing."

Before Laura could react, a middle-aged woman with a clipboard called for everyone's attention. The group quieted, taking their seats. "Welcome, everyone, to our September meeting."

Jasmine leaned toward Laura. "That's Melinda Winrow, the committee chair."

"Before we begin our regular agenda, I'd like to acknowledge we have a guest." Melinda gestured toward Laura. "Jasmine has brought Laura Evans, who manages the café at the General Store. Welcome, Laura!"

Laura gave a small wave as curious eyes turned toward her. "Thank you all so much for having me here this evening."

Melinda nodded. "Now, let's begin with a moment to acknowledge the passing of our valued member and friend, Vernon Reed." Her voice wavered. "Vernon served on the committee for five years and was a member for fifteen. His leadership in the Forest Initiative has been invaluable to our work in preserving local ecosystems."

A murmur of agreement rippled through the group. Laura studied the surrounding faces, noting the varying degrees of emotion—grief on some, polite solemnity on others, and a few neutral expressions.

"Vernon was passionate about protecting our natural heritage," Melinda continued. "He believed economic interests and environmental stewardship could work hand in hand, and he dedicated countless hours to proving that philosophy."

Warren shifted in his seat, his face impassive but his hands fidgeting with the edge of his jacket.

"In honor of Vernon's legacy," Melinda said, "the board has suggested we rename the spring sapling planting event the 'Vernon Reed Memorial Reforestation Day.' We'll vote on this proposal later in the meeting."

As Melinda moved on to discuss the immediate committee vacancy, a few people nodded in approval, while others exchanged doubtful glances.

———— ◦◦◦ ————

Later, the formal meeting adjourned, giving way to the gentle clink of teacups and the rustle of people moving to the refreshment table. It was an impressive spread—trays of homemade cookies, with slices of banana bread alongside the tea and coffee.

Laura accepted a mug of tea from Jasmine.

"This is when the real meeting happens," Jasmine said, nodding toward clusters of members who had broken into smaller conversations. "Come on. Let's chat to Leo."

Leo smiled as they approached. "Hello again."

"I'm so glad Jasmine convinced me to come tonight," Laura said. "I didn't know how much the Woodland Watch does for the community!"

Leo smiled. "That's true...but we all know the real reason everyone comes to these meetings. The treats! Just kidding! We love what we stand for and what we do." He sighed. "Though we're going to miss Vernon's contribution."

"I'm so sorry for your community's loss. Did you know him well?" Laura asked.

"Not particularly," Leo said. "We were on the board together but I wouldn't say we were friends. He was knowledgeable. Passionate. Not the easiest to work with, though."

Before Laura could probe further, a woman in her fifties with dark brown hair and red-rimmed glasses joined their circle. "Laura!" The woman extended her hand. "Anne Hughes, retired biology teacher. I run the Woodland Watch educational programs."

"Nice to meet you," Laura said, smiling, accepting the handshake.

"What brings you to Woodland Watch?" Anne asked.

"I've been looking to get more involved in town," Laura said. "Jasmine has told me great things about what you all do."

Anne nodded. "We can always use fresh faces. Especially now, with Vernon's position to fill." She glanced across the room to where Warren was standing alone, examining a map of conservation areas pinned to the wall. "Though I imagine Warren over there's relieved. One less battle to fight." Her voice lowered. "He must be glad Vernon's gone, given their infamous rivalry. It even spilled into our meetings."

"What do you mean?" Laura asked.

Anne shrugged. "Those two have been at odds for decades." She shook her head. "We had to schedule events to keep them apart."

Leo nodded. "It got worse the last few months."

Anne leaned closer. "A few weeks ago—mid-August, I think—there was a table setting mixup at our planning workshop. Warren and Vernon ended up assigned to the same breakout group. It got...theatrical."

"What happened between them?" Laura asked.

"They started discussing a trail restoration project," Anne said, "but it devolved into accusations about business practices."

"That must've been uncomfortable. Did anyone attempt to intervene?" Laura asked.

"Melinda tried," Leo said. "Warren was on his feet, pointing at Vernon, his face red."

"That's when he said it," Anne continued. "He told Vernon he was 'tired of this decades-long charade' and he'd 'end this rivalry one way or another.' Vernon just laughed it off, said Warren had been threatening him for years and never followed through."

"And when did this happen?" Laura asked.

"Three weeks ago, give or take," Leo said. Those two had been at each other's throats for years."

Anne excused herself and moved away to join in another conversation. Laura and Jasmine stayed with Leo. Across the room, Warren chatted to Melinda, gesturing toward the map on the wall. His hands moved as he spoke. Were those same hands capable of ending more than just a business rivalry?

She nudged Jasmine. "Do you think we should try to have a word with him?"

Jasmine nodded. "Let's just keep it low key."

They made their way across the room, but as they approached, Warren's gaze flicked toward them.

His expression tightened. "Excuse me, sorry, Melinda, I just remembered I need to check on something at the farm."

Before Laura and Jasmine could intercept him, Warren was already heading for the door, shoulders hunched.

"That was...obvious," Jasmine murmured.

Laura watched him leave. "He seems determined to avoid a conversation with us. That fact alone is interesting."

---

Jasmine's car moved along empty streets, the only sound the gentle hum of tires against asphalt and the soft rush of the wind through the trees.

"What a night," Jasmine said. "I've been a member for a while, and I've never heard people talk so openly about tensions within the group."

"It's understandable people are shaken by Vernon's passing," Laura said. She pulled out her phone. "May I quickly call Evelyn? I feel she would want to be updated on this development."

"Go ahead," Jasmine said. "Put her on speaker."

After three rings, Evelyn answered. "Laura? Is everything all right?"

"No need to worry," Laura said. "I'm with Jasmine. We finished up at the Woodland Watch meeting and wanted to share some information with you. And, I should mention, you're on speaker."

"Good evening, Jasmine," Evelyn said. "Tell me, what've you both uncovered?"

"It seems Warren Fisk and Vernon Reed indeed had a significant rivalry," Laura began, glancing at Jasmine. "Apparently, it was more intense than we realized. Anne Hughes, who's a member of Woodland Watch, mentioned just a few weeks before Vernon passed away, Warren threatened to settle the score, and he was tired of their decades-long dispute."

"All that happened during a heated argument at a planning workshop," Jasmine added, slowing the car as they approached a four-way stop. "We had to keep them separated at meetings because they clashed so often. I knew about their professional rivalry but didn't know their conflict had escalated to threats."

The car moved forward again.

"Good grief!" Evelyn said. "That sounds dramatic."

"Though Leo—a friend of mine who's also a member—pointed out they've had heated exchanges for years," Jasmine said.

"It's a detail we shouldn't overlook," Evelyn said. "Was there anything else you learned about Vernon?"

Jasmine hesitated. "Leo mentioned something interesting after Laura stepped away to visit the restroom. Vernon had withdrawn his yearly donation to Woodland Watch without explanation."

"When did this happen? Did he say?" Laura asked.

"Early August," Jasmine said. "It was unusual. Vernon had been one of our most reliable supporters for years, donating money and equipment."

"Did he say why he stopped?" Evelyn asked.

"That's just it—he didn't," Jasmine said, turning onto the alleyway that led to the rear of the Morrison Building. "He just said he wouldn't be making his usual contribution."

Laura frowned. "He might've been having financial troubles?"

"It's possible," Evelyn said.

The car slowed as they approached Laura's building. Jasmine pulled into a parking space, but neither woman moved to exit.

"I'll be accompanying Kathy to Warren's place tomorrow. It's for a routine supply pickup," Laura said. "I'm hoping I might notice something that could be helpful."

"Excellent," Evelyn said. "I'll make a few discreet inquiries into Vernon's finances. A change in donations could signal a shift elsewhere too."

Laura thanked Jasmine for the ride and said goodnight to Evelyn before ending the call. The night air bit at her cheeks as she fumbled with her keys. Above, the stars were obscured by clouds rolling in from the mountains—much like the truth about Vernon Reed, hidden behind layers of small-town secrets she was only beginning to peel back.

# CHAPTER TEN

Laura leaned forward in the passenger seat of Kathy's delivery van. It was a retrofitted microbus gifted to her by her family when she graduated college, and apart from Maggie, of course, her greatest love.

Laura took in the sprawling complex of buildings, making up Fisk Apple Works. It was a far cry from the rustic charm of Goldenleaf Apple Farm. Warren's place resembled a small-scale industrial facility. A large metal building housed the main production area, with gleaming stainless-steel equipment visible through wide windows. Nearby, a second structure—part office, part residence—stood on a gentle rise.

Kathy parked the van beside a loading area. "Vernon and Warren. Opposites in method and temperament."

As they exited the vehicle, a voice called out to them. "Morning!"

Laura turned to see Warren striding toward them from the production building. He wore a checkered flannel beneath a quilted vest, his face creased into a welcoming smile that didn't reach his eyes. "Kathy, right on time, as always." He extended his hand to Kathy before turning to Laura with raised eyebrows. "And...Laura Evans, isn't it? The new café manager? Don't see you on supply runs."

"It's important to me to learn about all areas of the business," Laura replied with a smile, shaking his hand.

His grip was firm, but not overpowering.

"Had a moment of clarity," Kathy said, pulling out her clipboard. "These errands are a logistical mess for one person. Laura stepped up."

Warren laughed. "Smart thinking. No sense throwing your back out when you've got extra hands available." He gestured toward the production building. "Order's ready inside. Follow me."

They trailed Warren into the facility. While Goldenleaf's operation had featured tools passed down through generations, Warren's cidery had modern implements and digital monitoring systems.

"What an impressive setup," Laura said.

Warren's chest puffed. "State-of-the-art. Invested in the juice press system three years ago—cuts energy costs by sixty percent and improves efficiency." He patted a large metal tank. "Cleaner process means purer flavor. Some folks are stuck in the past." Warren led them to a corner where several wooden crates were stacked, each bearing the Fisk Apple Works logo—a stylized apple, unsurprisingly. "Your usual order. Three cases of Honeycrisp, two Gala, two Golden Delicious."

Warren checked items off on his clipboard. Laura, Kathy, and Warren each grabbed a crate before heading to the van.

"I was wondering, how has production been for you recently?" Laura asked as they walked.

Warren's shoulders stiffened. "Production's been normal. The weather's been favorable so far. That's the only thing that has been lately." He sighed as they came to a stop in front of Kathy's vehicle. "The apple industry's been here for generations. One producer, no matter how…prominent…shouldn't change the fundamentals. Supply and demand continue. Nature doesn't mourn."

Laura caught Kathy shooting her a warning glance over Warren's shoulder as she put her crate down. She unlocked the van and opened the back.

"That makes sense," Laura said, loading her crate in.

Warren relaxed. "If you want to understand apple cider production, you're welcome to come to the tours we run. Much more informative than…some other operations in the area."

They collected the rest of the crates.

Warren settled his final crate into place, then did the same for Kathy, offering a few pointers on stacking them for the journey. As Kathy locked the van, Warren brushed his hands on his jeans and nodded toward the office building. "Let's head up to my office to handle the paperwork."

"Right you are," Kathy said.

<hr>

Warren's home-office combination struck Laura as a place designed to impress rather than comfort. They entered through a side door into a foyer with gleaming hardwood floors and walls adorned with framed certificates and industry awards. Not a speck of dust marred any surface, and the faint scent of lemon polish was present in the air—impeccable maintenance that matched Warren's production facility but lacked any sense of personality.

"My office is this way," Warren said, leading them down a hallway lined with more plaques—'Excellence In Agricultural Innovation,' 'Vermont Apple Cider Producer Of The Year,' 'Best In Category, Eastern States Exposition.'

A glimpse into the living room revealed barely used furniture—a sofa, a bare coffee table. No evidence of hobbies or interests beyond the apple business. They all filed into the office, and Warren took a seat behind his desk, gesturing for the two women to take the chairs in front.

"Now, about those contracts," Warren said.

Kathy pulled paperwork from her clipboard. "Maggie's proposed a few minor changes to the delivery schedule, but otherwise, the terms remain the same." She pointed to specific sections as Warren leaned forward.

"Bi-weekly deliveries instead of monthly," Warren murmured. "That could work."

While her boss and Warren talked, Laura's gaze drifted around the office before landing on a large wall calendar above a credenza. It displayed September, with handwriting filling many of the squares. What caught her attention was a date four days ago—the day of Vernon's murder. 'Industry Conference' had been written in black ink, now crossed out, with 'Competing priority' written beneath in blue. Competing priority? On that day? It was vague, a stark contrast to the precise scheduling around it.

On his desk, a cardboard box of promotional materials sat open, revealing glossy brochures featuring 'Fisk Apple Works: Silver Springs' Premier Apple Cider Producer' in bold lettering. The shipping label on the side of the box bore a date stamp from two weeks before Vernon's death. Beside the box lay a pamphlet tucked under a folder: 'Living with Chronic Pain: Burlington Support Network.' Laura's gaze lingered on the pamphlet for a moment. Chronic pain? What could that be about?

The shrill ring of a telephone interrupted Kathy and Warren's discussion.

Warren grabbed it from his pocket and glanced at the caller ID display. His expression changed—a tightening around the eyes. "I apologize. I have to take this. Give me just a moment." He stepped out of the office, pulling the door closed behind him.

Laura waited three seconds, then rose from her chair and moved toward the door.

Kathy's eyes widened. "Laura. What are you—"

Laura raised a finger to her lips and pressed her ear against the thin wooden door.

Warren's voice came through. "Yes, the spiced cider mix. I heard it wasn't as...original as he claimed." A pause. "I'm not surprised people are asking why Vernon went all 'innovative' after decades of tradition."

Kathy stared at Laura, shaking her head, before sighing. Warren's footsteps moved away down the hall, his voice fading. Another door opened and closed—he'd stepped into another room. Laura turned around to resume her position and found Kathy holding up her ever-present notepad. In neat block letters, she'd written: 'I'll pretend I didn't see that.' She gave Laura a wry smile. Laura had to stifle her laughter as she resumed her seat just as footsteps approached the office door.

Warren returned, his expression once again composed. "Sorry about that—supplier issue." He returned to his seat. "Now, where were we?"

They proceeded through the paperwork.

"These look good to me," he said, reaching for a pen from a polished wooden holder. With a flourish, he signed the contract.

As Warren dated his signature, a small collection of framed photographs on the side table caught Laura's attention. One depicted a much younger Warren and Vernon at an apple cider competition. Both held blue ribbons, their free arms slung around each other's shoulders, grinning. The genuine warmth and easy bond in the image seemed impossible, given what she'd learned about their relationship up until recently. What had happened in the decades between that moment and Vernon's death?

⸻◆⸻

The delivery van's tires hummed against the asphalt as Kathy steered them away from Fisk Apple Works, fields stretching on either side of the narrow country road. Neither woman spoke for the first few minutes, the radio playing in the background. Kathy had tuned the radio to her favorite station, Maplewood Airwaves, call sign WMWR, a local community station that played classic rock. The announcer came on after an upbeat song and talked about events for the coming weekend.

Kathy reached over, turned down the volume, and adjusted her grip on the steering wheel. "Worth coming along?"

"Absolutely," Laura said. "I saw on his calendar for the date of Vernon's death, he had 'Industry Conference' scheduled, but it was crossed out. Underneath, he'd written 'Competing priority.'"

Kathy raised an eyebrow. "Interesting timing."

"It makes me wonder. What could've been so significant he'd miss an important event?" Laura asked. "Another thing I observed was a box of new promotional materials on his desk. Brochures claiming his business was Silver Springs' best apple cider producer."

"Plenty of operations inflate their own significance," Kathy said, slowing as they approached a crossroads.

"I see your point," Laura said, "but the shipping label on the box showed they were ordered two weeks before Vernon died. Perhaps...he saw an imminent change in the local cider market?"

Kathy whistled. "Interesting." She signaled for a turn, checking her mirrors. "Warren has never lacked ambition. He and Vernon were locked in that power struggle for what—thirty years? Maybe longer."

Laura nodded. "That's what I keep hearing, but I can't help but wonder how much of it is true. And something else I observed on Warren's desk was a pamphlet for a chronic pain support group in Burlington."

Kathy frowned. "Strange. Never heard he had it, but I wouldn't say I know him."

The van bumped over a patch of rough road before smoothing out again. Through the windshield, Laura could see Silver Springs in the distance, nestled between hills.

"Did you catch what he said on the call?" Kathy asked. "Eavesdropping on our suppliers—bold move. Then again, I can't say I'm surprised."

Laura had the grace to look abashed. "He mentioned a spiced cider mix, saying it wasn't as innovative as Vernon claimed and acted surprised there was a discussion about Vernon's shift to innovation after such a long time keeping to traditional methods."

Kathy's eyebrows shot up. "That mix again! People at the café keep saying it's something to do with Vernon's latest product launch. Rumors are he lifted the idea from someone."

The van slowed as they approached the edge of town.

"One thing I'd like to find out is the truth behind that 'competing priority'," Laura said. "And those photographs in his office? They showed Warren and Vernon as young men, and they seemed to be friends."

"You'd be better off asking Maggie," Kathy said. "I haven't been around long enough to have the full picture."

Laura smiled and redirected her attention to the road ahead. "Two more stops, right?"

Kathy nodded.

———◆———

Goldenrod Roasters, their final stop, occupied one of the renovated spaces in the Old Ashford Lumber Mill at the edge of Silver Springs. On the drive over, Kathy talked about what she'd learned from Maggie about the Mill.

The family had sold their business to a larger company forty years ago, and the new owners moved the operations to their larger facility in another county. The place had fallen into disuse until the Braddocks had bought it, turning it into a series of rentable spaces for artists, small businesses, and community groups.

As Laura followed Kathy through the entrance, the rich aroma of roasted coffee enveloped her—earthy and nutty. This scent originated in the front section, a salesroom lined with burlap sacks of beans, displays of roasting equipment, and shelves packed with various retail blends. The rumble of machinery from behind a large glass partition suggested the day's roasting was well underway.

Samuel 'Sam' Walker, a man in his early fifties, with ash-blond hair in a short ponytail, looked up from the beans he was weighing. His face broke into a warm smile. "Kathy! Right on time." He set aside his scale and addressed Laura, his smile widening. "And you must be Laura! We've spoken on the phone about the General Store orders. It's good to put a face to the voice."

Laura returned his smile. "That's me. It's a pleasure to meet you, Sam."

He turned his attention back to Kathy. "The usual?"

Kathy nodded. "And more of the Silver Springs Breakfast Blend. Flew off the shelves in days."

Sam beamed. "That's what I like to hear." He hefted a box onto the counter, then turned to retrieve another. He stared at the packaging for several moments before letting out a sigh. "I still can't believe what happened to Vernon. This was his favorite blend. Such a shock."

Laura nodded, frowning. "I know, it's just terrible. How well did you know him, if it's alright to ask?"

"Well enough," Sam replied, checking items against an invoice. "He was one of my best customers for years." He paused, correcting himself. "Used to be, I should say."

Laura tilted her head. "I could've sworn you specialized in wholesale. Am I mistaken?"

"I do," Sam said, placing the final bag on the counter. "But I make exceptions for certain customers. Vernon was fond of coffee."

"Really?" Laura asked.

Sam nodded. "Every two weeks, he'd pick up a pound of the Breakfast Blend ground to his specifications. That's why it was so strange when he canceled."

"That seems a little out of the ordinary."

"It is! It happened a few months ago." Sam moved behind the counter, reaching for a notebook. He flipped through several pages. "Called out of the blue, said he didn't like the taste of coffee anymore and wouldn't be needing his usual order."

Laura filed this information away. First the withdrawal from Woodland Watch, now this.

"You're right to go," Sam said, returning to business. "Anything else for today?"

"All squared away," Kathy said. "Thanks, Sam."

⸺⬦⸺

Laura glanced at the clock—ten minutes until her break. The café door opened, bringing with it...Ramirez.

Laura pasted on her most professional smile. "Good afternoon, Detective Sergeant. What would you like to order?"

Ramirez gave a small nod. "Medium black coffee to go, please." As Eli moved to prepare the drink, Ramirez' eyes met Laura's. "Do you have a moment to talk?"

Laura nodded. "Of course. I'm due for my lunch break and thought I'd take advantage of the beautiful day outside if you'd like to join me."

Ramirez accepted her coffee from Eli and gave a nod. A little later, they sat on a bench beneath the apple trees behind the General Store. The dappled sunlight filtered through the branches, creating shifting patterns on the ground. Laura unwrapped her sandwich and took a bite.

Ramirez sipped her coffee before turning to face Laura. "I know you've been asking questions about Vernon Reed."

Laura considered her response. "It's amazing how people talk."

"Especially to the person who makes their morning coffee," Ramirez said. "You've done nothing reckless...yet, so I'm not here to tell you to stop. And...your help was...valuable on the Summer Cheese Festival case."

Laura raised her eyebrows. "Thanks, I appreciate that...I suppose?"

"It wasn't a compliment," Ramirez said, though a hint of a smile touched her lips before her expression turned serious again. "What I am here to say is whoever killed Vernon Reed isn't opportunistic or unassuming. This was premeditated, and that makes the killer dangerous."

"I understand," Laura said. "How are things progressing with the case?"

Ramirez raised an eyebrow. "You know I can't share that with you."

Laura nodded. "I wanted to tell you, there are rumors about Vernon possibly taking Warren's recipe for a spiced cider mix. Have you considered looking into that side of things?"

Ramirez' face remained neutral, but she didn't move to interrupt Laura.

"And I should also mention about three weeks before..." her voice caught, but she continued. "Vernon stopped donating to the local Woodland Watch group and canceled his coffee order with Goldenrod Roasters. He blamed it on not liking coffee anymore. It seems something changed for him."

Something flickered in Ramirez's eyes. "Interesting. How did you come by it?"

"The way news spreads around here, it's no wonder everyone knows everything," Laura said with a small shrug.

Ramirez gave a curt nod. "Just know we're pursuing all credible motives, including the...financial side of things." She finished her coffee and stood. "I appreciate that, and hearing anything else you might learn." She paused. "Come to me directly. Don't try to handle anything yourself."

"Yes, I'll do as you say," Laura said.

As Ramirez walked away, Laura remained on the bench, watching an apple detach from its branch and fall to the ground with a soft thud. The warning settled over her like the dappled shadows from the trees above.

⁕

Stepping through the sliding doors of the Silver Springs Public Library, Laura inhaled the warm, book-scented air. Her shift had just ended, and she was there to pick up the Vermont cookbook she'd reserved last week. At the front desk, Adult Circulation Librarian Joyce Adler helped an older patron find a large-print mystery. Laura waited, her gaze drifting to a bulletin board displaying upcoming events—a poetry reading, an author visit, a workshop on researching family history.

"Laura! So lovely to see you!" Joyce said.

"Hi, Joyce," Laura replied. "I believe you have something on hold for me?"

"No problem at all," Joyce said. "Your library card, please?"

Laura handed it over, pristine compared to her old, well-worn Boston one. Joyce scanned it and retrieved 'Vermont Gatherings: Classic Recipes With A Modern Twist,' its cover depicting a rustic table piled with local foods.

"Excellent choice," Joyce said. "There are some wonderful recipes."

"Thanks for setting this aside," Laura said, slipping the cookbook into her bag. "I'm excited to try them!"

Turning to leave, Laura noticed a display: 'Local History: Exploring Silver Springs' Agricultural Heritage.' An investigative lead she hadn't considered. At six-twenty-five pm, with the library open until nine, she had plenty of time and was already here.

A wooden sign etched with the town's founding date and sliding glass doors marked the Silver Springs Historical Society's entrance in the library's rear. Laura walked through, expecting to see Valeria 'Val' Del Solar, a volunteer, at the reception desk. Instead, an older woman sat there, poring over papers.

"Good evening," Laura said. "I was hoping to do some research tonight."

The woman looked up, her expression brightening. "Good evening! I'm Freya Romano, the Historical Society president. We've not met before. Welcome!"

"Pleased to meet you," Laura said, returning Freya's smile. "I'm Laura Evans. I'm the café manager at the General Store." She glanced around. "Is Val okay? I usually see her here."

Freya sighed. "Not well, I'm afraid. She's feeling under the weather today, so I'm covering her shift. Rarely get to sit at the front desk anymore—too busy with grant writing and preservation projects."

Laura nodded. "Please tell Val I'm thinking of her and wishing her a quick recovery. I'm hoping to learn more about the apple industry in Silver Springs. With the harvest season upon us, I thought it'd be good to understand more about such an important local tradition."

Freya's eyes lit up. "Wonderful! What specific aspect interests you?"

"I'm curious about shifts in the local industry," Laura said, "especially major growers or business relationships that made an impact."

"Perfect," Freya said, coming out from behind the desk. "Follow me."

The older woman led Laura through the doors to the wood-paneled reading room, directing Laura to settle in a chair facing the terminal, from which she could access the digitized records.

"Let me pull some materials for you," Freya said, sitting in the other seat and typing into the search bar. The results returned several files, and she pointed to each. "Here we have a timeline of major developments. This one contains profiles of significant local producers, including extensive documentation of Goldenleaf Apple Farm and Fisk Apple Works' operations."

Laura leaned forward. "People say there's a long-standing rivalry between them. Do you know if it was always like that?"

Freya shook her head. "They were friends, once."

"Do you mind telling me what happened?" Laura asked.

Freya sighed, opening a new window with another search. "It was all rather sudden. These newspaper articles might give you some context...but the only person who'd be able to tell you about it is Warren now."

Laura nodded.

Freya stood with a smile. "Happy researching! If you need any more help, I'm happy to provide."

Laura thanked her and the historical society president exited the room, leaving Laura alone. She scrolled through the digital archives, studying old photographs of Goldenleaf's founding. In one image from thirty years ago, in a newspaper article announcing their partnership, Vernon and Roy stood shoulder-to-shoulder. Both were young and eager, their faces bright with promise. She clicked through to the next series of photos, following the chronology of Goldenleaf's growth. A pattern emerged: as the business expanded, Vernon was pictured among the apple trees, with employees harvesting fruit, or chatting with customers at farmers' markets. Roy appeared less in the orchards and more in the production facilities and behind desks—less the apple farmer, more the business manager.

One article from the Maplewood Memo caught her eye—a business feature from fifteen years ago with the headline: 'Local Apple Operation Expands Distribution Beyond State Lines.' The piece praised Goldenleaf's growth under the 'complementary partnership of Reed's horticultural expertise and Beckett's financial acumen.' Several paragraphs in, among production statistics and expansion plans, was a brief mention of how Roy had 'reduced Goldenleaf's expenses while maximizing investment potential.'

She jotted quick notes, her mind already connecting dots as she continued searching.

# CHAPTER ELEVEN

Early Friday morning, as Laura set up for the day, she smiled as she watched Jesse at work behind the counter. They weren't just listing the day's specials on the large chalkboard, but had added an intricate border of falling leaves. Each leaf danced down the edge of the board, creating a frame for the menu items. Eli stood next to his colleague, warming up the espresso machine.

"That's gorgeous. I love how you've laid everything out," Laura said to Jesse, nodding toward the board.

Jesse glanced up, a smudge of orange chalk on their cheek. "Thanks."

"Wait, a second. Did you draw a little raccoon over there?" Laura asked, spotting a small masked face peeking out from behind the chalk-drawn word 'Specials.' "That's adorable."

"Anton found one trying to break into the trash cans yesterday," Jesse said with a chuckle. "Let's see how long he takes to notice."

As if on cue, Anton emerged from the kitchen. He looked around the café. His eyes narrowed. "Jesse," he said, voice flat but eyes betraying a hint of amusement. "Must you document my every misfortune?"

"Only the entertaining ones," Jesse said, adding a final flourish to the raccoon's whiskers.

Anton sighed and shook his head.

⸺⸺◆⸺⸺

The Friday morning rush at the café had settled into a comfortable lull. Laura wiped the espresso machine, her mind still processing everything she'd discovered in the Historical Society's archives last night. The bell above the door chimed, and she looked up to see Evelyn, Judith, and Martha entering. All three women wore light sweaters against the early fall breeze, and Martha carried her handbag, containing at least one book, a notebook, and her latest project.

"Good morning!" Laura called, setting aside her cleaning cloth. "Your usual table is all ready for you."

"Thank you, Laura," Evelyn said, leading her friends toward the corner table with the best view of the Village Green.

The three women settled in, arranging themselves with the comfortable familiarity of a long-established routine.

Laura approached with a tray of glasses and a jug of water, plus menus tucked under her arm, though she doubted they'd need them. Her shoulders relaxed as she reached their table—these three had become her friends over the past month or so, a welcome constant in her new life in Silver Springs.

"How are you all doing today?" Laura asked as she poured water into their glasses.

"Can't complain," Judith said. "Though my knees try to make me." As always, she'd retrieved her latest puzzle book from her bag, a cryptic crossword open on one page, half-filled in. She was a keen puzzle solver and constructor.

Martha peered up at Laura. "And how have you been since we saw you on Monday? Holding up alright? Especially since that..." She sighed.

Laura set the filled water glasses on the table in front of each woman. "I've been managing okay, thank you. I'm busy with work, of course." Her expression lightened. "I went to the library last night to pick up a book I had on hold."

Martha perked up. "What book did you get?"

"It's called 'Vermont Gatherings'," Laura said. "I've been wanting to learn more about local cooking traditions."

"How wonderful!" Martha clapped her hands. "I've been meaning to read that one. I'll have to put it on hold after you've finished with it."

Laura nodded. She glanced at Evelyn, who'd sat still, her fingers paused on the handle of her water glass. "You've gone quiet, Evelyn. Is something wrong?"

Evelyn blinked, then leaned forward. The other two women moved closer. "I'm fine. You mentioning the library just reminded me of something." Evelyn said, "I headed there last Tuesday—my usual day to exchange my mystery novels—and I saw something rather curious. As I approached the building, Warren Fisk stood at the return chute, shoving a stack of books inside, as if he couldn't get rid of them fast enough."

"Warren?" Judith's eyebrows rose. "Unusual. I didn't think he was much of a reader."

"That's not the interesting part," Evelyn continued. "He was in such a hurry he dropped one book. When he bent to pick it up, I got a look at the spines of the others in his stack. They were about succession planning and guides to writing wills."

Martha frowned. "How odd. Warren doesn't have any children."

Laura made a thoughtful noise. What strange timing. She recalled the 'competing priority' written in Warren's calendar on the day of Vernon's murder. "I should get your order started before Eli wonders where I've wandered off to. The usual for everyone?"

The three women nodded, and Laura left their table with a smile.

---

Laura had just delivered her three friends' orders when the front door flew open. Heads turned as a red-faced man in his sixties charged in, clutching the latest issue of the Maplewood Memo like a trophy. "It's been solved! They know who killed Vernon Reed!"

The peaceful Friday morning atmosphere shattered. Customers lowered their mugs, conversations halted mid-sentence, and necks craned toward the man with the newspaper. Laura froze beside one table, empty tray still in hand.

Someone called, "What's this about?"

"It's all here, front page!" The man waved the paper as he headed toward an empty table near the center of the café. "That theater fellow—the one who's always bouncing around town with his projects. He did it!"

A ripple of gasps and murmurs swept through the room. Two women abandoned their window table to join the man. Within moments, a small crowd gathered around him, pulling chairs from nearby tables.

Did he mean...Izzy?

Laura refocused. Table four looked ready to order, so she grabbed her notepad as voices rose around her.

"—fingerprints all over it—"

"—always seemed unstable—"

"—wonder when they'll arrest him—"

Laura took the order, which was right next to the growing crowd around the man. He'd positioned himself at the center, the paper spread out before him. If she edged past...

"Perfect timing!" The man had noticed Laura's attempt at an escape.

It took all the strength she had not to heave a sigh as she turned her attention to him. She pasted on what she intended to be a bright smile. "Good morning, and welcome. How may I assist you today?"

"We'll need a round of coffees," the man said. "Three regular, one decaf, and do you have any cinnamon rolls left?"

Laura nodded, jotting down the order. As she was about to leave, the man stopped her.

"Say, you're Laura Evans, right? The one who figured out that cheese festival murder?" He didn't wait for confirmation. "You won't need to solve this one." He tapped the newspaper. "Here, listen to this." He cleared his throat and read the headline aloud: "'Murder Weapon

Found: Amateur Actor's Hammer Sealed Victim's Fate.' According to sources, forensic analysis has confirmed the weapon used in the murder of Vernon Reed was a specialized bung hammer belonging to Isaac 'Izzy' Lennox. The hammer, discovered hidden near the crime scene, bears Lennox's fingerprints and traces of the victim's DNA."

Blood drained from Laura's face as the man continued reading.

"Lennox, known for his work with the Silver Springs Players community theater group, has exhibited erratic behavior in recent weeks, according to multiple sources. Kenneth Fraser, director of the Players' next production of 'The Wind In The Willows,' stated Lennox had become 'confrontational' during rehearsals." The man took a breath and resumed. "Fraser further noted Lennox was 'no longer affiliated with the production or the theater group' following a heated disagreement at their last rehearsal before Reed's death. 'His behavior had become unpredictable,' Fraser stated. 'We had no choice but to ask him to take a step back from the production.'" The man looked up at Laura. "He does the deliveries you get from Goldenleaf Apple Farm, right? Did you notice anything off about his behavior?"

Laura stood frozen, notepad clutched in her tight grip.

Jasmine appeared beside her, taking the notepad. "Why don't you check on the pastry situation, Laura? I'll handle this."

Laura nodded, stepping away as Jasmine took over, deflecting the man's questions. Behind the counter, Laura threw herself into the next task, taking deep breaths. She was a former restaurant manager with fifteen years of experience, for goodness' sake! She'd dealt with plenty of difficult customers before! Why was she letting this bother her? Laura had to admit…hearing a friend accused of something so terrible was enough to shake anyone up.

"You okay?" Jasmine asked shortly after, joining her. "That was pretty intense."

"I'm worried about Izzy," Laura said. "This doesn't make sense. I know him—he wouldn't—"

"Let's just hope nothing else happens," Jasmine said. "The Maplewood Memo isn't known for its journalistic integrity. Remember when they were so quick to cast suspicion on Maggie?"

Laura managed a weak smile.

The entrance brought forth Ramirez, who strode toward the counter. "Good morning Laura and Jasmine." She nodded toward the offending newspaper, her jaw in a tight line. "I see Sharon has delivered her verdict. It's convenient how she solved it in less than a week."

"Everyone's talking about it," Laura said.

Ramirez's eyebrow arched. "It's an obstruction. This sensationalist reporting can pressure witnesses, taint potential jury pools, and send my officers chasing shadows based on half-baked theories instead of facts. My phone hasn't stopped ringing. All asking why Izzy isn't in cuffs based on what this rag has printed. Never mind how I have to adhere to due process." She let out a controlled breath. "A black coffee to go, please, Jasmine."

As Jasmine moved to prepare the coffee, Ramirez's eyes met Laura's. "If you…have any credible information…let me know."

Laura nodded.

The bell over the door chimed again as Ramirez left, and Laura looked up to see a woman entering the café. She moved with the confident grace of someone accustomed to commanding attention, her designer business suit and coiffed hair standing out among the casual café patrons. The woman made a beeline for the counter.

"Laura, isn't it?" the woman smiled. "I'm Roxanne Beckett, Roy Beckett's wife."

"Good morning," Laura said. "Lovely to meet you. What will you be having?"

"A latte, please." Her expression softened. "I'm so sorry about poor Izzy's situation. Judging from how the patrons are acting..." She cast a discerning glance around the café. "They've seen the Maplewood Memo's latest issue. Before I went to law school, I trained in accounting. Numbers never lie, even when people and words do. Makes me good at spotting...irregularities." Roxanne leaned in. "You would be...looking into things, wouldn't you?"

Laura tensed as she prepared the latte.

Roxanne nodded. "Then you see things the way I do. Izzy doesn't deserve this. I have some connections in town. I'm trying to...correct any misunderstandings in this case."

"That's very kind of you," Laura said, steaming milk for the latte.

Roxanne sighed. "Things can be so complicated, don't you think? Vernon and my husband had their challenges. And now Nicky has been making such unfortunate choices."

"Did you say Nicky?" Laura asked.

"Our son," Roxanne's smile remained, but something flickered in her eyes. "If only he showed more interest in the business." She accepted the latte Laura handed over and took an appreciative sip. "Excellent, as I expected. Thank you, Laura." Her fingers traced the rim of the cup. "You know, that's why Vernon was so proud to be a vendor at your store. He appreciated the community spirit and dedication to craftsmanship. It's why we got along for so many years. Shared values. The understanding that sometimes tough choices must be made to preserve what matters." She straightened her blazer, glancing at her watch. "I should get back to th e office. Client meetings all day." As Roxanne turned to leave, she paused. "Do let me know if there's anything I can help with? For Izzy's sake. We all want what's best for Silver Springs, don't we?"

<hr>

The fluorescent lights of Northern Necessities cast a harsh glow over the checkout area as Laura fidgeted. Friday evening had brought the typical end-of-week crowd to the supermarket—people stocking up for weekend meals, exhausted parents with restless children, older couples comparing prices.

Laura's basket contained just the essentials: milk, eggs, bread, a package of chicken thighs, and the ingredients for a comfort-food pasta dish she planned to make that night. After the newspaper debacle this morning, she craved the simple normality of cooking dinner.

The line inched forward. Northern Necessities occupied a converted warehouse at the edge of town, its high ceilings and wide aisles giving it the spaciousness of a regional chain with the care of a local business: shelves of Vermont products and staff who knew most regular customers by name. She'd come straight from her shift at the café, hoping to get in and out quickly. The day had been draining, with customers buzzing about the Maplewood Memo's claims.

"Next in line, please," called a cashier at register three.

Laura moved forward, placing her basket on the counter and offering a tired smile to the young woman behind the register.

The cashier—in her early twenties with a short, bleached-blond asymmetrical haircut—looked up. "Hey, aren't you Laura Evans? From the General Store café?" She began scanning Laura's items.

"Good evening. Yes, that's me," Laura replied, reaching for her shopping bags.

The cashier's face brightened. "I thought so! You're the one who solved that murder last month during the Summer Cheese Festival, right? That was amazing."

"And yes, that's right," Laura said as her cheeks flushed.

"Wow, that's so cool." The cashier leaned forward, her voice soft even as she continued scanning. "I saw something the other day that'd interest someone like you."

"Really?" Laura asked. "What is it?"

The cashier glanced over her shoulder before continuing in a hushed tone. "It's about Dulcie Sanderson—she's the manager here. A week before that awful thing happened to her partner Vernon, I saw her in the hardware section testing out hammers."

Laura almost dropped the egg carton she was placing in her bag. "Wait, did you just say testing hammers?"

The cashier nodded, scanning Laura's pasta. "We carry a small selection of tools—nothing fancy, but the basics. She was picking up different ones, feeling their weight, checking their grip. Spent fifteen minutes doing it."

Laura tried to maintain a neutral expression. Dulcie testing hammers just a week before Vernon was killed with one? That had to be just a coincidence, because—

"It may sound only circumstantial, but I think at that point, she was still in the planning phase," the cashier continued, as if she'd read Laura's mind. "Because right before...she did it, she came up with a better idea. She used a hammer from the farm to frame that kid in the paper."

Keeping her features composed was near impossible now. Could...the young woman be right? Surely not. But still...Laura cleared her throat. "That's interesting. How much do I owe you?"

The cashier's shoulders slumped, but she gave Laura the price. Laura inserted her card into the reader.

"And she's been acting strange."

Laura nodded, watching the payment processing screen.

"She always talked about Vernon, you know? Not in a good way." The cashier's voice dropped even lower. "Once I heard her saying he was 'impossible to live with' and 'making everything difficult.' I just figured it was normal relationship stuff, but now..."

The terminal beeped, completing the transaction. Laura removed her card and gathered her bags, appearing only polite rather than focused. "Thank you so much for your help."

"No problem!" The cashier said. "If I notice anything else weird, should I let you know? I mean, since you solve murders and all."

"I'm only a café manager," Laura said, forcing a polite, self-deprecating smile. "If you notice anything else, I'd recommend telling the police."

As she walked toward the exit, her mind whirred. What if she was looking in the wrong direction? She reached her car, and placed her bags in the trunk and closed it, resolved to share this information with Jasmine and Evelyn as soon as possible. And Izzy. She needed to call him. She sat in her car and her eyes flicked back to the street as the ringtone echoed through the cabin.

"Hi, Izzy. Do you have time to talk?"

"Always good to hear a friendly voice." His attempt at cheerfulness fell flat, a weariness underlying his tone.

"I just wanted to make sure you're alright. How are you faring?" Laura asked.

There was a pause on the line. "Not great. The rumors are getting worse, thanks to that article. People look at me differently now."

"I'm so sorry you're going through this. Is there anything at all you need or I can do to help?" Laura asked.

"I'm okay for now," Izzy replied. "Just...don't be a stranger, okay?"

"I won't, I promise," Laura said. "And don't forget, the offer still stands."

After they said their goodbyes, Laura sighed. She had to uncover the truth before anything else happened.

# CHAPTER TWELVE

The quiche sitting in front of Laura looked and smelled delicious—Anton's spinach and salted cheese specialty—but even the rich aroma couldn't distract her from her swirling thoughts.

She was overlooking something...but what?

The buttery crust and creamy filling should've been comforting, but the flavors didn't register as her thoughts tumbled. She took another absent-minded bite. What about Warren and Vernon's old friendship that had deteriorated into fierce rivalry? Had something pushed their competition too far? Or Ruby's protective stance toward Dulcie—what was she hiding? Then there was Izzy. Laura couldn't believe he was capable of murder, but circumstantial evidence could make an innocent person look guilty. Or a guilty person look innocent.

Her phone vibrated on the break room table, making her jump. "Hi, Izzy?" she answered, dropping her fork with a clang. "How are you doing?"

His voice sounded thin and distant. "I've...been better. Just wanted to tell you I won't be seeing you when the deliveries come to the General Store anymore."

"What happened? Why not?" Laura asked.

A heavy sigh crackled over the line. "Got fired this morning. 'Can't keep someone on staff who's under investigation for murder,' and 'customers and vendors are uncomfortable' with me handling their products."

"That's so unfair! The police haven't brought any charges against you! It's just not right." Laura pushed her plate away, her appetite gone now.

"Roy mentioned the article in the Memo. Pointed out the hammer was a company tool. Said I'd lied about my whereabouts the night Vernon died. I tried to defend myself, but he kept repeating 'perception is reality' and 'I have to think of our customers.'" His voice caught. "And he pointed out my...family history, as if I'm just a carbon copy of my father waiting to explode."

Laura drew in a breath through her teeth. "It's ridiculous, Izzy. Anyone who's met you would never think that."

"That's just it," he said, his voice quieter now. "I thought people did. Now I'm getting strange looks in the street. And it's not just Goldenleaf. Kenneth Fraser called yesterday to make it official. I'm out of the Silver Springs Players too. Said my 'recent erratic behavior' and 'missed rehearsals' made me a liability to the production. After five years with them! I built half the sets for The Wind in the Willows myself. I tried to explain, to show him the evidence I was at the theater that night, but..." He paused. "You already knew that, if you've seen the article."

I'm so sorry about what you're experiencing. This is awful," Laura said.

"Theater was my..." His voice broke. "It was the one place I felt like I belonged. The only constant when things got rough." He cleared his throat. "Guess it just goes to show I can only depend on myself."

Laura closed her eyes. The small-town rumor mill at its worst. "Do you have enough to get by for a while?"

"I'll be fine," he said, though he didn't sound convinced. "I've got savings. The extension is almost finished, so at least I don't need to buy more materials. I can look for work in Burlington where people don't know me. Don't worry about me, Laura."

"Izzy—"

"I don't want to keep you. I just wanted to let you know, so you weren't expecting me on delivery day. That's all."

"Wait!" Laura said. "Something just came to mind."

He didn't reply, but he didn't hang up either.

"Kathy and Maggie have some work waiting at the Carriage House—repairs and such. Kathy usually does things herself, but she's been short on time. How about I see if they might take you on for the job?"

Izzy sighed. "I don't want to put Maggie and Kathy in an awkward position."

"Really, you'd be helping them out as much as they'd be helping you. It's been on their to-do list for ages. Let me at least ask them."

Another pause, then a sigh. "Fine. If they say no, I understand. And Laura...thank you."

After they hung up, Laura gazed at her half-eaten quiche. She couldn't eat another bite. She placed it in the fridge and hurried to Maggie's office.

The stairs to Maggie's office were steeper than usual as Laura climbed them, rehearsing her pitch in her head. Pausing at the landing, she inhaled and knocked on the wooden frame. She'd convince her boss. She had to.

"Come in," Maggie said.

Laura pushed the door open to find Maggie hunched over her computer, and her boss looked up. "Laura. Is everything okay?"

"I'm alright. I just wanted to ask you something," Laura said, stepping into the room. "Do you have time now?"

Maggie nodded and gestured for her to sit.

"It's Izzy and the situation he's in."

Maggie's expression shifted. "What about him?"

Laura struggled to keep herself in check. "Izzy just told me he lost his job at Goldenleaf Apple Farm, all because of what's in the Maplewood Memo. He's worried no one else around here will hire him after this."

"That's terrible," Maggie said. "But I don't see how—"

"I remember you and Kathy mentioning the Carriage House needs repairs," Laura continued. "Izzy has great woodworking and construction skills."

Maggie stared at her. "You want us to hire him?"

"It wouldn't have to be a long-term option, just until he finds something steady," Laura said. "He works hard, and he could use some help right now."

Maggie leaned back in her chair, fingers drumming against her thigh. "Laura, I appreciate your concern for him, but the General Store is a business that depends on its reputation. We can't afford to be associated with a murder suspect, especially not when the evidence seems so—"

The door opened, and Kathy stepped inside. "Maggie, really?"

Maggie blinked. "Kathy, what—"

"Izzy just texted. He's been fired," Kathy said with a heavy sigh. "And here you are, rationalizing why we can't help?" She moved further into the office, closing the door behind her.

"My love, it's not that simple," Maggie began.

Kathy shook her head. "You know what this feels like. Small-town pitchforks, rumors flying, everyone convinced you're a killer."

Maggie's face paled. "That was different."

"Was it?" Kathy asked. "Because it happened to you and not to someone else?"

Laura's attention bounced between her bosses. Maggie looked down at her desk, lips pressed into a thin line.

"We look after our own," Kathy said. "And Izzy is one of them. He didn't kill Vernon. Not a chance."

Maggie's shoulders sagged, and she rubbed her temples. "What if we lose business?"

"And if we gain it?" Kathy said. "You didn't inherit this place to turn your back when people need you. Your grandmother wouldn't have hesitated."

That struck home. Maggie was quiet for a long moment. "That's...true. Alright, then. But we keep it low-key. He can start on Monday with the interior work in the Carriage House, away from the customers."

Kathy nodded. "I'll message him the specifics."

"And," Maggie added, her tone firmer now, "if anything else comes out that makes his situation worse—"

"We'll reevaluate." Kathy leaned over the desk to kiss her wife's forehead. "The result will be worth it."

Maggie had to smile at that.

⸺⬥⸺

The Timberline Tavern was abuzz with activity. Live music night at the tavern was a Silver Springs tradition, with the crowd a mix of families, young couples, and groups of friends settling in for the evening.

"What a great crowd! I didn't expect to see so many people," Laura said as she and Jasmine, who'd invited her out that evening, entered the building.

"Every second Saturday," Jasmine said with a smile. "I love all the local bands."

The tavern's interior embraced its name with timber beams crossing the ceiling, polished wood tables, and a long bar crafted from a single piece of solid wood. At the far end, someone had set up a small stage area, where a man and woman adjusted microphones and tuned guitars.

"Let's see if we can find a table," Jasmine said, scanning the room. "They fill up fast on music nights."

As Laura followed Jasmine's gaze around the tavern, she froze. There, at the bar, sat Izzy. He was hunched, fingers wrapped around what looked like whiskey. Laura's stomach dropped.

"I just spotted Izzy over there," Laura murmured. "I'm going to see how he is."

Jasmine glanced over, her eyes widening. "No, we're both going. What on earth is he doing?"

They made their way through the crowd, weaving between tables and nodding at a few regulars they recognized from the café. Izzy looked up as they approached, his expression tensing before relaxing into a tired smile.

"Now, Izzy—" Jasmine began.

"Before you ask," he said, "it's ginger ale. Non-alcoholic."

"I wasn't going to—" Laura said, then stopped herself. "Okay. I was wondering."

"I know. It's fine." Izzy glanced around the busy tavern. "Clyde's one of the few people in town who hasn't treated me differently since the article. He helps the Players build sets. He's always been good to me."

As if summoned, Clyde Hastings, the tavern owner, appeared behind the bar, setting a bowl of soft pretzels in front of Izzy. He was a short guy in his fifties with grey hair and laugh lines around his eyes. "On the house." He noticed the two women and gave Jasmine a nod. "Evening, Jasmine. Who's this you've brought with you?"

Jasmine introduced Laura, and they exchanged greetings.

"I hope you enjoy music night. It's always fun," Clyde said before moving to serve another customer.

Laura turned back to Izzy. "Jasmine and I are going to grab a table by the window. Would you like to join us? The first band should start soon."

Izzy poked at the pretzels and shook his head. "I appreciate the offer, but I'm better off keeping to myself tonight."

"Izzy—" Laura began.

He held up a hand. "Laura, you've done enough for me today. Got me a new job within less than twenty-four hours. It means a lot." He nodded toward where the last few empty tables were. "Go. Enjoy the music. I'll be fine he re."

"Alright," Laura said. "If you need company later, we're here." Leaving Izzy alone made her uneasy, though she didn't want to impose. She shook herself a little and drew the attention of a bar attendant. "Can we please open a tab?"

The bartender nodded. "What would you prefer?"

"I'll have a burger and a soda," Jasmine said.

Laura ordered the same meal and a root beer. They took one of the few empty tables left over near the window, and the first musicians took the stage to scattered applause.

Laura nodded along, letting the music wash over her as the duo on stage began a folk rendition of a song she recognized. Despite her worry for Izzy, there was something comforting about the tavern's atmosphere—the ease with which conversations flowed around them, the appreciative nods at skilled guitar riffs, the sense that Saturday night would unfold at an unhurried pace.

⋅◦⋅

The second band had just finished their set, and Laura was halfway through her burger when the tavern door opened. A young man in his mid-twenties with neat, cropped curls stepped inside. There was something familiar about him—the set of his shoulders, pale skin, the tall, slight frame—but Laura couldn't place where she'd seen him before.

"That's Nicky Beckett," Jasmine said, following Laura's gaze with perhaps a little too much interest. She smoothed down her box braids and straightened her posture.

"Roy's son?" Laura asked.

"The same," Jasmine said. She studied Nicky for a moment as he made his way toward the pool tables. "This is an opportunity we shouldn't miss." Before Laura could respond, Jasmine was already half out of her seat, waving to catch his attention.

Nicky paused. His expression flickered between recognition and hesitation before he changed course and approached their table. A slight strain appeared around his mouth when he attempted a polite smile. "Hi Jasmine."

"Hi," Jasmine said, breathless. "Nicky, this is Laura Evans—she manages the General Store's café. Laura, this is Nicky Beckett." She lingered over his name like she enjoyed saying it.

"It's nice to meet you," Laura said, extending her hand.

Nicky's shoulders rose to his ears, but he tried to straighten, and accepted the handshake. What a strange...reaction. Had he...heard about the investigation?

"Same. You make a mean latte, according to my mom," Nicky said.

"That's high praise from Roxanne," Jasmine said, leaning forward with a bright smile. "Join us? We've got the perfect view of the stage for the next set." She gestured to a vacant chair at their table. "Order a drink if you like. Next round's on me. I owe you one. I mean, if you want t o."

Nicky glanced at the pool tables, where a game was still in progress. He shrugged. "That's kind of you, thank you. I could use a drink."

He headed up to the bar and returned a little later with a craft beer from a brewery in Burlington. His shoulders relaxed as he settled into their table, tapping his fingers against the wooden surface in time with the background music playing between acts.

"Kindling Company is up next," Jasmine said for Laura's benefit, nodding toward the stage where a trio was setting up instruments. "They do folk and bluegrass covers."

Nicky's gaze lingered on the musicians. A wistful expression crossed his face as the guitarist tested the microphone with a few muted chords. "I could've been up there. If things had gone differently."

Jasmine tilted her head. "What things?"

Nicky startled. He took a gulp of his beer. "Did pretty well in music back in school. I played guitar, some piano, and went to college for it."

Jasmine's eyes lit up. "I'd love to hear you play sometime. I mean, if you ever perform anywhere." She tucked a braid behind her ear.

"Maybe someday," Nicky said.

"But you didn't pursue it?" Laura asked.

"No one makes any money being a musician," Nicky said, the words sounding practiced, as if he'd repeated them many times. "Dad was thrilled when I came back to work at Goldenleaf Apple Farm. Everyone says how lucky I am to have something to come back to, a family business with my name on it." His fingers traced circles in the condensation on his glass. "I'm not so sure."

"Is the work not your thing?" Jasmine asked.

Nicky stared into his beer. "It's good work. Pays well. Stable." He shrugged. "Just not what I pictured for myself, you know?"

"What's stopping you from pursuing music now?" Laura asked.

Nicky shifted in his seat, his gaze sliding away from hers. "It's complicated." He took another long drink, then set his glass down with a thud. "Like everything else."

Laura nodded. "I'm so sorry about everything that's happened. It's been such a difficult time."

Nicky sighed. "It's been...strange for all of us. Complete shock."

"I can only imagine how tough it's been," Laura said.

Nicky's lips twisted. "If I'm being honest, some people are happy about it. Vernon wasn't the easiest person to work with. And it had gotten worse."

"Worse, in what way?" Jasmine asked.

Nicky sighed. "The last few months, he was different. More secretive. Aloof. He'd always been particular about operations, but he was shutting himself in his office, having private phone calls."

Laura exchanged a glance with Jasmine.

"And around three months ago, he started taking these business trips to Burlington," Nicky continued. "Every other Friday. Dad didn't go with him, which was weird, because they always handled major business dealings together. When I asked about it, Vernon said it was 'routine maintenance of business relationships' and changed the subject."

"Did he ever mention who he was meeting with?" Laura asked.

Nicky shook his head. "Never."

The band started playing then, a lively fiddle tune that made conversation more difficult.

Nicky glanced toward the pool tables and straightened, noticing his potential opponents signaling to him. "Looks like there's a free spot. Thanks for the drink. It was nice meeting you, Laura."

"You too," Laura said. "And don't give up on your music."

Nicky smiled. "Yeah, well...responsibilities, you know? Can't always do what we want." He reached for his wallet. "Let me pay for—"

"This one's on me, I've got it," Jasmine said.

Nicky huffed, then smiled, and this time, it reached his eyes. "Thanks, Jasmine. I'll see you both around."

"See you," Jasmine said, her voice quieter than usual.

She watched him walk away toward the pool tables before turning back to Laura with a sheepish expression.

"Don't say a word," Jasmine said, though she was fighting a grin.

"I wasn't going to say anything," Laura said. "Just you seemed...interested."

Jasmine shook her head, but her smile gave her away. It faded as her brow furrowed. "I'm telling you, Vernon was hiding something. What do you think he was doing in Burlington?"

Laura drank some of her root beer, her mind already racing with new possibilities. "We'll see."

The evening's third band had packed up their instruments, and the tavern crowd had thinned by the time Laura and Jasmine called it a night. They approached the bar, Laura fishing her wallet from her bag.

"Heading out already?" Clyde asked. "The night's still young."

"We'll pass," Jasmine said, smiling. "Some of us actually have to be awake and pleasant in the early morning."

"Fair enough." Clyde took the bill and began tapping on the register. "Enjoy the music?"

"It was wonderful," Laura said. "I had no idea Silver Springs had such talent."

"We're full of surprises," Clyde said with a wink. "That's why I started these nights three years ago. It gives the local musicians somewhere to play and keeps business steady." He glanced toward the door. "I saw you chatting with Nicky Beckett earlier. Nice kid. Has a good ear for music."

"He mentioned that," Laura said. "Said he studied music in college."

Clyde nodded. "Shame he gave it up for a position at Goldenleaf Apple Farm. But family businesses are complicated—take it from someone who inherited his dad's tavern." He ran the credit card Laura handed him. "Speaking of Goldenleaf drama, this place has been the hub for it."

Laura's ears perked up. "How so?"

"Couple weeks before—" Clyde glanced around and lowered his voice, "Before Vernon's death, he and Roy had quite the heated discussion right over there." He nodded toward a corner table. "I don't make a habit of eavesdropping, you understand, but when voices rise, it's hard not to notice."

"What were they disagreeing over?" Jasmine asked.

Clyde handed Laura her card back. "Something about 'the future of the business.' Roy kept saying, 'After thirty years, we deserve better than this,' and Vernon just kept shaking his head." Clyde shrugged. "Business partnerships are like marriages—sometimes they hit rough patches. Though that wasn't the strangest thing. About two weeks before...you know...Vernon was in here with someone I didn't recognize. City type, with a briefcase and everything. Had this unusual copper pin on his tie, shaped like a book, I think."

Laura tried to keep her expression neutral. "A business meeting?"

"Must've been," Clyde agreed. "They had a pile of papers spread out between them. Vernon looked...intense. Not angry, but focused. Dead serious." He straightened up, resuming his normal voice. "Anyway, thanks for coming. Always nice to see new faces enjoying music n ight."

"We'll be back," Jasmine said. "Thanks for everything, Clyde."

As they walked toward the door, Laura glanced back at the corner table Clyde had indicated. Who had Vernon been meeting with? And what was in those papers that had him looking so serious?

"So, what's your take?" Jasmine asked as they hurried to her car parked down the block.

"That gives us two new clues to work with," Laura said.

They reached Jasmine's silver car. Once inside, she turned on the engine and pulled away from the curb, the familiar hum of her compact SUV filling the comfortable silence between them. As Jasmine approached the alleyway at the back of the Morrison Building and parked, Laura gathered her things.

"I'll see if I can find out more about these Burlington trips," Laura said. "Evelyn might know something."

Jasmine reached over and gave Laura's arm a gentle squeeze. "Just be careful, okay? We're getting closer to the truth, and whoever killed Vernon won't want it uncovered."

Laura's lips curved into a smile as she opened the car door. "Thanks for tonight."

She stepped out and headed toward the building's back entrance, glancing back once with a small wave.

# Chapter Thirteen

Monday morning, Laura approached Evelyn's apartment door and rapped her knuckles against the wood. The scent of vanilla and cinnamon wafted down from her flat upstairs.

"Evelyn? It's Laura. Breakfast time!"

The lock clicked, and the door opened a fraction to reveal Evelyn in her dressing gown. "Hello Laura!" Evelyn's dark brown eyes sparkled. "What a lovely morning greeting. What's this about breakfast?"

Oscar's head popped out from behind Evelyn's shins, attempting to squirm past.

"Really, Oscar," Evelyn said, pushing him back. "A little decorum, if you please."

Laura bent down to give him a scratch under the chin, which only made him fight harder against Evelyn's grip.

"If you keep it up, there'll be no stopping him!" Evelyn said, smiling.

Laura laughed and stood. "I hope you haven't had breakfast yet because I'm just about to make pancakes."

Evelyn's face brightened. "That's so kind of you! And just when I was about to settle for scrambled eggs. Pancakes sound like a far better idea." She stepped back into her apartment. "Give me fifteen minutes."

"Everything looks wonderful," Evelyn said, settling into a chair. She'd changed into a dark green blouse and charcoal slacks, her silver-white bob styled. It'd been an effort to get her to sit without helping with the breakfast preparation, but she'd given in, at last. "Thank you very much for having me."

Laura placed the plate of pancakes down and retrieved the coffeepot, returning to fill two mugs. "I hope you're hungry."

"Famished," Evelyn said, accepting the mug with a grateful nod. Steam curled above the dark liquid. "This is just what we need before heading to Goldenleaf. Now, where are we with the investigation?"

Laura served pancakes onto their plates before taking her seat. "Jasmine and I attended Music Night at the Timberline Tavern on Saturday." She drizzled maple syrup over her stack. "And we saw Nicky Beckett there."

Evelyn added a dollop of jam to her pancakes and gave a shake of her head. "That boy."

Laura looked at her. "What is it?"

She shrugged. "He likes to be called Nicholas. If you're waiting for him to tell you that, you'll be waiting a long time."

Laura blinked a few times. "Jasmine introduced him as Nicky, though. He didn't correct her."

Evelyn added a dash of cinnamon to her pancakes before taking a bite. "If Nicholas lacks anything, it's the ability to stand up for himself."

"I should...call him Nicholas then?" Laura asked.

Evelyn nodded. "He won't say it himself, so it's left to us. So, what were you telling me?"

"According to...Nicholas, Vernon started taking regular trips to Burlington around three months ago—every fortnight," Laura said, cutting into her pancakes.

Evelyn set down her coffee mug. "Peculiar timing. It feels like a significant change occurred for him."

Laura leaned forward. "Exactly! It lines up with other changes in Vernon's behavior—withdrawing his annual donation to Woodland Watch, canceling his regular coffee order with Sam at Goldenrod Roasters."

Evelyn nodded, motioning for her to go on.

"He told the other staff they were business trips, but he was secretive about them. Nicholas said Vernon called them 'routine maintenance of business relationships,' but wouldn't elaborate. What's strange is that nobody went with him, not even Roy."

"Now, that's something to consider." Evelyn took a bite.

Laura nodded, setting down her fork. "There's more. When Jasmine and I paid, the owner, Clyde, he mentioned seeing Vernon meeting with someone he didn't recognize about two weeks before he died. He described them as a 'city type' carrying a briefcase and said they had documents spread out between them."

Evelyn's eyebrows rose. "A business meeting?"

"Perhaps," Laura said. "Clyde also said he overheard Vernon and Roy having a heated argument. Roy said they deserved better after thirty years." She took another bite of her pancakes, then reached for her coffee. "And there's the spiced cider mix. During my visit to Warren's farm with Kathy, I overheard him on the phone. He seemed convinced Vernon had stolen the recipe."

"Several potential motives are emerging," Evelyn said. "Money troubles, possible stolen ideas, secret gatherings...yet still so many things unanswered."

"Exactly! We don't know why Dulcie was testing hammers," Laura said. "Or why Ruby is so protective of her."

Evelyn looked up. "This case is becoming more complex by the day."

Laura set her fork down with a sigh. "There's something else. Izzy called me yesterday. He's been fired from Goldenleaf because of the accusations in the Maplewood Memo."

A knot formed in her stomach. Izzy had been so kind when she'd moved to town. Seeing him punished for something he hadn't done made her blood boil.

"Good grief," Evelyn said. "And how is he managing?"

"About as well as to be expected," Laura said. "I got him some work with Maggie and Kathy, doing some finishing jobs on the Carriage House. The only good thing about all this is he'll have income while this blows over."

"That was thoughtful of you," Evelyn said.

"It was the least I could do," Laura said. She wrapped her hands around her coffee mug. The memory of his voice breaking over the phone still echoed in her mind, and she sighed. "And the Silver Springs Players have removed him from their production. Kenneth Fraser, the director, kicked him out, citing missed rehearsals and 'erratic behavior'. Izzy was devastated—said the theater was the one place he felt he belonged."

Evelyn's expression softened. "Yes, I saw the article. Theater groups can be rather...dramatic, even offstage."

"I need to find out what happened there," Laura said. "Something's not adding up."

Evelyn dabbed at her lips with a napkin. "I know someone who might help. Liz Andrews serves on the Silver Springs Players committee. She's a retired drama teacher who's been with the group since its inception."

Laura's eyes brightened. "Could you introduce me?"

"Better than that," Evelyn said. "The costume department is forever in need of an extra hand. Can you hand sew?"

Laura nodded.

"Splendid! I'll ring her and let her know you're free for the next rehearsal. You'll likely meet the actors, though the costume team is the chattiest lot of all. She'll understand your schedule if I explain."

"That'd be perfect," Laura said. "Thank you."

"I'll call Liz this afternoon," Evelyn said. "Though you should prepare yourself—theater people can be protective of their own."

"I'll be subtle," Laura said.

Evelyn nodded. "What we need is more direct information. And now we have a plan to get it."

<hr>

The road leading to Goldenleaf Apple Farm revealed golden-hued orchards, their branches heavy with ripening fruit against the clear blue September sky. Laura's small blue car hummed along the familiar route. The dashboard clock read eight-twenty-eight am—perfect timing before the day's operations kicked into high gear.

"It's been years since I've visited Goldenleaf Apple Farm," Evelyn said. "It's such a shame I'm returning under these circumstances." She set her face in a determined line. "We will be the ones to figure out what happened."

Laura pulled into the parking area. Several vehicles were already there—Roy's four-wheel drive with the Goldenleaf logo painted on the door, a couple of employees' cars, and a delivery van. No burnt orange pickup truck. Her chest tightened.

"Ready?" Laura asked, turning off the engine.

Evelyn nodded, gathering her handbag. "Remember our cover story—we're here about the historical items Vernon promised to loan for the 'Harvest Season' library exhibit."

"Right," Laura said, opening her door. "And I'm accompanying you because you need the help."

Evelyn stared at her for a second, a twinkle in her eye. "Need? I assure you, I'm a spritely sixty-eight-year-old! I only asked you along because I enjoy your company."

Laura laughed as they stepped out of the car. In the distance, figures moved about the cidery, and closer, a worker emerged from a storage shed, their arms laden with supplies. Everything appeared to be operating normally, despite the loss of one of the farm's owners.

"This is the perfect opportunity to gather more information about Vernon's behavior in the months prior to his death," Laura said. "We should pay attention to Roy's reaction when we mention the Burlington trips."

"Indirectly, of course," Evelyn said. "Perhaps a casual mention of the exhibit featuring the history of apples growing throughout Vermont, including Burlington, should do the trick."

Laura smiled. "Good idea."

* * *

As they approached the office, there was movement inside. The old porch creaked under their weight as they climbed the steps.

"Evelyn, Laura," Roy greeted them as he ushered them in. "What brings you to Goldenleaf this morning?"

Roy's office spoke volumes about the current state of Goldenleaf Apple Farm. What had once been an orderly space now showed signs of hasty reorganization. Files piled up in precarious towers, Vernon's nameplate still sat on the adjoining desk though his chair had been pushed against the wall, and a calendar with multiple crossed-out appointments. Roy was as disheveled as his surroundings, his normally neat appearance undermined by dark circles beneath his eyes and a coffee stain on his flannel shirt front.

Evelyn stepped forward. "Good morning, Roy. Forgive the interruption. We're here regarding the historical pieces Vernon offered for the library's 'Harvest Season' showcase. I understand if this isn't a good moment—"

Recognition flickered across Roy's face. "Yes, of course." He gestured toward a cardboard box sitting near the door, labeled 'Library Exhibit,' in precise handwriting. "Vernon had everything ready to go. He was particular about what pieces would best represent Goldenleaf's heritage."

Laura studied the box. "You remembered the exhibit? That's thoughtful, given everything you must be managing now."

Roy's shoulders slumped, a sigh escaping him. "Keeping up with Vernon's commitments is...challenging. He kept records of everything, thankfully." He moved to the box, running a hand along its edge. "We'd been business partners for thirty years, but I'm still discovering projects he had in the works. The man never slowed down." His fingers fidgeted with a heavy ring on his right hand—a college ring. "Everything has been difficult lately, with..." Roy trailed off as he straightened a pile of bank statements on his desk.

"I can only guess how hard this transition must be," Laura said. "My life felt like that after my maternal grandmother passed away. So many things she'd left unfinished."

Roy nodded. "That's it. Vernon had his way of doing things. Some mornings I come in and just...stare at his empty desk." He gestured to the abandoned workspace.

There was a photograph on the wall—Roy and Vernon, much younger, standing in front of the cider house.

"How long had you two been working together?" Laura asked.

"It would've been thirty-one years this spring," Roy said. "Vernon had the family land and traditions. I had the business degree and marketing ideas." A ghost of a smile crossed his face. "We were going to revolutionize Vermont apple products."

"And indeed you have," Evelyn said. "Goldenleaf's reputation extends far past Silver Springs."

Roy leaned against his desk, arms crossed. "Vernon was the heart of this place. His passion for quality, for tradition..." He trailed off, his gaze drifting toward the window where the cider house was visible in the distance. "Though, he'd been...different."

Laura inclined her head.

Roy debated whether to continue, then sighed. "More secretive. Less present. He started questioning everything." He twisted his ring. "Thirty years of mutual trust, and suddenly he needed to verify my every decision. It hurt."

Laura nodded, trying to look sympathetic.

"And for someone who had never missed a production day in three decades, suddenly he was taking regular time off. Trips to Burlington every two weeks to visit his mother. After avoiding her for years, these visits became a priority."

"Family reconciliations can happen," Laura said. "Especially as people get older."

As she spoke, Laura couldn't help but wonder what had prompted the visits. Was it just family ties, or was there something else in Burlington that required his attention?

"True," Roy said, shrugging. "Vernon was never one to discuss personal matters."

Evelyn leaned forward. "Thank you for assisting with the exhibit. The library is excited about featuring Silver Springs' apple growing heritage. Such a rich tradition you both helped continue."

Roy's expression darkened. "Traditions matter in this business. Innovation without respect for the past leads to trouble. Vernon understood that. At least, he used to."

Evelyn nodded. "We're grateful you've honored Vernon's commitment to the library exhibit. It'll mean a great deal to the community."

Roy gave a solemn smile. "The community meant everything to Vernon. More than—" He paused as his phone chirped with an alert. Pulling it from his pocket, he glanced at the screen, his expression shifting. "I'm sorry. I forgot about meeting with a manufacturer. They're making equipment that will streamline our bottling process in town. I'm already late." He ran a hand through his hair, further disheveling it. "Thank you both for coming."

Evelyn collected her things, and Laura picked up the cardboard box. Roy ushered them out of the office, locked the door behind them, and sped off.

They reached the parking lot by the time Roy had gotten into his four-wheel-drive and started the engine.

Laura put the cardboard box in the car, making a show of arranging it in the back seat. Then she raised her hand in a friendly wave as she got into the car. Roy offered a distracted return of the gesture, reversed, and pulled forward with more speed than caution would suggest, disappearing down the driveway toward the main road.

Once he'd gone, both women looked at each other.

Evelyn stroked her chin. "Why would he say business to some, and family to others?"

"Maybe they're a cover for something else," Laura said, glancing toward the visitors center. "Ready for part two of our plan?"

Evelyn nodded. The September sun had climbed higher in the sky, though the morning air still held a hint of fall crispness as they walked back toward the main buildings. They entered, and Nicholas stood behind the front counter. He looked up, his expression shifting from professional welcome to recognition upon seeing Laura.

"Laura, wasn't it? Good morning." His gaze shifted to Evelyn, a polite smile forming.

"Morning, Nicholas," Laura said.

The reaction was immediate. He almost choked on something non-existent, startled by the sound of his full name, and stared at her. Then a ridiculous smile blossomed across his features. Laura hid hers. Amazing, the power of calling someone what they preferred.

"We just spoke with your father about some items Vernon had promised to the library," Laura said.

"Right. The exhibit box." Nicholas said, spluttering. He wore the Goldenleaf Apple Farm uniform—a green shirt with the company logo embroidered on the pocket—but somehow made it look rumpled.

"I'm guessing you already know Evelyn," Laura said, gesturing to her companion.

"Everybody does," Nicholas said, extending his hand. "It's good to see you."

Evelyn shook it with a warm smile.

"Did you find everything you needed with my father?" Nicholas asked.

"We did, thank you," Evelyn said. She glanced around the visitors center. "I was just telling Laura that despite living in Silver Springs most of my life, I've never taken a proper tour of Goldenleaf Apple Farm. Though this has been a terrible situation for your family and the business. I understand if tours aren't operating right now."

Nicholas sighed. "We're...still figuring things out. Dad's keeping everything running as normally as possible, but...I'm not sure when—or if—regular tours will begin again this season. We're still getting our feet un der us."

Disappointment crossed Evelyn's face, though Laura suspected it was at least partially manufactured. "Of course. I should have realized. Perhaps another time, then."

Nicholas glanced around the empty visitors center, then at his watch. His expression brightened. "While you're here, I could give you a quick look around if you'd like. Nothing fancy, like our usual tours, but enough to see the basics of the operation."

Evelyn looked surprised. "I couldn't impose—"

"It's nothing," Nicholas said. "Dad's off at a meeting. The senior employees don't start until nine, and I doubt anyone will come in here in the next twenty minutes. Nothing to do here except rearrange these apple caramels to make them look 'more appealing to impulse buyers,' whatever that means."

"If you're certain it's no trouble," Evelyn said.

"None at all," Nicholas said, moving toward a door. "We'll just do the abbreviated version—cider house, pressing room, bottling area. Should only take fifteen minutes."

"That would be wonderful," Evelyn said. "Thank you. I've always been curious about how the process works."

Laura caught the gleam in Evelyn's eye—this was what they'd hoped for. An opportunity to see more of the operation, perhaps speak with other employees.

———◆◦◆———

The production area of Goldenleaf Apple Farm hit Laura with a wave of sensory information—as it had last time—the sweet scent of fresh apple juice, the steady hum of equipment, and the massive press that dominated the center. Workers moved between stations, checking gauges, adjusting valves, and monitoring the transformation of apples into amber cider, sweet and hard.

"We harvest from about two thousand trees," Nicholas said, leading them along a marked pathway designated for visitors. "Some varieties are picked early in the season, others will ripen later, giving us a steady supply through November."

An older man looked up from a control panel and nodded at Nicholas. "Morning, Nicky. Showing folks around?"

Nicholas winced at the use of his nickname, resisting the urge to heave a sigh, but maintained a polite smile. "Just a quick tour, Casey. This is Evelyn Chan and Laura Evans from the General Store café."

Casey tipped his cap to them. "You picked a good day—first major pressing of the season, and the sugar content in these early varieties is excellent."

"Does that mean things are going well?" Evelyn asked.

"Better than average," Casey replied. "Higher sugar content makes for better cider and means less work in the fermentation process for our hard cider varieties."

Laura studied the press, watching as the apples moved through the crushing and pressing stages, releasing their juice. "How long does the process take?"

"From tree to bottle, about twenty-four hours for a batch this size," Nicholas said. "It takes twenty pounds of apples to make a gallon of cider." He guided them toward the far end of the room, where the bottling area was separated by a glass partition. Two women operated a small-scale bottling line, filling and capping decorative glass bottles with the amber liquid. "That's our specialty packaging line. Standard bottles go through a larger operation in the next building, but gift sets and limited editions are handled here."

One woman glanced up and smiled. "Just finishing the remainder of the special reserve Vernon set aside before—" She stopped, her smile faltering. "Well, you know."

"Special reserve?" Laura asked.

The woman nodded. "He'd been experimenting with a spiced cider mix. Something about fermenting the cider with specific spices to create unique flavor profiles."

Nicholas cleared his throat. "That's part of what Dad's meeting is about today—figuring out if we can continue the new product line without..." He sighed. "So much has changed so fast. All these weird things happening..."

"So many things! Vernon had been coming in at the strangest hours these past few weeks," the woman said. "Sometimes I'd arrive early and find him already here, going through papers in his office. Just staring at them and making notes. Never seen him so interested in the admin side before."

Nicholas shrugged. "My dad usually handles all that."

The door from the hallway banged open, cutting him off mid-sentence. Ruby stood in the doorway, her expression shifting from purpose to shock.

"Nicky!" Ruby called, striding toward them. "I was looking for you." Her gaze hardened as it settled on Laura. "What are they doing here?"

Nicholas screwed up his face and straightened. "I'm giving Evelyn and Laura a quick tour of the facility. Evelyn is interested in learning about the process for—"

"Enough," Ruby said. "You two are sticking your noses where they don't belong."

Laura maintained a neutral expression despite her surprise. "Ruby, there's been a misunderstanding. We're just here about the library exhibit items and—"

"Save it," Ruby snapped. "Things are bad enough with Vernon gone. Need I remind you we had to stop production for a day so Ramirez and her team could question every one of us? And don't get me started on the media! They're hassling everyone, especially Dulcie." Her voice cracked. "The last thing we need is amateur detectives stirring up more trouble."

Nicholas stepped forward. "Ruby, I don't think that's fair. They haven't asked anything inappropriate."

Ruby turned on him. "Maybe not, but if Roy finds out, he won't be happy his son is indulging people who are sniffing around where they aren't welcome."

The production room had grown quieter, workers casting sideways glances while pretending to focus on their tasks.

Evelyn touched Laura's arm. "We should go. We've imposed enough on Nicholas' time."

"That's right," Ruby said. "Get out if you want me to stay quiet about this." She stepped closer to Laura. "And don't come into the yarn store while I'm working. I mean it."

Laura nodded, turning to Nicholas. "Thank you for the tour. It was very informative."

Nicholas looked torn. "I'm sorry about this. Let me walk you out."

"That won't be necessary," Ruby said.

⸺⬦⸺

They raced toward Laura's car. As soon as they jumped inside, Laura started the engine and sped out of the parking lot, back toward town. Evelyn exhaled a long breath.

"Ruby's reaction was out of proportion. She's hiding something." Laura sighed. "So much for talking to the Goldenleaf employees."

Evelyn tapped her fingers against the dashboard. "Her reaction confirms we're asking the right questions. And she mentioned Dulcie again—she seems protective of her."

"Protective enough to threaten us," Laura said. "Which makes me wonder what Dulcie knows Ruby is so desperate to hide."

"Perhaps," Evelyn said, "it's time we stopped reaching Dulcie through intermediaries."

Laura groaned. "Ruby made us promise not to go to her house, and we agreed."

Evelyn nodded. "Let's think about that. We shouldn't let this spoil the rest of your day off."

# Chapter Fourteen

Evelyn's characteristic simple elegance was reflected in the lunch she'd prepared. After they'd returned from Goldenleaf and dropped off the items for the library exhibit, Laura had wanted to get straight back into the investigation. Evelyn had insisted she take the morning to recenter, and they'd discuss it over lunch. Laura had tried to relax, doing her crochet project and listening to an audiobook...her mind wouldn't stop turning everything over. It was still working overtime as they ate leftover chicken and broccoli pasta bake, complemented by a salad.

"I can't believe we went all that way just to be chased off by Ruby," Laura said after several mouthfuls. Like everything else Evelyn cooked, it was delicious. "It feels like we're going in circles."

Evelyn paused. "I wouldn't say it was fruitless. We confirmed Nicholas' story about Vernon's Burlington trips contradicts Roy's explanation for them. And we learned about Vernon's spiced cider experiments from that worker."

"That's true," Laura said. "I just wish we could've learned more before Ruby showed up."

"Ruby's reaction was telling," Evelyn said, reaching for her water glass. "People rarely respond with such hostility unless they're protecting something—or someone."

Laura nodded. "You're right."

Evelyn sipped her drink. "How do you plan to spend the rest of your day off?"

"I'm attending the Maplewood Woolgatherers meeting this afternoon," Laura said, brightening. "Beverly invited me last week when she came into the café. Once she discovered I like crocheting, she thought I might enjoy seeing what they do."

"The Woolgatherers? What a wonderful idea," Evelyn said. "They're a lovely group—skilled artisans, all of them. Beverly has been spinning her own yarn for decades."

"Do you attend?" Laura asked. "I didn't realize you were a member."

Evelyn chuckled as she reached for the bread. "I'm what they call an honorary member. My Monday afternoons are reserved for Mahjong at the Silver Springs Senior Center. I've been playing with the same group for ten years. I tried convincing Martha to join me, but the weekly bingo club happens at the same time."

Laura smiled. "I hope you win a round. While I'm there, I'll work on my project and untangle our investigation. Crochet helps me think—something about the rhythm of it seems to organize my thoughts." The mantel clock in Evelyn's living room chimed once, and Laura glanced up. "I should head out soon. The Woolgatherers meeting starts at two-thirty, and I want to stop by Red Trillium Bakery to pick up some cookies to t ake."

"Beverly has a particular weakness for apple walnut sticky buns," Evelyn said. "Layla usually has them on Mondays."

"Thanks for the tip!" Laura said. She finished the delicious pasta bake and gathered their dishes. "And thank you for lunch."

"My pleasure," Evelyn said, rising too. "Let me know if you hear anything…interesting at the meeting."

Laura smiled as she carried their plates to the kitchen. "I'll keep my ears open. With any luck, I might pick up a new skill and a new lead all in one afternoon."

---

Beverly's two-story home sat on Hill Street, its pale yellow exterior brightened by flower boxes filled with late fall blooms. Laura climbed the steps to the porch, balancing a box from Red Trillium Bakery in one hand while adjusting her tote bag with the other.

The door swung open a minute after she knocked, and Beverly stood in the entryway, her white hair pulled back in a loose bun, wearing a hand-knit sweater in varying shades of purple. Her face broke into a wide smile. "You came! How wonderful!" She stepped back to let Laura inside. "And you brought treats? You didn't have to do that, but we'll enjoy them. Thank you."

"Apple walnut sticky buns from Red Trillium," Laura said. "Evelyn mentioned they're your favorite."

"Evelyn knows me too well," Beverly said with a laugh. "Come in, come in. Everyone's already settled in the living room."

Laura followed Beverly through a hallway lined with framed photographs of Vermont landscapes and Beverly's fiber creations—intricate weavings in natural colors and textures.

The large living room was arranged for comfort and function, with several armchairs and a long sofa positioned to capture natural light from the large bay windows. There were about ten people, settled in the space, each engaged in some form of fiber art. The room hummed with conversation and the rhythmic sounds of spinning wheels, the soft click of knitting needles, and the thump of a small loom being worked in the corner. Skeins of yarn in every conceivable color filled baskets around the room. A floor-to-ceiling bookcase housed not books, but cubbies of sorted fleece, roving, and prepared fibers, their natural hues ranging from creamy white to deep chocolate brown, with some dyed vibrant colors. The air carried the faint, pleasant smell of lanolin and herbal tea.

"Everyone," Beverly said, setting the box of buns on a side table, "I'd like you to meet Laura Evans. She's Evelyn's friend who's interested in learning to spin."

All eyes turned toward Laura, some faces lighting with recognition, others with polite curiosity.

A woman with dyed bright red hair and nimble fingers spoke first. "You're the General Store's café manager! Your lattes are divine."

"Thank you," Laura said, feeling a touch of warmth in her cheeks.

Another woman, working at a small loom in her lap, paused her movements. "Any friend of Evelyn's is welcome here. We enjoy it when she can make it."

"Which is rare," Beverly said with a grin. "Nothing comes between Evelyn and her tiles."

A middle-aged man with chestnut-brown hair looked up from his latch-hooking. "Take a seat anywhere that looks comfortable, Laura. We're an informal bunch."

Laura nodded. She scanned the space, absorbing the various activities: two women carding wool by hand, another spinning on a small, portable wheel, and yet another working with tiny needles on the finest lace Laura had ever seen. "I brought Red Trillium's sticky buns." Laura gestured to the box Beverly had set down. "Apple walnut."

The woman with the portable spinning wheel perked up. "Delicious. Thank you!"

Laura stood for a moment, unsure where to situate herself.

"Laura will sit with me," Beverly said, returning to Laura's side. "I promised to teach her the basics of drop spindle spinning. It's more beginner friendly than the wheel." She gestured to an empty cushioned chair beside her setup.

The group returned to their activities and conversations as Laura made her way to the indicated chair, setting her bag down beside it. The rhythm of the room enveloped her—wheels turning, shuttles passing, needles clicking, voices murmuring.

"Is this your first time trying any fiber arts?" asked the silver-haired knitter as Beverly gathered materials.

"I crochet," Laura said, "but I've never tried spinning before."

"You'll love it!" the woman said. "It's fiber magic."

Beverly handed Laura a wooden drop spindle and a cloud of soft blue fiber. "We'll start with the basics. By the end of the afternoon, you'll be making your very own yarn." She settled into her chair beside Laura, the wooden drop spindle with its whorl and shaft balanced in her palm like an elegant toy top. The blue roving—a term Laura now understood meant prepared wool with the fibers loosely aligned, ready for spinning—rested on Beverly's lap.

Laura nodded, watching as Beverly manipulated the tool. "You make it look so easy."

"That's the beauty of it," Beverly said. "People have been spinning with tools like this for thousands of years." She tore off a small section of the blue roving and showed how to attach it to the spindle's leader thread. Her fingers pulled and teased the fibers into a consistent thickness.

"This is called drafting. You want to pull out just enough fiber at a time to create an even yarn. Too much, and your yarn becomes thick and lumpy. Too little, and it becomes too thin and breaks." She held the fiber with one hand while the other sent the spindle spinning with a flick. "The twist travels up into the fiber and creates your yarn. You control how far the twist travels by pinching above it."

The spindle dangled and twirled, looking as if it were dancing in midair. Laura watched, fascinated, as the unstructured fluff transformed into a coherent strand.

"Now you try," Beverly said, stopping the spindle and handing it to Laura. She tore off another piece of the blue roving and passed it over. "Feel it first—get to know your fiber."

Laura took the soft mass between her fingers with a slight lanolin scent that reminded her of specialty hand creams. The blue was variegated—ranging from sky to deeper navy. Following Beverly's instructions, Laura attempted to draft a thin section of fiber while setting the spindle in motion. The spindle wobbled as it rotated, and her drafted fiber section was inconsistent—thick in some places, thin in others.

"It's falling apart," Laura said as the spindle came to a premature halt, her uneven yarn lacking sufficient twist to hold together.

"That's normal," Beverly assured her. "Everyone's first yarn looks like that. Here, let me show you again."

From across the room, the knitter called out, "When I did it the first time, I thought I was spinning yarn, but I invented a new form of abstract sculpture! Keep going."

Laura laughed, the tension easing from her shoulders as she tried again. Beverly guided her hands, showing her how to pinch and control the fiber supply while maintaining a consistent draft.

"Let the spindle do the work," the man doing the latch hooking suggested. "Don't fight it."

On her third attempt, Laura created a short length of consistent yarn before the spindle touched the floor.

"Good!" Beverly exclaimed. "Now wind that onto the spindle shaft and keep going."

Laura followed the instruction, proud of her small accomplishment. Each attempt brought improvement.

Later, Beverly and the knitter went into the kitchen, bringing back a tray bearing an ornate teapot and vintage cups and saucers, while others cleared space on the central table for people's contributions for afternoon tea.

"These sticky buns look marvelous," said the woman who had been working at the loom, opening the Red Trillium box. The rich aroma of cinnamon and apples filled the air.

"Layla outdid herself as always," Beverly said, pouring steaming tea into cups.

Laura accepted a teacup and saucer painted with delicate blue cornflowers. She bit into a sticky bun, savoring the spiced apple sweetness.

"Ginny, show everyone what you found at that estate sale in Burlington," the man said.

Ginny reached inside her bag and took out a small wooden tool with metal teeth. "A genuine Victorian wool picker, perfect condition. The family didn't know what it was—thought it was some kind of kitchen implement."

Appreciative murmurs followed as people passed the tool around for inspection. The conversation flowed, touching on upcoming fiber festivals, a new sheep farm outside town, and the best methods for setting dye colors.

"Speaking of color," said a woman with curly gray hair, "did anyone else see Ruby and Dulcie having a heated discussion outside Northern Necessities yesterday? Ruby's face was the same shade as her name."

Laura paused mid-sip of her tea.

"I saw that too," said the loom weaver. "Around noon, wasn't it? Ruby looked like she was about to explode."

"What were they arguing about?" asked Ginny, selecting a second cookie.

The curly-haired woman shrugged. "I couldn't hear much, but Ruby kept gesturing with her hands—you know how she is—and Dulcie just stood there with her arms crossed, shaking her head."

Beverly nodded, refilling their teacups. "Ruby can be dramatic, but it's not surprising they're both stressed, considering what happened to Vernon."

"Everyone connected to Goldenleaf is under tremendous pressure right now," the man said. "Between the police investigation and keeping the business running during harvest season…it can't be easy."

"Vernon had been acting strangely in the months leading up to his death anyway," said Ginny, her knitting needles resuming their clicking. "I sometimes saw him in town, and he'd gone down at least a size in clothing."

"He'd been rather odd," the woman with the spinning wheel said, lowering her voice, "did anyone hear about Izzy's situation?" Without waiting for anyone to answer, she continued. "Apparently, Vernon turned down his request for a raise last month, even though Izzy was practically running half the production line."

"That seems unfair," Beverly commented, drafting her wool. "Especially since Goldenleaf has been flourishing, though given what's just come to light, I'm not surprised."

"Money troubles make people desperate," Ginny murmured. "He's been living in that same little caravan for years, while everyone else at his level has moved on to better things."

"Vernon's always been tight with money," Beverly said.

Laura focused on her drop spindle, careful not to react. Was it significant? Or just ordinary workplace friction? The timeline was becoming clearer: something had changed for Vernon around June. The conversation shifted back to lighter topics. Laura took part, but her mind remained fixed on this new information.

◆◇◆

Later that evening, needles clicked and gentle conversation flowed around Evelyn's living room, where the members of the Maplewood Crafters Club had settled into their usual spots. Oscar, Evelyn's dark-brown Burmese cat, had claimed Laura's lap, while his bluish-gray brother Monty observed the proceedings with a regal detachment from his perch on the windowsill.

"That's where we stand," Laura said, picking up her mug of chamomile tea. "We've gathered plenty of rumors and circumstantial evidence, but we can't seem to get close enough to anyone at Goldenleaf to verify anything. Ruby's made it her mission to keep us away from Dulcie."

Evelyn nodded. "It's frustrating because Dulcie is our best source of information about Vernon's personal life and recent changes in behavior."

Martha leaned forward, setting aside the embroidered napkin she'd been working on. "What we need is someone who can get into Goldenleaf without raising suspicions. Someone with a legitimate reason to be there asking questions."

"Someone not connected to Laura or Evelyn," Fran said. "Since Ruby's already warned the staff about you two."

Christopher set down his mug. "I might have a solution. Given I run The Whittled Word..."

"I know!" Jasmine said from her window seat perch. "You could do a memorial piece about Vernon!"

"That would give you legitimate reason to interview everyone at Goldenleaf," Evelyn said, her eyes brightening.

Christopher nodded. "I've featured local businesses before, and Vernon was a notable figure in Silver Springs. A tribute article would seem natural."

"Would you be comfortable doing that?" Laura asked. "Using your newsletter for our investigation?"

"Sure," Christopher said. "The Whittled Word might be small, but people around here trust it. I've always tried to highlight the best of our community—and helping solve this terrible situation qualifies." He pulled out his phone. "I'll call Goldenleaf first thing tomorrow morning to set up some interviews."

"This is brilliant," Martha said. "No one would question Christopher asking about Vernon's life and work for a memorial piece."

"And since Ruby doesn't know you're working with us on the investigation, she won't be on guard," Fran said.

Christopher's expression grew serious. "I'll need to be careful how I phrase my questions—keep them appropriate for a tribute while looking for anything unusual. What specific information should I focus on?"

"Changes in Vernon's conduct in the months preceding his death," Evelyn said.

Laura nodded. "And his relationship with others at Goldenleaf. Also, anything about his trips to Burlington or that spiced cider mix."

"Got it," Christopher said, making notes on his phone. "I'll say I want to capture the full picture of the man behind Goldenleaf's success—his recent projects, aspirations, and relationships with colleagues. All reasonable for a memorial article."

"Well done," Evelyn said. "We need all the information channels we can get."

"The spiced cider mix!" Judith said. "I've been hearing rumors about it being a product Vernon was working on, which seems odd, considering his focus has always been pure apple cider. The more concerning rumor is that he stole the idea from someone else."

"From Warren Fisk?" Laura asked, recalling his phone conversation.

"That's what I thought," Judith said, her eyes narrowing. "I've also heard it might've been someone from outside Silver Springs."

"That could explain the secretive Burlington trips," Jasmine said. "Meeting with the actual creator of the recipe."

Martha shrugged. "Perhaps."

Judith's eyes widened. "I saw Roxanne Beckett entering the Maplewood Memo office recently. Marched straight past the receptionist as if she owned the place!"

Martha raised an eyebrow. "And this is related to the investigation...how? Besides, Roxanne specializes in business law, handling legal matters for several local businesses. She was probably there on behalf of a client. You know that!"

Judith conceded, not without adding, "I never did like that woman. She always seemed...strange."

Fran straightened. "I might have an answer to the...Dulcie situation. I walk Gus every evening around Mossridge Nature Preserve and often see Dulcie walking her dog. You could come along."

Laura nodded, jotting down the details. "Perfect. Between Christopher's interviews at Goldenleaf and our 'chance' encounter with Dulcie, we should break through this information barrier."

"Speaking of that..." Judith said, not looking up from her knitting. "I've been doing some...reconnaissance."

"What?" Martha asked, a warning tone in her voice.

Judith smiled. "Let's just say I might have something substantial to share soon." She met Laura's questioning gaze with a secretive wink.

"Just be careful," Christopher said. "And that goes for you too, Laura."

"Me? Not careful?" Judith scoffed. "I'm just an old woman who's in the right places at convenient times. No one pays any attention to someone my age."

Laura reassured Christopher, but her mind was elsewhere. Tomorrow would bring revelations. She was certain of it.

# CHAPTER FIFTEEN

Laura slipped out the General Store café's back door, headed across the courtyard toward the Carriage House. It stood at the rear of the property. A two-story structure that had once housed carriages for the original Brook's Inn, it was now renovated into living quarters for Maggie and Kathy. As Laura approached, she could hear a rhythmic thud inside. She knocked on the door as she stepped into the entryway. The repeating thunk stopped, and footsteps approached from the adjoining room.

Izzy appeared in the doorway, a fine layer of sawdust dusting his pants. "Hey, Laura! Come on in—just mind the drop cloths."

Laura navigated her way around stacks of materials and tools. The air smelled of fresh cut wood and paint. The main living area was mid-renovation, with installed crown molding and half-completed wainscoting along one wall. He was half-way through the skirting-boards around the wall edges.

"How's it going?" she asked.

Izzy nodded, setting the nail gun on a workbench. "Keeping my hands busy helps keep my mind off...other things. Kathy had all the materials ready to go. She knows what she wants—makes my job easier."

"It looks beautiful," Laura said.

Izzy wiped his hands on a rag tucked into his back pocket. "Thanks for coming by. Checking to make sure I haven't fled? Good news is I haven't. Don't plan to."

"No, I wasn't checking up on you like that," Laura said. "I wanted to see how you were doing. That article in the Maplewood Memo was—"

"Character assassination?" Izzy said with a wry yet strained smile. "Yeah." He turned back to the wall where he'd been installing the skirting boards. "This helps. Having somewhere to be, something to do. Appreciate Maggie and Kathy taking the risk."

Laura tried to lighten the mood. "I'm going to get a book I ordered from Mountainside Stories. I thought I'd check if you needed anything while I'm out."

Izzy huffed a laugh. "I swear, Laura, at this rate, I'm going to lose track of how many favors I owe you. Still...since you asked. I'm running low on these finishing nails." He handed her a small box. "Ashby Hardware should have them. I'd go, but..."

"I get it," Laura said.

"Appreciate it, thank you."

Laura tucked the box into her bag. "No problem at all. Anything else?"

Izzy shook his head. "Nope, that's it." He picked up the nail gun again, settling it in his hand. "Better let you get to it—lunch breaks don't last forever."

He measured a piece of skirting board, the concentration on his face as he marked the cut line with precise movements. His steady hands contradicted the Maplewood Memo's depiction. Izzy might be enthusiastic and over-excitable, but unstable? Violent? She couldn't see i t.

He saved even the smallest wood scraps, setting them aside rather than discarding them. She remembered the careful way he'd portioned their dinner that night at his caravan—generous enough to be hospitable but with no excess. The patches on his clothing. The way he'd mentioned repairing rather than replacing his ancient truck. Was this frugality by nature or necessity?

"I'll be back with those nails," she said, heading toward the door.

"Thanks, Laura." Izzy's voice followed her.

<hr>

She'd jumped the first time she'd entered Mountainside Books, three weeks ago. It was on the Morrison Building's first floor, and she'd been there to order a hardcover collection of the Sherlock Holmes stories. As soon as the doors opened, a cheerful man's voice had announced: "You made it! Now let's get lost—in a story." Even stranger, she'd seen no one else inside the shop.

It was Jay Wilson's signature greeting, triggered by a motion sensor above the door—just one of the bookshop co-owner's charming eccentricities. The recorded greeting played as she entered, making a few browsing customers smile. Laura loved the place's character—the oak shelves that reached toward the stamped tin ceiling, the rolling library ladders that creaked when moved, and the handwritten recommendation cards tucked beneath select titles. Jay had preserved the original medical office features when converting the space—the built-in cabinets that once held medical supplies now displayed special editions, and the examination room had become a reading nook.

The shop featured an ever-changing soundtrack of nature recordings mixed with classical pieces. Today's selection was birdsong accompanied by violin concertos.

She approached the counter, looking around for Jay. He remained unseen, yet his appearance was inevitable.

"Excuse me," Laura called out. "I'm here to—"

"Perfect timing!" Jay said in his New Jersey accent as he rose above the counter and drew himself up to his full height, a tall six-feet-four-inches. He wore his signature paint-splattered overalls, and despite being indoors, an emerald green trapper hat. "Good on you for not keeping your book waiting any longer."

"I got your message," Laura said. "I wasn't expecting it until next week."

Jay nodded with a grin. "It couldn't wait to meet you, of course!" He held up one finger and vanished into the back room with long, loping strides.

"Does he always talk about books like they're alive?" asked a customer browsing nearby.

"Always," replied another.

Jay returned carrying not just a book but a small paper bag with the Mountainside Books logo stamped on it. "Here we are! Just retrieved from the Booklovers Vault—which my husband Trenton insists on calling 'the cluttered back room.'"

Laura couldn't resist smiling. "Thank you. I've been wanting a copy for so long."

"Sir Arthur Conan Doyle. A giant among mystery writers! 'The Speckled Band' is the best, in my expert opinion," Jay said with a wink. "Though 'The Red-Headed League' comes close. I've read them all at least a dozen times."

Laura laughed. "You've read it?"

"Every mystery that passes through these doors gets a thorough inspection from yours truly." Jay tapped his temple. "A vital part of running this establishment, of course." He handed her the paper bag. "And this is a little welcome-to-the-bookstore gift from Trenton and me."

Laura opened the bag to find a small, handmade booklet—filled with nature photographs. 'Silver Springs Through the Seasons,' the cover read in elegant typography, with 'Photography by Jay Wilson' beneath it.

"These are breathtaking," Laura said, flipping through images of mist-shrouded mountains, close-ups of apples ripening on branches, and shots of the creek reflecting the sunset. "I didn't know you were a photographer."

"Amateur enthusiast," Jay said. "I believe in documenting the world from unexpected angles. Trenton's the real artist—he made the bookmark."

Laura looked down, seeing a thin package beneath the small booklet. She unwrapped it to find a printed bookmark on a thick cardstock with a literary-themed design. "This is too generous."

"Nonsense. Good customers deserve good treatment," Jay said.

Laura slipped the book, booklet, and bookmark into her bag. "Thank you, Jay."

<hr>

"If it isn't Laura!" Pete's voice boomed from behind the counter of his hardware store. "What brings you in today?"

"Hi, Pete, how are you? I need these nails, if you have them." Laura held up the empty box Izzy had given her.

Pete took the box, examining it. He turned it over and paused, his thumb running across a faded pencil mark on the bottom. Something flickered in his expression. "Two-inch galvanized finishing nails," he said, already moving toward the fasteners section. "Follow me." Pete navigated the crowded aisles, stopping at a wall of bins. "Here we are." He scooped up what he was looking for and directed her to follow him back to the counter. "Working on a project at your place?"

"Just replacing what the General Store ran out of," Laura said with a smile.

Pete studied the box again. "Interesting. I remember this box." He tapped the pencil mark. "Sold it last week to Izzy Lennox."

Laura hesitated a moment too long. "What a coincidence."

Pete sighed as he told her the amount. "Not much of a coincidence in a town this size."

Laura set her bag on the counter. "Is something wrong?"

"These are for skirting boards, aren't they?" Pete asked. "At Maggie and Kathy's place? I heard they hired Izzy for renovation work."

Laura blinked. "How did you—"

"Small town," Pete said, shrugging. "And I know my nails. These are for trim work." He rubbed his jaw. "Look, Laura. I feel like I should mention something that's been bothering me."

Surely he wouldn't talk about the Maplewood Memo accusations. Those were just rumors. She nodded and motioned for him to continue.

"Three days before Vernon was killed, Izzy came in here. He bought an axe, a handsaw, a splitting maul, and specialized wood chisels. Paid cash—over three hundred dollars, all in twenties."

Laura waited, sensing there was more.

"Now, I know he does woodworking," Pete continued. "That's not what concerned me. It was how he acted. Kept checking over his shoulder, asked if I'd seen Vernon lately—which struck me as odd since they work together. When I asked what the project was, he got evasive." Pete's frown deepened. "Then he asked me about weight-bearing requirements for different woods, and whether oak could 'hold up under pressure.'"

Laura's stomach tightened. "That...could mean anything."

"True," Pete said. "But combined with him asking about Vernon, and the way he kept looking at his phone like he was expecting a call...maybe I'm overthinking it. Izzy's a good kid. But that day felt different."

A crash from the back room interrupted their conversation, followed by a muffled "Sorry!" that could only belong to Ben Ashby, a youth in his early twenties, and Pete's son. He emerged a moment later, his expression brightening when he spotted Laura.

"Laura! Great to see you," he said, setting the box down with a thud. "Wait, Dad—you're not telling that story again, are you?"

Pete's face reddened. "Ben, I was just explaining—"

"Dad, you know how fast stuff gets around," Ben said. "Blink and everyone's heard it."

"It's Laura, though," Pete said, and Ben had to concede the point.

Laura gave an abashed smile. "If I might ask...what happened?"

Pete sighed. "It wasn't intentional. Maisie Watkins came to pick up an order for her husband, and she asked how business was. When she mentioned the murder, I said something about having an 'unsettling interaction' recently. I never gave details." His shoulders sagged. "But Maisie kept pushing. I should have kept my mouth shut, but I mentioned it involved someone who worked at Goldenleaf."

Ben's expression softened, gaze directed at Laura. "And Maisie put two and two together and of course she went straight to the Memo about it."

Pete nodded. "By the time the story came out, my 'unsettling interaction' had become 'suspicious behavior' and 'damning evidence.' I never said he was guilty of anything! I was just...concerned."

"Next time you're 'concerned,' check in with the person first, okay?" Ben said, shaking his head in a mixture of fondness and exasperation.

Pete nodded before flashing a sheepish smile at Laura, handing her the nails. "I hope...whatever happens, it gets solved soon. Let me know If I can help."

"Thank you, Pete," Laura said, as she put the box in her bag. "Enjoy the rest of your day, the both of you."

Ben waved and rolled his eyes behind his father's back.

She walked toward work. The nails were a small weight in her bag, but Pete's information was a heavier burden. Could what had happened...mean anything? Surely not. She'd prove Izzy's innocence.

Laura pushed open the door to the Carriage House. In her absence, Izzy had made impressive progress—the skirting boards now lined the entire north wall. The gentler sound of sandpaper on wood had replaced the nail gun's distinctive rhythm as Izzy knelt in the corner, smoothing a seam where two pieces met.

He wasn't alone.

"Laura," Ramirez said with a curt nod. "We were just finishing up." She closed her notepad, her expression unreadable.

Izzy's gaze remained focused on his work, his neck stiff.

Laura tried not to look...anything, really. She pasted on a polite smile. "Good afternoon, Detective Sergeant. I was just...delivering some finishing nails Izzy needed."

She clamped her mouth shut. Now Ramirez would sense Izzy didn't feel comfortable around town. Would she interpret that as a sign of incessant rumors, or...further evidence of suspicious behavior?

Like the excellent police officer she was, Ramirez gave nothing away. She just nodded. As she was about to exit, she paused at the doorway. "Izzy has been helpful in clarifying certain timeline discrepancies." Her tone carried a warning edge. "I trust you'll both continue to be forthcoming if we have additional questions." She didn't give either of them a chance to reply as she left.

Izzy sighed deeply as he set aside the sandpaper, looking up at her.

"Is everything alright?" Laura asked. "Did she—"

Izzy shook his head. He didn't look shaken or distressed, just...thoughtful. She hadn't given him the ninth degree, at least. "Just needed a few clarifications on my work history, Vernon and Roy's business relationship, the rivalry he had with Warren..." He trailed off, shaking his head. "Not that I know much about the last two."

Nothing out of the ordinary, except his admission. Had Vernon always kept secrets from Izzy? If so, what?

Laura nodded, trying to lighten the mood by smiling. "So...I have a special delivery for you, as promised."

She pulled the box from her bag and placed it on the ground next to his other tools.

Izzy's face brightened. "Much appreciated!"

Laura shifted. "How's the job going? Do you need anything else?"

"All good thanks. Are you still...investigating?"

She stared at him. "Yes, why?"

Izzy looked thoughtful, picking up a measuring tape. "I don't know if it counts, but as I mentioned to the Detective Sergeant, Nicholas—Roy's kid and a wonderful fellow—transitioned to working part-time instead of full-time a few months ago." He measured a length of wood, marking it with a pencil. "I always thought Nicholas was as dedicated to the business as I was."

Laura's brow furrowed. Nicholas, not Nicky. Had he mentioned it to Izzy? Or had Izzy just picked up on Nicholas' discomfort? And the timing for Nicholas changing his hours—it lined up with when Vernon's behavior changes started.

Laura made a non-committal noise. "Nicholas mentioned Vernon started making regular trips to Burlington every other Friday around the same time. Did you know about those?"

Izzy nodded, selecting a piece of skirting board and placing it against his workbench. "Vernon told all the staff they were business trips—something about special clients."

Laura tilted her head. "Strange. Roy told us they were visits to Vernon's mother."

Izzy's hand slipped, and the board clattered against the workbench. "His mother?" He adjusted his grip on the wood, not meeting Laura's eyes. "I hadn't heard that."

"So Vernon was telling two different stories about the same trips," Laura said. "Don't you find that strange?"

Izzy shrugged. "Maybe he didn't want the staff knowing. Some folks are private about family matters." He busied himself with arranging tools with a stiffness in his shoulders and too-deliberate movements.

"Izzy, what aren't you telling me?" Laura asked.

"What? Nothing." He turned to face her and tried to smile, but it was the first time she'd ever seen him have to force it. "He...liked his secrets, that's for sure."

"I should get back," Laura said, straightening up. She moved toward the door, pausing with her hand on the knob. "You know you can talk to me if there's anything bothering you, right? I want to help."

A flash of what might've been guilt crossed his face before he managed a smile. "I know. Thanks for the nails—and for believing in me when most of the town doesn't."

Izzy was hiding something. But was it guilt, or knowledge that might lead to the killer?

⸻◆⸻

Mossridge Nature Preserve glowed with the soft light of early evening, the setting sun casting long shadows across the leaf-strewn trail. Tall pines stood along the path, their branches swaying. Laura walked beside Evelyn and Fran. Just ahead, Gus—the ever-energetic Bernese Mountain Dog—bounded along, tugging Fran's arm as she kept a firm grip on his leash.

"Gus, slow down," Fran said. The dog did as asked, looking back at his owner with what Laura could only describe as a canine grin, before continuing along at a more moderate pace. "I swear he thinks every outing is a brand new adventure."

"Finding joy in the familiar—we could all learn from that," Evelyn said.

Laura nodded, though her thoughts returned to her encounters earlier that day. "I spoke with Izzy this afternoon. He seemed nervous when I asked about Vernon's trips to Burlington. And Pete at the hardware store told me Izzy bought an axe, saw, and other tools just days before Vernon's murder."

Fran frowned, adjusting the collar of her light jacket. "That doesn't sound great."

"It doesn't," Laura said. "especially with how The Maplewood Memo has twisted the facts. However, he has a legitimate reason for those tools. I've seen the extension he's building. And Izzy mentioned something interesting—Nicholas Beckett switched from full-time to part-time work at Goldenleaf around three months ago. The same time Vernon started his Burlington trips."

"The timing correlates with other shifts in Vernon's behavior," Evelyn said.

Laura tilted her head. "It's like all these small changes are connected."

Fran nodded. "Reminds me of how birds behave when something significant is about to change. A shift in patterns, subtle but definitive. Speaking of which, from the way you've described Roy, he reminds me of a bald eagle."

Laura stared at her. "How so?"

"Impressive and commanding presence, respected by the community," Fran said. "They'll fish for themselves, sure, but they swoop in when it suits them. They're strategic about when to exert their authority."

"And what about Warren?" Evelyn asked, amused by the comparison.

Fran considered this. "A blue jay. Makes a lot of noise, seems aggressive, but mostly it's for show. Underneath, they're quite intelligent and adaptable."

"Ruby?" Laura asked.

"Northern cardinal," Fran said without hesitation. "A fiercely protective, brightly colored personality that stands out in a crowd, and makes distinctive alarm calls when threatened."

"And Dulcie?" Evelyn asked.

"Mourning dove," Fran said. "Quiet, overlooked, but with a haunting call that carries farther than you'd expect."

"What about me?" Evelyn asked.

Fran studied her. "Cedar waxwing. Sociable, elegant, travels in groups but with a distinct presence. Plus, they have excellent taste in berries."

"I like that idea," Evelyn said. "And Laura?"

Fran tilted her head, considering. "Barred owl. Observant, sometimes active during daylight unlike most owls, asks all the right questions. 'Who cooks for you? Who cooks for you all?'" She mimicked the owl's call perfectly.

"That's uncanny," Laura said.

"Birds reveal a lot about people," Fran said, shrugging. "Both humans and birds are creatures of habit, territorial, and social in their own ways. The difference is birds are honest about their intentions." She paused, pointing to a tree where a small warbler was flitting between branches. "Yellow-rumped warbler. They're everywhere this time of year, gathering in flocks before heading south. Reminds me of how this town comes together when something happens."

"Flocking together for safety?" Evelyn suggested.

"More like strength," Fran said. "No single bird can change the season, but together, their migration is one of nature's great spectacles. Much like no single person can hold a community together, but collectively, we manage."

Their conversation paused as Gus lifted his head, ears perked toward the curve in the trail ahead. A moment later, a medium-sized dog with a liver and white coat appeared around the bend, followed by a woman in a light olive parka.

"Charlie," Fran said. "That's Dulcie's English Springer Spaniel."

Gus let out a bark and strained forward on his leash.

Fran tightened her grip as the two dogs stretched toward each other. They engaged in a flurry of enthusiastic sniffing, tails wagging as they circled as far as their restraints would allow.

"Gus, settle down," Fran called, then shrugged toward Dulcie. "Sorry about that—he thinks every dog is his best friend."

"It's fine," Dulcie said, her voice softer than Laura had expected. "Charlie loves the company." She tried to pat her dog, but he was too busy with Gus to notice.

"I'm Francesca 'Fran' Palermo," she said, extending a hand. "We've seen each other around but haven't met. These are my friends, Evelyn Chan and Laura Evans."

Dulcie shook Fran's hand, then Evelyn's and Laura's. Her eyes widened. "Yes, I—remember you. You were there when..." she trailed off, color rising in her cheeks.

"We're very sorry about Vernon," Evelyn said. "Such a terrible tragedy."

Dulcie nodded, her fingers fidgeting with Charlie's leash. "Thank you. It's been...difficult." Her gaze settled on Laura. "Wait, you're the café manager who solved that murder during the Summer Cheese Festival, aren't you?"

Laura shifted. "I wouldn't say I solved it. I just asked some questions that helped point things in the right direction."

"I'm glad someone in this town is asking questions instead of just spreading rumors," Dulcie said. She glanced around, then stepped closer. "There's something I've been wanting to tell someone. I found something while going through Vernon's things at home. Something that might explain why he—"

"Dulcie!" The sharp voice cut through the peaceful evening like a whip crack.

All four women turned to see Ruby charging up the path from the same direction Dulcie had come, her face flushed with exertion or anger—both.

Ruby's eyes narrowed as she took in Laura and Evelyn. "I might've known," she muttered, hurrying to Dulcie's side and taking her arm. "We need to go. Your lasagna will be overcooked."

"I was just telling—" Dulcie began.

"Nothing that can't wait," Ruby said. "Charlie needs his dinner too, don't you, boy?" She whistled for the spaniel, who disengaged from his play with Gus.

Dulcie gave an apologetic look. "I'm sorry, I should go."

"By all means," Laura said, keeping disappointment from her voice. "Enjoy your evening."

As Dulcie and Ruby walked away, Ruby glanced over her shoulder at Laura and Evelyn. With her free hand, she pointed two fingers at her eyes, then jabbed toward the women—the classic "I'm watching you" gesture.

Laura, Evelyn, and Fran were left standing in stunned silence. Gus whined.

Fran raised an eyebrow. "She's not winning any awards for subtlety."

"Ruby is determined to keep Dulcie from speaking with us," Evelyn said, her brow furrowed. "But Dulcie wants to share something."

Laura nodded. "We need to speak with her alone."

"Ruby can't monitor her twenty-four hours a day," Fran said.

"Come on," Laura said. "Let's finish our walk and make a plan. If Ruby thinks her intimidation tactics will work on us, she's wrong."

# CHAPTER SIXTEEN

E velyn's apartment glowed with warm lamplight. She lived alone in the Morrison Building's second story in the apartment she'd once shared with her late husband. The floor below had once been his medical practice. Laura leaned against the windowsill, watching dusk settle over the Village Green while Jasmine paced the rug, her box braids swinging with each turn. The meeting had started well enough, but after an hour of circular conversation, frustration hung in the air like the scent of Evelyn's earl grey tea, which sat cooling in cups scattered around the living room.

Oscar appeared from wherever he'd been napping, stretching before hopping onto the coffee table. The cat sniffed at the papers, his whiskers twitching.

"Not now, Oscar," Evelyn murmured, nudging him away. "And not on the table!"

Oscar, undeterred, batted at a small index card with 'Warren Fisk' written on it, sending it skittering across the table to land next to 'Ruby Callahan'.

"Hey!" Laura protested, reaching for the card, but she paused. "Wait a minute..." She looked from the cards to the cat and back again. "What if there's a connection there?"

Jasmine rolled her eyes as she moved Oscar off the table, shaking her head. "I can't believe you're taking investigative advice from a cat." Despite herself, she had to crack a smile, but snapped back into seriousness as she dropped onto Evelyn's floral settee. "Dulcie was about to tell you something significant. And Ruby stopped her. The question is why and is Ruby protecting Dulcie or herself?"

Evelyn made a thoughtful humming sound.

"We need to get Dulcie alone," Laura said, returning to her seat in the armchair opposite Evelyn. "But how?"

"What about creating a diversion?" Jasmine said. "Something that would draw Ruby away long enough for one of us to approach Dulcie? But if Ruby realizes we're behind it, she'll be even more vigilant."

"What about contacting Dulcie?" Laura said. "A phone call or a note?"

"We don't have her details," Evelyn said.

The conversation continued in this vein, each suggestion less practical than the last. Then the apartment's intercom buzzed.

Evelyn rose from her chair. "Strange. I'm not expecting anyone else." When she returned, she addressed Laura and Jasmine. "It was Christopher. He says he has news."

A few minutes later, a knock sounded at the apartment door. Evelyn opened it to reveal Christopher, windblown and cheeks ruddy. He wore his usual flannel shirt under a light jacket, and his expression was triumphant.

"Evening!" he said, stepping inside as Evelyn ushered him in. "Sorry to interrupt your dinner, but—" He stopped when he saw Jasmine and Laura, and his face split into a grin. "Perfect! I was going to give this to Evelyn to show you both, but you're already here."

Evelyn smiled. "We were just discussing our investigation. Would you like some tea? It's still warm."

"No thanks, I won't stay long," Christopher said. He sat in an armchair and slipped the manila envelope from under his arm. "I've been researching that memorial article for The Whittled Word."

"You've finished the interviews at Goldenleaf already?" Laura asked.

Christopher nodded. "Spent most of the afternoon there, interviewing staff for the tribute piece. I started by asking about good memories. Something to honor Vernon. Once people started talking, it was clear there were other undercurrents. They seemed to need to get it off their chests, especially with everything that's happened. I typed up several pages of notes about what the employees said that I thought might be of interest to you. Of course, these won't be included in the tribute."

"That's wonderful," Jasmine said. "Thank you."

Christopher grinned and handed the envelope to Laura. "Better you read it yourselves. I've included direct quotes from most of the staff."

Laura accepted the envelope, sliding out several typed pages to read aloud: "Casey Jennings, Acting Production Supervisor: reports increasing tensions between Vernon Reed and Roy Beckett in the months preceding Reed's death. Quote: they'd worked together for thirty years, but they couldn't agree on anything. It was tearing the place apart."

She looked up. "That confirms what we've heard about their disagreements."

She continued reading: "Janet Collins, Administrative Assistant: states Vernon Reed became secretive about three months ago, locking his office door during phone calls, a behavior she described as out of character. She noted Vernon began taking Mondays off, something unprecedented in her ten years at Goldenleaf Apple Farm."

"The timeline matches," Jasmine said.

Laura nodded and flipped to the next page: "Malik Rivers, Seasonal Worker: reported witnessing a heated argument between Isaac 'Izzy' Lennox and Vernon Reed in Reed's office four days before Reed's death. Quote: 'I was delivering supply invoices to Janet when I heard shouting. The door was ajar, and I could see Izzy waving his arms. Vernon was seated at his desk, looking more annoyed than angry. I heard Dulcie's name mentioned several times. Izzy said something like, 'You can't do this to her' and 'She trusted you.' Vernon kept saying, 'It's none of your business, Izzy.' When Vernon noticed me, he slammed the door shut.'"

Quiet enveloped the room.

"Izzy never mentioned this argument to me," Laura said.

"And he talked about Dulcie," Jasmine said, her expression troubled.

Laura continued reading: "Gwen Foster, Neighbor to Goldenleaf Apple Farm: reported seeing Dulcie Sanderson and Vernon Reed engaged in what looked like an argument out the back of their property one week before Reed's death. Quote: 'I was on my way out to the stables to feed my horses, when I saw them. Dulcie was upset, gesturing at papers she was holding. Vernon kept shaking his head. Dulcie crumpled the papers and threw them at him before storming off toward her car. I thought little of it at the time—people argue. But given what happened later...'" Laura set the pages down, her mind racing. "These accounts put Izzy and Dulcie in conflict with Vernon before his death."

Christopher cleared his throat. "That's not all. I have something I saw today."

Three pairs of eyes turned toward him.

"I was at Warren Fisk's farm this morning," Christopher said. "Silver Springs Woodworkers had been looking for affordable materials, and Warren mentioned he'd collected a fair amount of off-cut wood over the years—scraps from various projects on his farm. He wanted to clear out space in his barn and offered to let us take what we could use."

"That's generous of him," Evelyn said.

Christopher nodded. "I thought so too. I swung by this morning to collect the wood. When I arrived, no one was out front, so I figured everyone was out in the orchards harvesting."

"Busy time for apple producers," Jasmine said.

"Exactly. I started walking around, looking for Warren or one of his workers. As I rounded the corner near the equipment shed, I heard voices." Christopher leaned forward. "I couldn't see who was speaking, but I caught fragments of their conversation. Things like 'we have to keep this secret' and 'I appreciate you doing this' and 'no one can find out.'"

Laura's heart rate quickened. "What did you do?"

"I'm not proud to admit it, but I got curious. I peeked around the corner of the shed and saw Warren talking with someone—a young man wearing a hoodie pulled up and dark sunglasses."

"Who was it?" Jasmine asked.

Christopher couldn't resist a grin. "I'm getting to that. The young man handed Warren what looked like cash. They shook hands, and then the lad turned to leave. So I backed away and tried to make it look like I was just arriving." He paused. "But I collided with him. I didn't see him coming around the shed. His sunglasses slipped, and I got a clear look at his face."

"And?" Laura asked.

"Nicky Beckett," Christopher said. "Roy's son."

Laura exchanged glances with Jasmine and Evelyn. Nicholas had mentioned being unhappy at Goldenleaf Apple Farm, trapped in the family business when he'd rather be pursuing music. What was he doing paying Warren—his father's competitor—in secret?

"How do you know him?" Laura asked.

Christopher shrugged. "Back when I ran my carpentry business, I made Roy some furniture. Nicky looks like his dad."

"He prefers being called Nicholas," Evelyn said. "And did he recognize you?"

"Does he? That's the first I'm hearing. Fair enough. And I don't think so," Christopher said. "I pretended not to know who he was. He mumbled an apology and bolted. Warren looked rattled when I greeted him, but he relaxed once I asked about the wood. We loaded up my truck, and I left without mentioning what I'd seen."

"This is significant," Evelyn said, counting off on her fingers. "Nicholas paying Warren, Izzy arguing with

Vernon about Dulcie, Dulcie confronting Vernon with papers..."

"You try to carve out some sense from all these disconnected pieces," Christopher said. "And every time you think you've got it nailed down, another clue pops up."

Jasmine nodded. "It feels like we're missing something."

"You need to sand away the rough edges of this case," Christopher continued. "Whittle down the suspect list to reveal the true grain of this mystery."

Laura grinned, suppressing a chuckle, and looked at Evelyn, who was failing to maintain a straight face. "Are you...making woodworking puns?"

Christopher's expression remained innocent. "We can't let the culprit chisel their way out of this."

Jasmine snorted. "Please stop," she said, though she was smiling.

Christopher held up his hands, bursting into a grin. "Don't worry. I wooden dream of continuing."

Everyone groaned as he rose from his chair.

"I'll leave you to piece it together. I thought you should know about...Nicholas right away. It seemed important."

"It is," Laura said, as all three walked him to the door. "Thank you, Christopher."

"Before I forget," he said, pausing. "What did the detective say when she found the missing luggage?" He waited, eyes twinkling. "Case closed!"

Laura couldn't help but smile despite herself. "Another one for The Whittled Word?"

"You know it," Christopher replied. "I like to bring a little levity to the newsletter. People say it's their favorite section, though I suspect they're just being kind."

After Christopher had left, Laura snapped her fingers. "I've thought of something. Roy told us Vernon was visiting his mother in Burlington, but that contradicts what he told the staff about business meetings. What if we can speak to his mother? Maybe she knows something about these changes in Vernon's behavior."

Jasmine nodded. "It's worth checking out."

"The question is," Evelyn said, returning to her armchair, "where in Burlington would we find her? And how would you make time to visit? Burlington is over an hour away."

Laura sighed. "I don't know. Given Vernon's age, I'd assume she may be in an assisted living facility or perhaps a nursing home. And between my shifts at the café and everything else..." she trailed off.

Evelyn's eyes lit up. "Judith might know." She reached for her phone. "She's usually arguing with Edward about what'll happen next in the book they're reading at this hour. It couldn't hurt to interrupt."

Laura laughed.

With a knowing smile, Evelyn gave a slight shake of her head. "They've had a two-person book club forever. The most argumentative one I've seen, though. I'll call her."

After three rings, Judith answered. "Evelyn! Perfect timing. Since you've already read—"

Evelyn chuckled. "I'm not playing referee in your literary spats, Judith."

A man's voice, tinged with a distinct rhythm, flickered down the line. "You disappoint me, Evelyn! Just when I thought I could get you on my side."

Judith spoke again with mock admonishment. "Need I remind you, Edward, she was my friend first?"

Evelyn heaved a theatrical sigh. "If you're finished, I have Laura and Jasmine here with me. Judith, I need to ask a favor."

Rustling crackled through the phone. "Alright, Edward, shoo! This is Maplewood Crafters Club business." More static suggested she'd moved into another room. "So, what thrilling adventure may I help you with?"

Laura leaned toward the phone, smiling despite it all. "Hi, Judith. We believe Vernon had been visiting his mother in Burlington in the months before his death. She might have information that could help us understand what was happening in his life."

"The problem is," Jasmine said, "we don't know where she lives or how to find her."

There was a pause. "Vernon's mother...Lavinia Reed, if I'm not mistaken. Let me think."

Laura exchanged hopeful glances with Jasmine and Evelyn.

"Yes!" Judith said. "She's at Lakeside Pines Assisted Living. My dear friend Agnes moved there last spring. I've been meaning to visit her for weeks now."

"That's perfect!" Laura said. "If you were planning to visit anyway—"

"Are you suggesting I could do some investigating while I'm there?" Judith asked, her tone brightening. "I'd be delighted to help."

"I was thinking I might accompany you," Evelyn said, meeting Laura's eyes.

"That'd be wonderful!" Judith said. "We could make a day of it. I could introduce you to Agnes—she's a marvelous woman, used to be a concert pianist. And we could speak with Lavinia Reed."

Jasmine grinned. "That sounds perfect! When do you think—"

"I'm free on Friday," Judith said.

Laura exchanged a stricken glance with Jasmine. That was four days away!

Judith sensed their silent disappointment. "I know it's pressing, but I must remind you, once you reach retirement, you'll have never been so busy in your life! Besides, Agnes is a social butterfly, she'll need a few days' warning. I'll let her know we're coming. And I'll check to see which room Lavinia is in."

"Just be careful," Laura said. "This needs to look like a normal social visit."

"Don't worry," Judith said with a laugh. "Evelyn and I will be the picture of innocuous older visitors."

They ended the call.

Laura collapsed onto the sofa with a sigh. "I wish I could go with you, but I can't take time off work."

"You're needed here," Jasmine said. "Besides, Evelyn and Judith will blend in better without us."

Evelyn nodded. "We'll call as soon as we learn anything. Now, we could all use a proper meal and a break from murder investigations. Would you both stay for dinner? Nothing fancy, but I have some fresh salmon I'd planned to prepare."

Jasmine's eyes brightened. "That sounds wonderful."

"I'd love to," Laura said, realizing how hungry she was. "How can I help?"

They followed Evelyn through the archway that connected her living room to the kitchen—white cabinets with glass fronts displaying delicate teacups and dishes, well-used wooden spoons in a ceramic holder, and copper-bottomed pots hanging from a rack. Plants with hand-lettered tags thrived on the windowsill—Agatha, Dashiell, and Dorothy. Evelyn had named all her houseplants after mystery authors.

Oscar and Monty had followed, but Evelyn pushed them out of the way, shutting the door, shaking her head with a smile. "Sorry, gentleman, but the kitchen is closed to you." She opened her refrigerator and pulled out a package wrapped in brown paper. She set it on the counter and turned to Jasmine. "Would you mind rinsing the rice? Three cups should be enough. The colander is in that drawer." She pointed, then turned to Laura. "And you could chop the vegetables? There's bell pepper, snow peas, and water chestnuts in the crisper."

Laura nodded, pulling open the refrigerator drawer. "What size for chopping?"

"Bite-sized will do," Evelyn said, unwrapping the salmon fillets.

Jasmine measured rice into a bowl. "Who taught you to cook, Evelyn?"

"My mother," Evelyn said as she prepared the salmon. "She worked as a secretary but somehow put a home-cooked dinner on the table every night." She reached for a small ceramic jar. "This ginger-soy glaze was her recipe. I've made a few adjustments over the years, but the essence is hers." She paused. "Hand me that little grater, would you, Laura? It's hanging just above you."

Laura reached up and unhooked the requested item, passing it to Evelyn, who zested an orange over the glaze mixture. The citrus scent brightened the kitchen.

The kitchen filled with delicious aromas as Evelyn brushed the salmon with her glaze and set it in the oven.

Laura finished chopping the vegetables and watched as Jasmine measured water for the rice. There was something soothing about the three of them moving around the kitchen together.

"Shall we set the table while everything cooks?" Evelyn said. "The dishes are in that cabinet."

Laura opened it to find delicate porcelain dishes with a blue flower pattern, and removed three dinner plates. "These are beautiful."

"My wedding china," Evelyn said with a small smile. "Charles and I received them as a gift."

"Are you sure we should use these?" Laura asked.

"Good food and company are always worthy of good dishes," Evelyn said, her eyes twinkling.

They carried everything to the dining room table.

"This feels like dinner at my grandmother's," Jasmine said, smoothing a napkin. "She always made us use proper place settings, even for weeknight meals."

"Wise woman," Evelyn said, appearing with a pitcher of ice water. "Small rituals give meaning to everyday life."

Later, they were seated around the table, steam rising from the platters of cooked salmon, fragrant rice, and stir-fried vegetables. Oscar had positioned himself under the table, hopeful for scraps.

"This looks amazing," Laura said as Evelyn served her a portion of the glazed salmon, its surface caramelized to a rich amber.

"Wait until you taste it," Jasmine said, having already taken a bite. "It's incredible."

The three women ate with appreciation and the conversation flowed, touching on favorite books and places they hoped to visit someday. As they finished their main course, Evelyn disappeared into the kitchen, returning with a serving dish of warm poached pears, their flesh tender and infused with honey, cinnamon, and vanilla.

"These look delicious," Laura said, accepting a pear half drizzled with the poaching syrup. "Where did these come from?"

"Just something I prepared this morning," Evelyn said with an innocent expression.

"You were planning this dinner all along, weren't you?" Jasmine asked, raising an eyebrow.

Evelyn flashed a secret smile.

After the last bites of the tender, spiced pears had been savored, and the dishes cleared, Evelyn led them back to the living room. She moved to a cabinet in the corner, extracting a wooden box she placed on the coffee table.

"I thought we might play a game of Mahjong," she said, opening the lid to reveal rows of polished tiles. "A beginner one, mind you."

Laura peered at the tiles—ivory-colored rectangles with intricate engravings.

"I'd love to learn," Laura said. "Though I warn you, I'm terrible at games."

"Nonsense," Evelyn said, beginning to arrange the tiles face down on the table in a rectangular formation. "Everyone starts somewhere."

Evelyn arranged the tiles into what she called 'walls.' "Mahjong has been played for centuries. The version we'll play tonight is a simplified American variant. The basic goal is to create sets of tiles—either three or four identical tiles, or sequences of three consecutive numbers in the same suit. "Don't worry about memorizing everything at once. The game is learned through practice, not instruction."

They began with Evelyn dealing thirteen tiles to each player. Laura followed Evelyn's instructions, and patterns emerged from the chaos. She discarded a tile, and the game progressed with each woman taking turns.

"Pung!" Evelyn said at one point, taking a tile Jasmine had discarded and revealing three matching tiles from her hand.

"Is that good?" Laura asked.

"It means I've made a set," Evelyn explained. "When someone discards a tile, you need to complete a set. You can claim it and reveal the set."

As the game continued, Laura became absorbed in the rhythm—draw, decide, discard. When Jasmine knocked several tiles over with her sleeve, they all burst into laughter. Monty, who'd been sleeping nearby, raised his head to observe.

Evelyn laid down her final combination of tiles. "Mahjong."

Laura examined Evelyn's revealed hand. "That looks...impressive?"

Evelyn couldn't resist a smile. They helped Evelyn tidy the living room, straightening cushions and returning teacups to the kitchen.

"Thank you for dinner," Laura said as she prepared to leave. "And for teaching us Mahjong. It was what I needed."

Jasmine echoed the sentiment and gave them both a hug goodbye. After seeing Jasmine to her car, Laura climbed the stairs to her apartment. As she unlocked her door, she smiled. In Boston, her work had defined her life. Here in Silver Springs, she'd found something different—a community that balanced the weight of responsibility with connection.

# CHAPTER SEVENTEEN

The back door in the General Store swung open, and Izzy entered, a canvas bag of tools slung over his shoulder. He bounded over to Laura, his smile more subdued than usual, but still present. "Good morning!

"Hi, Izzy," she said, smiling. "You're here early."

"Nothing like the motivation an early start brings," he said, then glanced around the café before spotting Eli behind the counter. Over he went. "Morning, plant whisperer!"

Eli looked up from the espresso machine, surprise crossing his features. "Hey, Izzy. Didn't see you there."

"Remember that Aloe I mentioned last week? Still hanging on by a thread." Izzy placed a small brown paper bag on the counter. "Brought you some of those butterscotch discs you liked from Honeybell Sweets as a bribe for more plant wisdom."

Eli smiled. "You really didn't have to, but I'll make sure you've got a care plan."

"Wonderful!" Izzy said. "My caravan will no longer look like a plant hospice."

Both Laura and Eli had to smile.

That morning, at ten-fifteen, Pete should've lumbered through the Silver Springs General Store's doors, desperate for his usual two-shot espresso to rejuvenate him...now Ben appeared instead.

"Morning, Laura!" he said as he approached the counter. "Wouldn't you know? My father, dependent on coffee for the past twenty years, declares himself not in need of it." He rolled his eyes. "Love the man, but he's hopeless, and the last thing I need is him falling asleep on the job. So, I'm here to get his coffee."

"Is he alright?" Laura asked, head tilting.

"Yeah. Just still embarrassed. He means well, but self-awareness isn't his strong suit," Ben said. "Can I get the usual to go?

Laura smiled and turned to Eli. "A coffee for Pete."

Eli nodded. She didn't have to say anything else. Eli remembered the preferences of all their regulars.

As she turned back to Ben, who'd fished cash from his pocket, the young man leaned in. "By the way, are you back on your amateur sleuth game or what?"

Laura hesitated, then nodded.

Ben grinned. "Excellent! I shall keep an eye out for you then."

"Ben..." she sighed. "You know the gravity of this, right? Don't do anything dangerous."

Ben scoffed. "Please. I brave wobbly ladders and geese, so a little light spying? Child's play. Trust me, I can gather information with the best of them."

The afternoon lull had settled over the General Store café like a comfortable blanket. Laura wiped down the espresso machine, enjoying the momentary quiet after the lunch rush had ebbed away. A few regulars remained, scattered among the tables—a schoolteacher grading papers in the corner, a pair of hikers refueling before heading back to the trails, and two middle-aged women deep in conversation by the window, their half-empty mugs of tea forgotten as they leaned toward each other, voices lowered but animated. Laura glanced at the clock—three-thirty-five pm. Less than three hours until closing, and then she could continue pursuing leads in Vernon's case.

"Are the pastries passing inspection?" Jesse asked, appearing beside her with a tray of clean mugs.

"Selling well," Laura said, moving to the display case where she rearranged the remaining items—scones, apple cinnamon muffins, and chocolate chip cookies, all from Red Trillium Bakery. "Not much left."

Jesse nodded, shelving the mugs. "Midweek blues. Sweet treats are the only answer."

A young mother with a toddler entered and Laura greeted them, taking their order for hot chocolate and a cookie. Eli then prepared their drink. As the mother settled her child at a table near the counter, Laura began wiping down the coffee preparation area, gathering stray sugar packets and organizing the condiment station. Her position gave her a clear view of the two women by the window, their conversation growing more animated as one of them gestured.

"—mortified," the woman in the plum-colored cardigan was saying. "There I was, sitting in Denise's waiting room, ready for my weekly massage, when who should walk out but Vernon Reed!"

Laura's hands stilled on the counter.

"Vernon Reed?" the other woman said. "Getting a massage?"

"The same! Looking as uncomfortable as a cat in a bathtub," the woman continued with a shake of her head.

"That's strange," her companion said, stirring her tea. "Remember what Cynthia said about dating him? He could barely stand holding hands in public."

Laura moved closer to their table, pretending to check the sugar dispenser nearby. The women continued their discussion.

"That's what I thought!" the first woman nodded. "A woman from my book club used to work for him—said his head would hit the ceiling if anyone touched his shoulder to get his attention. Yet there he was, at a massage place."

"When was this?" the other woman asked, reaching for her mug.

"About a week before he died," the woman telling the story said. "I remember thinking how strange it was he'd scheduled another appointment for the following Wednesday."

Laura's pulse quickened. Another piece of the puzzle. How did it fit?

"All good, or should I worry?" Jesse asked.

"Fine," Laura said, offering a smile that didn't reach her eyes. "Just thinking."

She returned to her tasks, serving customers and preparing for the after-work crowd, but her mind continued whirring.

<hr>

That afternoon, Laura and Jasmine walked down the sidewalk along Main Street toward the Maplewood Credit Union. The pavement was dappled with sunlight filtered through the turning leaves—gold, russet, and amber overhead, with crisp-edged shadows at their feet.

A pair of window washers worked across the street, one whistling as they wiped down the panes of the Quartermark Inn's bay windows. A trio of tourists with camera bags pointed toward a mountain ridge peeking between rooftops. Laura carried the General Store café's daily cash deposit in a sturdy zippered bank pouch tucked inside her bag. Her arm pressed it against her side, elbow angled just so.

The red brick building that housed the credit union stood at the corner. The lobby was small but well-appointed, with polished wooden counters and local artwork adorning the walls—watercolors of Vermont landscapes and black-and-white photographs of Silver Springs' historic buildings. A row of four teller stations stretched along one wall, three occupied by staff members helping customers.

Laura and Jasmine joined the short line, taking their place behind an older woman clutching a deposit slip. At the front of the line, a familiar figure stood at the first teller station—Warren Fisk, his cap clutched in his hands, shoulders hunched as if making himself smaller. His fingers drummed agains the desk as the teller counted out a substantial amount of cash.

Warren peeked over his shoulder. When his gaze met Laura's, he startled, turning back to the teller. He signed a receipt with hurried motions, then scooped the cash into a manila envelope, which he tucked inside his jacket. The doors shut behind him with a soft hydraulic hiss as he raced o ut.

"Next customer, please," the teller said.

Laura stepped forward, unzipping the bank bag, and handed over the bundled money. "Daily deposit for the General Store, please."

As the teller processed their transaction, Jasmine leaned close to Laura. "Did you see how much cash he took? Had to be at least two thousand dollars."

Laura nodded, waiting until they received their receipt and stepped away from the counter before responding. "He couldn't get away fast enough. Something's off."

They exited the credit union.

"You don't think..." Jasmine began, frowning as they returned to the General Store, "someone's pressuring Warren for money? Blackmail?"

Laura considered this. "But Christopher saw Nicholas paying Warren, not the other way around. Why would Warren be withdrawing cash if Nicholas was paying him?"

"Unless Warren is a middleman," Jasmine said. "Nicholas pays Warren, Warren pays someone else. Or there are multiple transactions happening."

They walked in thoughtful silence, each turning over theories in their minds.

That evening, Laura entered her kitchen, switching on the kettle before retrieving her crochet project from the side table. The rhythmic motion of a hook through yarn had become her thinking ritual. The kettle switched off, and Laura prepared a mug of chamomile tea, carrying it and her crochet work to the comfortable armchair near the window.

Her phone rang, vibrating against the coffee table. Laura glanced at the screen—Unknown Number. Her hand hesitated above the device. She'd always ignored unidentified callers, but with the investigation ongoing, it could be someone with information.

Laura set her crochet aside and picked up. "Hello?"

Silence followed, then a shaky exhale. "Is this Laura Evans?"

"Yes, this is Laura."

Another pause. "It's Noah. I work at Goldenleaf Apple Farm. I..."

Laura sat up straighter, reaching for a notepad on the side table. "Hi, Noah. How are you doing? Is everything okay?"

"Not really..." Noah trailed off, then gathered himself. "That's not why I'm calling. There's something I need to tell you, something I was too scared to tell the police."

Laura's pulse quickened. "I'm listening."

"First," Noah said, "you have to promise not to tell anyone else."

"I promise to keep your information confidential," Laura said, though uncertainty flickered through her mind. If this information proved critical, she might need to share it with the police, and Evelyn and Jasmine, of course.

"Okay." Noah took a deep breath. "The day before Vernon was killed, I was walking past the old storage shed—the one near the north apple grove. It's unused now, except for some seasonal equipment." His voice lowered further. "Izzy was there. Alone."

Laura frowned, jotting notes. "What was he doing?"

"He was talking to himself. Pacing back and forth, gesturing with his hands. I couldn't hear everything, but it sounded like he was rehearsing some kind of confrontation with Vernon."

Laura's stomach tightened. "What makes you think it was about Vernon?"

"Izzy was saying things like, 'You can't keep doing this' and 'She deserves better.' He seemed worked up," Noah said.

Laura recalled what Christopher's notes had mentioned—Izzy's argument with Vernon in his office, with Dulcie's name being mentioned. The pieces aligned.

"Had Izzy and Vernon argued publicly before?" Laura asked.

"Several times in the months before—" Noah broke off. "I have to go."

"Wait," Laura said. "Is there anything else you remember? Anything that might help us understand what happened?"

"Just...Izzy looked...different that day. Not his usual cheerful self. Dangerous. I was going to tell the police, but I was afraid this would make things worse for him."

Silence. Had he hung up?

He spoke again. "There was something else—Vernon had been asking Izzy strange hypothetical questions. Like one day I overheard him ask what Izzy would do if he discovered someone close to him stealing something. Izzy looked almost terrified. He stammered about confronting them. Vernon just nodded. It was a really weird conversation."

"I understand," Laura said. "Thank you for trusting me with this. Please call again if you remember anything else."

"I will," Noah said. "I should go now. Please be careful."

The line went dead before Laura could respond. She placed her phone down, staring at the notes she'd taken as unease built in her chest. She was about to reach for her crochet project when her phone rang again, startling her. This time, the caller ID displayed a name she recognized: Judith Yoon.

"Hi Judith. How are you?"

"Laura," Judith's warm voice came through, though there was an undercurrent of excitement. "I hope I'm not disturbing your evening, but I've heard something about Dulcie that might apply to your...investigation."

"You're not disturbing anything," Laura said, reaching for her notepad. "What've you heard?"

"You know how information travels in Silver Springs," Judith said, a rustling suggesting she was settling into a more comfortable position. "My friend Josephine Kirby's daughter, Mia, works as a cleaner. Dulcie hired her to help sort through Vernon's belongings. Mia was there today while Dulcie was out running errands. She was organizing bedroom closets when she came across something...concerning."

Laura tucked the phone between her ear and shoulder, poised to take notes. "What did she find?"

"A photograph," Judith said. "It was tucked in Dulcie's nightstand drawer. A picture from last year, showing Dulcie, Vernon, and Ruby together at a summer barbecue. Vernon's face had been crossed out with a black permanent marker."

Laura frowned. "That's...unsettling. Was there anything else unusual?"

"Yes, and this is even stranger," Judith said. "According to Josephine, Dulcie had given Mia instructions to gather all Vernon's remaining clock pieces for donation to the thrift store. Said she couldn't bear to look at his projects anymore."

"Clock pieces," Laura said, writing it down. "That's what I saw in the garage. Was Vernon a hobbyist?"

"Yes, he enjoyed fixing old clocks," Judith said.

"Did Mia mention anything about Dulcie finding something specific among Vernon's belongings after his death?" Laura asked, thinking of Dulcie's almost-confession at the nature preserve. "Something that might've upset her?"

"Not specifically," Judith said. "Though she mentioned Dulcie seemed concerned about going through his papers herself rather than letting Mia handle them. Had them all gathered in boxes in the dining room."

Laura made another note. "This is really helpful, Judith. Thanks so much for calling."

"I thought you'd want to know," Judith said.

After a few more minutes of conversation and promises to keep each other updated, Laura ended the call. She set her phone down and stared at her notes.

More pieces of the puzzle. So how did they all fit?

# CHAPTER EIGHTEEN

Northern Necessities hummed with the quiet industry of a small-town supermarket. Laura guided her shopping cart down the produce aisle. Laura selected a carton of vegetable stock for soup, placing it amongst the other items in her cart. Between the investigation and everything else, she'd been living off café breakfasts, rushed lunches, and whatever sandwich she could throw together while flipping through her notes.

Twenty minutes later, her basket filled with the essentials she needed, Laura approached the checkout area. She heaved a sigh as she recognized the cashier at the only register without a line. Early twenties. Short-cropped bleached-blond hair. Laura considered pretending she'd forgotten something and circling back through the store, but the young woman had already spotted her.

"Evening, Laura," the cashier called with a wave. "No line over here."

With a resigned sigh, Laura wheeled her cart to the register and began unloading her items onto the conveyor belt. "Hello. Working late today?"

"Short-staffed, as usual." The worker began scanning items. "Dulcie called in sick again. Not that I blame her."

Laura arranged her reusable bags at the end of the counter. "How is she holding up?"

The cashier glanced around before leaning across the scanner. "Between you and me, I think there's more to Vernon's death than anyone's letting on."

Laura kept her expression neutral despite the sudden acceleration of her heartbeat. "What do you mean?"

The young woman scanned a carton of eggs, checking them for cracks before placing them in a bag. "I think Dulcie was poisoning Vernon before she lost patience and—" she made a quick hammering motion with her hand. "Bop. Finished the job more directly."

"Poisoning him?" Laura repeated, struggling to keep her voice even. She handed over her loyalty card. "What makes you think Dulcie would do something like that?"

The young woman swiped the card and continued scanning. "Vernon loved his ribeye. Starting a few months ago, Dulcie wasn't buying as much as she used to." She bagged Laura's vegetable stock carton with an emphatic gesture. "When I asked her about it, she said, 'Vernon's not eating as much.' That's when I started paying attention. Classic slow poisoning."

Laura's mind raced. "Did Vernon ever come shopping with her? Did he look ill to you?"

"Hardly ever saw him in the store, except to pick up Dulcie after her shifts sometimes." The young woman rang up Laura's total. "But the few times I did, he looked...different. Thinner, but also distracted."

Laura slid her card into the reader. "That doesn't mean Dulcie was poisoning him."

The cashier shrugged, bagging the last of Laura's groceries. "Maybe. But it's strange."

Laura gathered her bags. "Thanks for your help."

"Anytime."

---

Later that evening, at the library, Laura went to the front desk, where Joyce Adler sat cataloging a stack of new arrivals. She looked up as Laura approached. "Laura, hello!"

"Hi, Joyce. I'm here for some quiet reading," Laura said. "I needed somewhere different."

Joyce nodded. "The library has always been my thinking sanctuary. Something about being surrounded by all these stories helps put one's thoughts in perspective." She pushed the stack of books aside. "How are things at the General Store?"

"The café keeps me busy. I'm enjoying getting to know Silver Springs better," Laura said.

"This town has a way of growing on you," Joyce said with a fond smile. "Even with its complications."

Laura was about to ask what Joyce meant when the older woman's expression shifted, her smile tightening at the corners. Joyce's gaze moved past Laura's shoulder toward the library entrance. A woman in her late forties with hair in a French twist wearing a sharp charcoal pantsuit strode through the doors. Her heels clicked against the hardwood floors—loud enough to draw annoyed glances from several patrons without breaking library etiquette.

"Good evening, Sharon," Joyce said, her tone professional but cooler than when she'd greeted Laura.

The woman gave an imperious nod and a tight smile as she passed the desk. "Joyce. Busy night?" Her gaze swept the almost empty room before she continued toward the Historical Society archives without waiting for an answer.

"Who's that?" Laura asked, keeping her voice low.

Joyce sighed. "Sharon Winters. Editor of The Maplewood Memo. She's always here, researching local history for her 'Silver Springs Then & Now' column. Sometimes, she uncovers something important, holds people accountable. Other times...it's just sensationalism. Give me Hazel Thorton's 'Local Lowdown' any day. She at least makes town happenings sound amusing, not scandalous."

Laura made a split-second decision. "I'll go introduce myself."

Joyce raised an eyebrow but didn't comment as Laura moved away from the circulation desk. She found Sharon in the archives' reading room at the terminal.

"Excuse me, and good evening," Laura began, extending her hand. "I'm—"

"Laura Evans, café manager at the General Store," Sharon finished for her, not looking up from the computer screen. "Purveyor of coffee and...amateur insights."

Laura withdrew her unshaken hand, heat rising in her cheeks. "I wanted to talk to you about your article on Izzy Lennox. You've unfairly—"

"Reported the facts?" Sharon turned from the screen, exhaustion etched in the lines around her eyes. "Or connected dots that the police seem unwilling to connect themselves?"

"Izzy isn't guilty," Laura said. "Your article is based on speculation and—"

"Rumors?" Sharon held up a hand. "I have the forensics report—leaked, yes, but accurate—about the hammer and bracelet. Fraser's statement about Lennox's behavior that day." She rubbed her temple. "What I don't have is time to wait three months for Ramirez while evidence disappears."

Laura crossed her arms. "And destroying an innocent man's life in the process?"

Something flickered across Sharon's face before her expression hardened again. "You think I enjoy this? It's about survival. Not just mine."

Laura studied her. "And if you're wrong about Izzy?"

Sharon's fingers stilled on the keyboard. "I've been wrong before. I may push boundaries, but I'm not without conscience."

"But the damage—"

"Is why I triple-check everything now. The Fraser quote? I have it on tape. The forensics? Verified with two sources. The timeline? Three witnesses." She pulled out a small recorder. "I even tried to interview Lennox."

Laura frowned. "Can you blame him for not wanting to talk?"

"No. But silence reads as guilt to the public." Sharon sighed. "I noted in the article he declined to comment—didn't say he refused or avoided me. Words matter. You think I'm a vulture? Fine. But I've lived here for thirty years. I've seen what happens when powerful people's secrets stay buried."

"Even if you drag innocent people through the mud?"

Sharon's jaw tightened. "Sometimes being necessary is more important than being liked. The truth will come out. It always does."

Laura started to protest, but Sharon held up a hand to silence her.

"You don't know about Callahan's interesting background, do you?" Sharon asked. "Or Sanderson's unfortunate history. Or how 'helpful' a certain apple farmer has been with providing information about Vernon."

Laura frowned. "What do you mean?"

"Let's say Callahan didn't come to Silver Springs just for the charming scenery or job opportunities," Sharon said. "As for Sanderson...you'll find out soon enough. So if you wouldn't mind, I must get back to work." She gave Laura a thin smile. "When the full story breaks, you're welcome to come have an official interview about your amateur sleuthing. It might make for an interesting sidebar."

Sharon returned her attention to the terminal, dismissing Laura with the wave of her hand.

Laura stood there for a moment, heat rising to her cheeks. Amateur sleuthing? A sidebar? She opened her mouth to respond, then closed it again. Engaging further would only feed Sharon's apparent hunger for drama.

With a deep breath, Laura turned and walked away, her steps measured despite the indignation bubbling inside her. She returned to the reading area she'd claimed earlier, sitting in her chair with more force than necessary. The book she'd brought lay open where she'd left it, but the words blurred as her mind replayed Sharon's remarks.

"Unbelievable," she muttered, forcing her attention back to the page.

Laura's phone buzzed with a text from her mother: "Saw another article about your town online. Call me."

She dismissed the notification without responding. The last thing she needed right now was Bridget's commentary. Some battles weren't worth fighting, especially when she was already fighting to solve an investigation. Even as she tried to lose herself in the story, questions about Ruby's background and Dulcie's 'unfortunate history' lingered. Perhaps there was more to discover after all.

# CHAPTER NINETEEN

Laura balanced three plates along her left arm as she navigated through the lunchtime crowd. Coffee, soup, and sandwich aromas filled the air as Jesse delivered Anton's daily specials and Eli made drinks. Every table was full, conversations overlapping—business discussions, friendly catch-ups, and the occasional burst of laughter.

A roast turkey club went to a middle-aged guy in a flannel shirt at table five. The second, a veggie wrap with extra hummus, found its way to a woman in a bright blue scarf who thanked her with a smile. And the soup and half sandwich combo got placed before a young woman with textbooks spread across the table.

The doorbell chimed.

Laura glanced up to see Marcela joining the line at the counter. Her undercut touched up, and her blazer suggested she'd come straight from the Town Clerk's building. Their eyes met, and Marcela offered a small wave.

Laura returned the gesture with a smile, making her way behind the counter to relieve Jesse. "Would you please check the pastry stock? I think we're running short on Layla's apple cinnamon scones. I'll continue taking people's orders."

"On it," Jesse replied, slipping into the back.

Laura served three customers before Marcela reached the front of the line.

"Hi, Marcela! It's always nice to see you outside the Crafters Club meetings."

"Good afternoon," Marcela returned the smile, though her eyes held a certain intensity. "Do you always get this busy for lunch?"

"Friday's special brings them in," Laura said, gesturing to the chalkboard where 'Maple-Dijon Chicken Salad Wrap' was written in Eli's handwriting. "What can I do for you today?"

"I'll take the turkey and avocado on sourdough to go, please," Marcela said. "Also, I've remembered something that might be useful for the...thing you're looking into."

Laura's attention sharpened, though she maintained her professional smile. "Really?"

"It's...something I've observed at PTSA meetings that seems odd in retrospect," Marcela said. "It'd take too long to explain now, so I'll text you later with the details."

"That'd be great, thank you," Laura said, processing the payment while her mind ran at an equal speed.

Marcela nodded, accepting her receipt. With a subdued goodbye, she turned to stand in the waiting area. The lunch rush continued unabated, keeping Laura too busy for extended contemplation. With every order taken, food served, and table cleared—her anticipation grew.

---

Laura pulled out the General Store's P.O. Box key. As ridiculous as it sounded, checking the incoming mail was a task she enjoyed. She pulled open Box two-four-seven's narrow door. Inside was the usual assortment—utility company envelopes, a restaurant supply catalog, and a business newsletter. Laura gathered everything into her bag.

She still had time to sort through the mail and pick up the parcel her grandmother had sent. Gran's occasional care packages were a tradition that had followed her from Boston to Vermont, each containing a letter and a small item. Sometimes it was a knitted scarf for the colder weather, other times it was a scented candle her friends at the assisted living facility insisted 'her granddaughter must try.'

How she looked forward to them.

Laura claimed a space at one of the form-filling counters along the side wall and began sorting through the General Store's mail, creating neat piles—bills for Maggie, catalogs for Kathy, and miscellaneous items.

Someone worked at the adjacent counter space—a distinguished older man in a charcoal suit with subtle pinstripes, filling out certified mail forms. He was pale, made more so by the unflattering light overhead, but he was a person you could only characterize as a gentleman.

As he leaned forward to write, something captured her eye—a book-shaped copper tie pin.

Laura's breath caught.

The memory of Clyde's words from the Timberline Tavern echoed in her mind. He'd seen Vernon there with someone, carrying a briefcase, and wearing a pin...just like that one. She hesitated, not wanting to intrude, but this was too important to ignore.

"Excuse me," she said, keeping her voice low. "I don't mean to interrupt, but I couldn't help noticing your tie pin. It's lovely."

The man looked up from his paperwork with a surprised smile. "Why thank you! It was a gift from my father when I passed the bar exam. All the Lancaster attorneys wear one—a family tradition." He studied her face. "You're...Laura Evans, aren't you? The café manager from the General Store. I heard about your help during that unfortunate business at the Summer Cheese Festival."

"That's right," Laura said, surprised he knew her. "And you're...?"

"Malcolm Lancaster, probate attorney here in Silver Springs." He extended his hand for a handshake. "I enjoy visiting your café when I get the chance—the cranberry scones are exceptional."

"I love Layla's baking too!" Laura said as Malcolm smiled. She hesitated. No, she had a chance. Time to take it. "I hope you don't mind me asking, but that copper book pin you're wearing...someone mentioned seeing a gentleman at the Timberline Tavern with Vernon Reed, who had one just like it."

Malcolm raised an eyebrow.

Laura continued. "I've been...looking into some things about Vernon's death. It was such a terrible loss for our community, and with so many rumors swirling, I want to set things right. So, I wondered if you knew him?"

Malcolm paused mid-signature, considering her words. His expression grew thoughtful. He glanced around, then lowered his voice. "That was me, yes. Vernon requested we meet somewhere less formal than my office." He hesitated. "I can't share specifics, but I can tell you he changed his will a fortnight before his death. After fifteen years with the same arrangements." He gave her a meaningful look. "The timing might be significant." He reached into his jacket pocket and slid a business card across the counter. "If you learn anything concrete, I'd appreciate a call. Vernon was more than just a client—he was a friend."

"Thank you, and I'm sorry for interrupting," Laura said, gathering the store's mail. "Have a great rest of your day."

Malcolm nodded. "Not at all, and thank you."

As Laura collected her grandmother's package, her mind raced with new questions. Vernon had changed his will just days before his murder. What had he known? What had he been preparing for?

⸺⧫◯⧫⸺

Back from the post office, Laura claimed a small table in the far corner of the break room, setting down her lunch—avocado on two slices of rye toast, topped with a sprinkle of everything bagel seasoning. The sounds of the café continued at a distance, though the lunch rush had tapered right off.

Laura stared at the phone. Come on, show a notification! When it buzzed, at last, she grabbed it so quickly she nearly dropped it.

Marcela's name appeared above a message that began, "Sorry for the delay. So, what I meant to tell you was…"

Laura tapped to open the full text. It was an audio message, so Laura put on a pair of earphones.

"Sending this as a voice clip because it's running too long. I'm in the Parent Student Teacher Association at Silver Springs High—my twin girls are juniors. Ruby Callahan's a member too. Her son Arlo is in the same grade. I've known her for almost three years through school stuff. She used to be super outgoing—volunteering, baking for meetings, chatting with everyone. But when Dulcie moved to town, Ruby changed. She still shows up, but keeps her distance. The weird thing is how she talks about Dulcie. At least once a month she brings up how lonely Dulcie is or how she's struggling to adjust here. I've tried suggesting Dulcie come to stuff, but every time Ruby shuts it down. Says Dulcie's too shy, wouldn't enjoy it, like Dulcie can't decide for herself. It's been bothering me. And now, with what happened to poor Vernon...I don't know. It feels off."

Laura put away her earbuds. The image of Ruby at the nature preserve came to mind—her angry approach, the territorial way she'd taken Dulcie's arm, the threatening gesture as they'd left. What Marcela described fit with that behavior, but extended it back much further. She took a thoughtful sip of her water. What was Ruby's motivation? Was she hiding something about Dulcie's past?

Laura took notes on her phone, adding Marcela's message to her growing web of connections. She considered what she knew about Ruby—part-time at The Village Skein, working at Goldenleaf Apple Farm during harvest season, and Dulcie's best friend. Each role provided opportunities for Ruby to have learned something significant about Vernon.

Laura typed a response to Marcela: "I appreciate you sharing this with me. It's good to know."

# CHAPTER TWENTY

Nicholas entered the café that afternoon, which was unusual enough. But what caught Laura's attention was the change in his bearing—the familiar strain had melted away, replaced with nervous energy.

He approached the counter, his hands shoved deep in the pockets of a denim vest Laura hadn't seen before. Gone was the Goldenleaf Apple Farm shirt he always wore, but he'd kept his work boots. Even his expression had shifted—the furrow between his brows had smoothed.

"Good afternoon, Nicholas," Laura said, setting aside some take away containers. "Are you ready to order?"

"A black coffee, please," he replied. The effect of hearing his full first name—what he preferred to be called—still hadn't worn off. That ridiculous smile bloomed on his face for a split second before his expression went neutral again. "And a minute of your time, if you're not too busy."

Laura glanced around the quiet café and paused for a moment. "Of course. Let me prepare your drink for you."

A little while later, Nicholas leaned on the counter, sipping the coffee Eli had made for him, as Laura prepared afternoon tea for a customer. He kept his hands wrapped around the mug, staring into the dark liquid. "I quit. This morning. I walked into my dad's office and told him I'm done."

Laura couldn't hide her surprise. "I imagine that wasn't easy. How did your father react?"

A humorless laugh escaped him. "About as well as you'd expect. Called me ungrateful, shortsighted, irresponsible—the usual Roy Beckett greatest hits. Said I was abandoning the family legacy." His fingers tensed around the mug. "He started ranting about how I was throwing away my birthright. Dad mentioned the will, said Vernon had 'guaranteed' my future. As if I ever wanted that." Nicholas stared into his coffee. "You know what's ironic? I told Vernon exactly how I felt about the business three months ago. He listened, unlike my father, and got this strange look on his face."

"That's...interesting timing," Laura said. "That must've been difficult—your father planning your entire future without considering what you wanted. What do you think that strange look Vernon gave you meant? And what made you decide now was the time to leave?"

Nicholas hesitated, eyes darting to the café door as if checking who might enter. "I don't know. Maybe he was surprised? A confirmation of something he'd already known? I've wanted to quit for years. Vernon's death just...clarified things for me." He set his mug down. "Life's too short to spend it fulfilling someone else's dreams, you know?"

"I do," Laura said, thinking of her recent move from Boston to Silver Springs. "What'll you do next? Music?"

A smile flickered across Nicholas's face. "You remember that? Yeah." His smile faded. "I've got some ideas I'm working on. Just need to figure out the finances."

Laura recalled Christopher's account of seeing Nicholas passing an envelope of cash to Warren Fisk. "I hope things go okay. Starting fresh can be expensive, especially in a creative field."

Nicholas' posture stiffened. "I've been saving! And there are opportunities if you know where to look."

Perhaps...he was referring to Warren Fisk?

Laura nodded. "I'm so glad you've taken that first step. Being...honest with others around you about what you want out of life...takes courage."

Bravery she hadn't found yet. Especially with her mother. She recognized the irony. Here she was, encouraging Nicholas to stand up to his father's expectations while she still fielded weekly phone calls from her mother about "when you'll settle down and start a real life."

Nicholas set down his cup and gave her a knowing, gentle smile. "I appreciate that, and you taking the time to listen. I should get going. Thanks for the coffee."

"Nicholas," Laura said as he turned to leave, "I hope things work out for you."

He paused. "Thanks. I hope so too."

As he left, Laura added this development to her mental map of the case. Nicholas had just removed himself from the family business at a critical moment. And he knew more than he was saying.

Laura reviewed her closing checklist behind the counter. Between inventory counts, she bagged leftover muffins for the Meals That Matter program.

Kathy marched in from the back rooms, toolbelt jingling, and headed straight to the tables with their upturned chairs, hunting through them. She grabbed one. "Found the culprit! Just needs ten minutes of attention."

From her stepstool perch, where she wiped the top shelves, Maggie groaned. "Kathleen Quinn! Wasn't the plan to replace those old things, not patch them up again?"

"Why replace what I can fix?" Kathy's hand drill whirred to life.

"The last time you 'fixed' something quickly, you were limping for a week," Maggie said.

Kathy studied the broken chair leg. "Doesn't count. That was a dresser."

Laura pressed her lips together, suppressing a smile.

Maggie sighed. "Eight years together and she still thinks she's a professional carpenter."

"Eight years," Kathy said, measuring the leg, "and she still thinks I'll let good furniture go to waste."

Laura couldn't hold back her grin any longer.

She only had one task left, then, home time. There was a session of crocheting and listening to an audiobook with her name on it. The soft click of the door to the back rooms opening made her look up. Ben's head poked in, his eyes darting around the empty café before he stepped inside.

"Hi, Ben," Laura said. "Need a hand with something?"

"Yeah, do you have a second?" Ben asked. "I overheard something kinda major for...the big-deal mystery project."

He approached and drummed his fingers against the counter. "I was at Hearthstone Legal Services today. They needed their gutters cleaned. I was up on the roof, and I overheard something through an open window."

"Really? What did you hear?" Laura asked.

"There were these two voices chatting," Ben said. "I couldn't spot them, but it was all 'Izzy this, Izzy that.'"

"Izzy?" Laura said. "What were they saying?"

Ben grimaced. "Nothing good, trust me! One of them, a woman, said 'that theater kid' was poking his nose in where it didn't belong, and then she goes "thanks for taking care of the problem." It gave me the absolute creeps, Laura!"

Laura's mind raced. "Could you tell who either voice belonged to?"

Ben shook his head. "The woman's voice was...I don't know, proper? Educated? The other person was quieter. I tried to peek in, but nearly lost my balance, so I didn't see them. By then, they'd moved to another room."

Perhaps...it had been Roxanne? But she'd offered Izzy legal help. And why would she have it out for Izzy? It didn't make sense.

"Can you recall anything else they said?" Laura asked.

"I wish I could say more," Ben said.

Laura chewed her lower lip. "Thank you for telling me about this. It could be important."

"I thought so!" He grinned. "Didn't I say I'd come in handy? What's next, a midnight stakeout? Hidden cameras? Should I go back and pretend the gutters need additional work?"

Laura had to suppress a smile. "Let's take this one step at a time. Just stay observant, and be careful, please."

"Don't worry! Danger is my middle name," Ben said with a grin.

Laura smiled. "I thought you said it was Wilbur."

He nodded. "Alright, you got me! One more thing. While I was there, Roxanne, if that's her name, was talking to someone about their books, saying something about 'reconciling the accounts' and 'adjusting the entries.' Sounded like accountant-speak to me. Isn't she a lawyer?"

Laura shrugged. "She has a background in accounting, too."

"Makes sense. Night, Laura!" He paused at the door. "You're going to crack this case wide open. Just wait and see."

The Silver Springs Community Theater's front doors swung open with a theatrical creak as Laura stepped inside, leaving the September warmth behind. Unlike the sleek spaces of Boston's theater district, this converted church embraced its century-old bones—exposed wooden beams arched overhead like protective ribs, while mismatched vintage seats faced a stage framed by deep red curtains. Voices carried from somewhere beyond the house, actors warming up with vocal exercises that echoed through the space with haunting musicality.

Laura clutched her small sewing kit as she made her way down the center aisle. A woodland scene was taking shape on the stage—half-painted flats depicting riverbanks and weeping willows, with props scattered on a side table. She'd come to a rehearsal at Evelyn's suggestion, volunteering with the costume department to gather information about Izzy and his dismissal from the production. She needed to understand if there was more to the story.

"I insist you consider the consequences of your actions!" A man in a partial costume—a tweed vest and a fake nose attached by elastic—paced across the stage, gesticulating at a shorter woman in a garish green coat who stood with arms crossed.

"Badger, old fellow, where's your sense of adventure?" the woman replied.

"Cut!" A bearded man in his fifties with russet-brown hair clapped his hands from the front row. His pale skin flushed with exertion, despite only sitting and waving his arms around. "Terri, remember Toad's posture—chest out, chin up! You're not just eccentric, you're fabulously deluded about your capabilities!"

Laura reached the edge of the stage, hesitating.

A silver-haired woman sitting a few seats away from the director noticed her. "Can I help you?"

"I'm Laura Evans. Evelyn Chan arranged for me to help the costume department tonight? She mentioned Liz Andrews..."

The woman's face brightened. "You're Evelyn's friend? Wonderful!" She jumped to her feet and exited the row, stopping a few paces away. "I'm Elizabeth Andrews, but please call me Liz." She extended a hand, which Laura shook. "Perfect timing. The costume team is working in the hall through that side door. Follow that corridor and you'll find about four frazzled people surrounded by animal costumes and fabric scraps. Tell them I sent you."

Laura thanked her and headed toward the indicated doorway. Following the sounds of conversation and the whir of sewing machines, she emerged into a cramped room bustling with activity. Racks of partially completed costumes lined one wall, while long tables overflowed with fabric, fur trim, and various accessories. Four women worked at different stations—one operating a sewing machine, two hand-stitching details onto costumes, and another sorting through piles of materials.

A woman in her sixties with a tape measure draped around her neck looked up as Laura entered. "Please tell me you're the help Liz promised."

"I am," Laura said. "I'm Laura Evans."

"Thank goodness for that," the woman said. "I'm Amelia, the costume coordinator, or perhaps more accurately...the chaos coordinator. Do you sew?"

"I can't use a machine, but I can hand sew," Laura said.

"That'll do!" Amelia said, gesturing to a table piled with woodland creature vests. "Do you know the shank method?"

Laura nodded.

Amelia slumped with relief. "The universe is being kind for once. Each of the vests already has the button placement marked. You'll just need to sew them on. I'm happy to help if you get stuck."

Laura settled at the assigned table, picking up a small brown vest with a pattern suggesting otter fur, preparing her items from the sewing kit she'd brought. "I'd be happy to sew on those for you! I'll let you know if I need anything."

She began sewing on the buttons, and the group worked in comfortable silence. Amelia spoke with another woman in the corner. Laura's ears pricked.

"The insurance renewal notice came in yesterday," Amelia said. "It's gone up again."

"How much do we have in the fund so far?" the woman asked.

"Twelve-fifty. We're still two-fifty short, and the deadline's next month." Amelia sighed. "We've been doing bake sales and passing the hat after every rehearsal, but it's been slow going."

Laura's fingers paused on the button she was sewing. Two hundred and fifty dollars—not an impossible amount, but a struggle for a community theater group already stretched thin.

"How's everything been going?" Laura asked.

A younger woman with red hair in double buns snorted from her position at the sewing machine. "It's been going great until Kenneth forgets his department and tries to get involved."

Laura looked up. "Is Kenneth the director?"

"That's him," the young woman said with an eye roll. "He's a perfectionist with grand visions and little patience."

Amelia shot the woman a warning look. "Romy! No gossiping."

"It's not gossip if it's common knowledge," Romy said, feeding green fabric through her machine. "Besides, the production is still recovering from Kenneth's drama and Izzy being forced out."

The atmosphere in the room shifted.

"Poor guy got a raw deal," a woman working on what seemed like a weasel mask said.

Amelia sighed. "Poppy, please. We have work to do."

"It applies to our situation," Poppy said. "We wouldn't be so behind if Kenneth hadn't thrown Izzy off the production. He built half the sets!"

"Was he not good at his job?" Laura asked, threading her needle through the fabric.

"The opposite," said an older woman. "I'm Kirsten, by the way. Izzy was one of our most dedicated members—passionate about every project he took on."

"Too passionate, according to Kenneth," Romy said with a groan. "He called Izzy 'temperamental' and 'difficult to work with,' but we know that's not true."

"Izzy cared about the quality of the work," Kirsten said. "He stayed late, came in early."

Laura nodded. "So what happened? Why was he asked to leave?"

"It was sudden," Kirsten said, lowering her voice. "Kenneth announced Izzy was no longer part of the production. Called him a disruption to the creative process."

"Which was complete nonsense," said Poppy. "I've worked with Izzy on three productions, and he was always professional, if enthusiastic."

Romy inhaled sharply. "You all act like it was unexpected. It was planned."

Kirsten paused. "How so?"

Romy took far too long to respond. "I overheard Kenneth on the phone at the previous rehearsals before he made his announcement. Jabbering with someone about 'taking care of that Izzy problem.'"

Poppy groaned. "And you're just mentioning this now?"

Amelia clapped her hands. "That's enough gossip! We have costumes to finish, and The Wind in the Willows opens in two weeks. Laura didn't come here for theater drama."

But Laura had. Or at least, she'd come for this information. She bent her head over her sewing, feigning concentration. Was someone...else involved in Kenneth's decision? Who?

The door swung open, and the man who'd been instructing the two actors earlier strode in. "Amelia, how are we coming with Toad's transformation outfits? And the prison guard uniform still needs work."

"We're on schedule, Kenneth," Amelia said, doing a remarkable job of keeping a steady voice. The subtle frown lines on her forehead gave her away, though. "Everything will be ready for the dress rehearsal."

He had the audacity to huff, his gaze sweeping over the room before landing on Laura. "You must be the new helper. I'm Kenneth Fraser, the director."

"Laura Evans," she said.

"Are you new to Silver Springs? I don't recall seeing you around before." Kenneth asked.

"Yes, I am. I moved here early last month," Laura said. "I heard wonderful things about your theater group. Particularly about the craftsmanship of your sets."

A tension appeared in Kenneth's jaw. "Yes, we've had some...personnel changes. Creative differences, you understand."

"Yeah right," Romy muttered.

Kenneth's expression hardened. "As I've said before, Romy, Izzy Lennox was unpredictable and hard to work with. We can't have someone who thinks themselves more important than the production."

"I commend you on your levels of delusion," Romy said, raising an eyebrow.

Kenneth drew a deep breath. "I need to get back to rehearsal." He nodded to Laura. "Nice to meet you." The door slammed behind him.

Amelia covered her face with her hand, letting out a sigh. "Romy, how many times have I told you—"

Romy somehow interrupted her with a shrug. "His ego can afford to be taken down a peg. Or five." She turned to Laura with a grin. "Don't worry, Kenneth and I are the only tetchy ones. Will you come see the play when it opens? I'm biased, of course, but I know you'll enjoy it."

"I'd love to come," Laura said as she continued sewing.

Romy nodded. "Great! And since Kenneth didn't have the manners to thank you—"

"Romy—" Amelia said with a warning tone.

"We appreciate you coming and helping." Romy finished, ignoring Amelia. The other costume volunteers voiced their agreement, and Laura smiled.

# Chapter Twenty-One

The Morrison Building welcomed Laura with the familiar creak of its century-old floorboards as she climbed the stairs to Evelyn's second-floor apartment. The scent of something savory—a stew, perhaps—wafted down the hallway. Laura knocked on Evelyn's door.

"Laura, perfect timing!" Jasmine said as she appeared in the entranceway, her box braids held back with a blue paisley scarf.

Oscar greeted Laura at the door with an insistent meow. Monty sat on the corner bookshelf, his amber eyes tracking her movement across the room. Inside, Evelyn stood by the stove stirring what Laura recognized as her signature lamb stew—a recipe Evelyn claimed had sustained her through forty Vermont winters. Never question Evelyn's culinary wisdom.

Judith appeared from the kitchen, clutching a basket of Red Trillium Bakery bread. "There she is! Now the Council of Concerned Citizens can convene."

"The...council?" Laura asked with a smile.

"A strategy session sounds too formal," Judith said with a dismissive wave. "And 'gossip gathering' doesn't have the right tone of authority."

Evelyn laughed. "A proper dinner might help us organize our thoughts. We've been gathering information, and it's time to put it together."

Evelyn set the dining table with her blue-flowered china. Oscar and Monty observed from their respective perches—Oscar curled on the windowsill, Monty sitting on the corner bookshelf. The women settled around the table as Evelyn served the steaming stew—chunks of lamb and root vegetables fragrant with rosemary and thyme. The rich aroma filled the room as they passed around the bread basket and butter dish.

"Now," Evelyn said once everyone had been served. "Judith and I have news from our Burlington excursion today."

"Not just a trip, an investigative assignment!" Judith said, buttering a slice of bread. "And I must say, Lavinia Reed is a formidable woman, even at eighty-two. Sharp as a tack, too."

"She saw right through our reason for dropping in," Evelyn said. "But that didn't stop her from telling us what we needed to know."

"Did she mention Vernon's recent visits?" Laura asked.

Evelyn and Judith exchanged a glance before Evelyn replied. "That's where things became interesting. According to Lavinia, she and Vernon had a complicated relationship at best. They'd been estranged for a decade—barely speaking beyond obligatory holiday phone calls."

"She called him 'headstrong and secretive, like his father,'" Judith said.

Laura took a taste of the rich stew, savoring its warmth as she considered this information. "So, if their relationship was strained, why did he visit her?"

"That's what puzzled Lavinia," Evelyn said. "She said Vernon appeared unannounced about three months ago."

"That timeframe keeps appearing in everything we learn," Jasmine said.

Judith nodded. "Lavinia commented he looked 'diminished.' He dismissed her concerns."

"The most revealing part," Evelyn said, "was Vernon began...making a genuine effort. One time, he brought her favorite chocolates, and another, old family photo albums he'd found."

Laura's spoon paused halfway to her mouth. "Did she have any theories about what prompted this change?"

Evelyn sipped from her water glass. "She believes Vernon had received bad news. Or, he was proving he was still a good person after having done something wrong."

Judith frowned. "It's not much, but it's something."

Laura nodded. "Thank you both for going."

Judith grinned. "Give me a few more assignments, and I might discover my true calling as the next Sherlock. Except...we all know who the Sherlock in this room is. And Doctor Watson."

"Who's that?" Laura asked.

"Evelyn, of course," Judith said, smiling.

Jasmine's expression took on one of mock affront. "Why am I not included?"

Judith let out a light laugh, shaking her head. "My mistake. You'll have to split the honor of being Dr. Watson between the two of you."

Jasmine grinned.

Turning to Laura, she asked, "Did you learn anything at the theater?"

Laura nodded. "Before I mention that…I learned something interesting at the Maplewood Woolgatherers meeting that might be relevant." She took another bite of the rich stew.

Evelyn tilted her head.

"They were discussing Izzy," Laura said. "Apparently, he asked Vernon for a raise in August and was turned down, even though Goldenleaf Apple Farm has been doing well this year."

"That seems unlike Vernon," Jasmine said, frowning. "I thought he was always fair with his employees."

"That's just it," Laura continued. "Several members mentioned Izzy has been struggling financially."

"Financial pressure can be a powerful motive," Evelyn said.

"Especially combined with resentment," Jasmine added. "If Izzy felt undervalued after years of dedication…"

Laura shook her head. "But it doesn't fit with Izzy's character. From everything I've seen, he's passionate about Goldenleaf Apple Farm. Why kill Vernon when he could find another job?"

"Perhaps there's something we're still missing," Evelyn said.

Laura nodded. "And as you know, Izzy was removed from the Silver Springs Players. A woman doing the costumes, Romy, said she overheard the director, Kenneth Fraser, on the phone discussing 'dealing with that Izzy problem.'"

Evelyn's seriousness sharpened. "How…interesting."

"So, someone else might've influenced Kenneth's decision?" Jasmine asked.

"It appears so," Laura said. "But...why?"

Judith frowned. "How dastardly!"

"The perfect scapegoat," Jasmine said.

The four women ate in thoughtful silence for a moment.

"That reminds me," Laura said. "I ran into Malcolm Lancaster at the post office today."

"The named partner at Lancaster & Porter? How did you recognize him?" Evelyn asked.

"I didn't, but I saw the tie pin he was wearing," Laura said. "Do you remember what Clyde mentioned, Jasmine?"

Her friend raised an eyebrow. "I remember Clyde said...something about Vernon meeting with someone?"

Laura nodded. "He also said the person Vernon was with was wearing a tie pin. I noticed Malcolm wearing it this afternoon and went to ask about it. He mentioned Vernon changed his will for the first time in fifteen years, just a fortnight prior to his passing."

Jasmine's eyes widened. "How strange. What made him decide to change? And what changes?"

Laura took a sip of water. "That's what we'll have to find out. And what about you, Jasmine? Anything new?"

"Yes," Jasmine said, pulling a small notebook from her pocket. "I spoke with Melinda Winrow yesterday. She mentioned something interesting—Vernon had withdrawn from the habitat restoration project a month ago. It fits with what we know so far, but—she said Warren Fisk had stepped up to take over Vernon's responsibilities in the project, even though those two could barely stand each other."

Laura sighed. "Warren again. He's connected to so many threads in this investigation."

"Speaking of investigative threads...I also have news," Judith said.

All eyes turned to her.

"I've long suspected Dulcie of hiding something," Judith said. "Those furtive looks, the way Ruby shields her...there was always a piece missing. It bothered me. So this morning, I followed her."

"Judith!" Evelyn said. "What? Why? You can't...do that!"

"I can and I have," Judith said, straightening her cardigan. "I discovered Dulcie gets every second Friday off from her job at Northern Necessities. So...I made a plan."

"And?" Jasmine asked, eyes wide.

"This morning, I tailed her around town. First to the post office, then the credit union—nothing unusual. Then," Judith said, her voice dropping, "she went to the Quartermark Inn for morning tea. Not in the dining room, mind you, but the garden patio at the back."

Laura stared at her. "What was she doing there?"

"She was meeting someone, a man I didn't recognize," Judith said. "Tall, well-dressed. They chose the most secluded table—tucked in the corner, trying not to be seen."

"Did you overhear anything?" Jasmine asked.

Judith nodded. "Not everything, but enough. They spoke in hushed tones, but I heard her say, 'he almost found out,' and the man replied something like, 'I'm glad he didn't.'"

The room fell silent.

"All this time," Judith said, "we've been assuming Vernon was the one keeping secrets. What if it's Dulcie who's been having an affair? What if Vernon discovered it?"

Laura frowned. "Ruby implied Vernon was having an affair, not Dulcie."

"Perhaps that's what Ruby wanted us to believe," Evelyn said.

"It'd explain Ruby's overprotectiveness," Jasmine added. "And why Dulcie has been so distraught—not just grief, but guilt."

"And perhaps," Evelyn said, "a motive for murder."

Laura leaned back, the stew forgotten as her mind raced with this new possibility. The puzzle pieces were shifting again, forming a different picture.

"We have to identify this man," Laura said. "And if Vernon knew about him."

"I got a good look at him," Judith said. "I could identify him again. Distinguished-looking, silver at the temples, carries himself like someone used to being in charge." She turned to Laura, her eyes gleaming. "Where next, Sherlock?"

Laura buried her face in her hands and groaned. "Please don't start."

Judith laughed, and the other two joined in.

"Sounds like we have a new lead to pursue," Evelyn said. "And...there's something else. I saw Sadie Evers yesterday at Style Revival—Bethany Clarke's hairdressing salon. Sadie is Toby Evers' wife, the vegetable farmer. They live across from Warren Fisk."

Laura and Jasmine exchanged glances.

"Sadie mentioned something odd," Evelyn continued. "The night Vernon was killed, she was walking her dog past Warren's house. She heard raised voices—like people arguing."

"Was someone with him?" Jasmine asked.

Evelyn nodded. "She couldn't see, but it sounded like it. Then he got in his truck and drove off, which contradicts what I heard. He claimed he was home alone doing Sudoku puzzles all evening."

"Perhaps we should ask him," Jasmine suggested. "If he has nothing to hide..."

Laura nodded. "It's worth looking into. Though it might have nothing to do with Vernon's murder."

"Or everything," Judith said.

Evelyn smiled. "Now, let's finish our dinner before it gets cold."

The women dug back into their meals, their chatter drifting between theories and quiet observations. But Laura's mind wasn't on it. She kept returning to Dulcie—and that secret meeting. Was that what Dulcie had almost confessed at the nature preserve? And more importantly...was it tied to Vernon's death?

# Chapter Twenty-Two

Laura flipped the chairs from their upturned positions on the tables, each one landing with a soft thud against the floor. Outside, dew glittered on the village green, the temperature having dipped overnight.

"We've got about forty-five minutes until we open," Laura said, glancing at the vintage clock on the wall. "Did Layla mention when she'd drop off today's delivery?"

When Jasmine didn't respond, Laura looked over. Her friend leaned against the counter, her box braids pulled back into a ponytail, eyes narrowed and fixed on the newspaper spread before her.

"Jasmine? Is everything okay?"

Jasmine looked up. "Not exactly. Have you seen this morning's paper?"

Laura shook her head, setting down the last chair. "What happened?"

"It's about Dulcie." Jasmine pushed the newspaper across the counter as Laura approached. "Sharon Winters' latest exposé. It's...you should read it."

Laura pulled the paper closer, her breath catching as she read the headline: 'Death Follows Dulcie: Vernon Reed's Former Partner Has Suspicious Past.'

Her eyes widened as she read further.

'The woman known to Silver Springs residents as Dulcie Sanderson arrived here three years ago, presenting herself as a quiet newcomer seeking small-town tranquility. However, an exclusive Maplewood Memo investigation has uncovered this woman was formerly Portia Wetherington of Connecticut—a person with a troubling history of being the last person to see her loved ones alive.'

'Public records show her previous husband, Gregory Castor, died from what authorities ruled an accidental fall down basement stairs in their home five years ago. Mere months later, her mother, with whom she lived after her husband's passing, suffered a sudden death. In both cases, she was the sole beneficiary of substantial insurance policies.'

'Within weeks, she changed her name to Dulcie Sanderson and moved to Silver Springs, where she soon became romantically involved with Vernon Reed—who now joins the list of deceased individuals connected to this mysterious woman. And given her reclusive behavior, and reports of her testing the weights of certain hammers at Northern Necessities shortly before the death...one can't help but wonder.'

Laura met Jasmine's worried gaze. "Is this verified information or just Sharon's sensationalism?"

"I checked online while you were reading," Jasmine said. "I can't find evidence of the name change, but there are local news articles from Connecticut about both deaths, and they were ruled accidental."

Laura put her fingers to her temples. "So she's now...connected to three deaths?"

"And they all benefited her financially," Jasmine said, retrieving mugs from beneath the counter and arranging them in neat rows. "Vernon's will hasn't been executed yet, but surely it'd include her."

Laura paced behind the counter, her mind racing. "That could explain Ruby's protective behavior. Maybe she knows about her friend's past and is shielding her from scrutiny." She paused. "Or perhaps Ruby is complicit? She arrived in town first, but they knew each other from college."

"What could she gain from Vernon's death?" Jasmine positioned the salt and sugar containers on various tables. "Money is the obvious answer, but Vernon wasn't wealthy. Comfortable, yes, but not enough to kill for unless she was desperate."

Laura nodded. "There's also whatever she found in Vernon's possessions after he died. If Vernon discovered something about her past…"

"It could've given her a motive to silence him," Jasmine said. "Or what if someone's framing her? Using her to direct attention away from themselves?"

"Either way," Laura said, "we should speak with her."

Jasmine nodded. "Agreed. But after this article, she'll be even more guarded! How do we get to her?"

"I'm not sure," Laura said. "We'll find a way. If Dulcie's been eliminating people close to her, we have to understand why. And if she's being framed, she deserves a chance to defend herself."

The store's phone rang, and Laura moved to answer.

It was Layla, waiting outside, with her delivery of baked goods. As Laura helped unload apple turnovers and cider donuts, the weight of the morning's revelation stayed with her. Once Layla had left, and Laura began restocking the jam jars, she noticed a familiar figure across the street.

Ruby stood outside the Town Hall where a newspaper dispenser sat, clutching what appeared to be the morning's edition of the Maplewood Memo. Laura could just make out Ruby's intensity, the way she kept reading and re-reading the front page, her lips moving as if she were arguing with the words themselves.

Ruby crumpled the paper, then smoothed it out again. Her shoulders shook. Anger or tears? Laura couldn't tell. Ruby pulled out her phone, then stopped, shoving it in her pocket. Her head snapped up, scanning the street. When her gaze fell on the General Store, she hesitated, took a step forward, then stopped.

She pressed her palm against her forehead, then folded the newspaper with sharp, angry movements and strode away. Dulcie Sanderson—and her former self—had just moved from a person of interest to a prime suspect in their investigation. The only question was, where did Ruby fit into all this? What did she know?

* * *

The morning wore on, heading into the afternoon. The Maplewood Memo's latest edition made its rounds—more than one customer poured over the front page, then leaned toward their companions.

"Have you seen this?" A middle-aged woman in a navy cardigan tapped the newspaper as Laura delivered her coffee. "About Vernon Reed's partner? I always thought she was too quiet. The quiet ones are the ones you have to watch."

"Sounds like there's a lot going around today," Laura said. "Would you like anything else?"

The woman shook her head, disappointed, but said nothing more. Thankfully.

Laura offered a noncommittal smile and moved away.

She had a list of errands she'd meant to tackle during her break, but she made a quick lunch and retreated to the staff room. The last thing she needed was more questions—or more reminders of the latest scandal.

She'd tried something new today, a Warm Grain Bowl, with farro, quinoa, kale, roasted beets, and feta with a lemon-tahini dressing. She'd barely taken a single mouthful when her phone buzzed in her pocket. It didn't let up.

A call? Was it Evelyn? Or Izzy? To her surprise, it was The Village Skein. Why would they ring her now, especially while she was working? She hadn't ordered anything in.

She picked up. "Hi, this is Laura."

"Laura. It's Ruby Callahan."

Laura almost dropped the phone. Ruby's voice sounded strained, lacking its usual assertive edge.

"Ruby," Laura said. "This is...unexpected."

A momentary quiet stretched between them.

"I need to speak with you. In person. Today, if possible," Ruby said.

Laura put her head in her free hand, mind spinning. After Ruby blocked any contact, this sudden reversal was suspicious at best, dangerous at worst.

"May I ask what this is about?" Laura asked.

Ruby's exhale was audible through the phone. "Dulcie found something. Among Vernon's things. She wants you to see it. And...there are things we need to say. Both of us."

A chill ran down Laura's spine.

"I see," Laura said. "This...seems like something that might be better discussed with the authorities."

"No. Not yet. That's not how this works," Ruby said. "It's...messy. Dulcie insisted we go to you first."

Laura frowned. "Why should I come?"

Ruby sighed. "Because it matters. Obviously."

Laura said nothing more.

Ruby gave a groan. "Fine! Look, you won't get it unless you see it for yourself, but what I can say now is Dulcie...testing those hammers? It's a pure coincidence."

"How so?" Laura asked.

"Dulcie and I were working on a DIY project," Ruby said. "Converting an old dresser into a bench seat with storage. Vernon had been acting weird for months—Dulcie needed a distraction. We found plans online. She was comparing hammers because I hadn't told her what we specifically needed. That's all!"

Laura sighed. "Then how do you explain the photo of you, Vernon, and Dulcie, with Vernon's face crossed out?"

Ruby gasped. "Excuse me?"

"At Dulcie's house," Laura said. "A photo from last year, showing you, Dulcie, and Vernon at a summer barbecue."

"How did you—you know what, never mind. I...that was me, but not for the reason you think!" Ruby spluttered a few times before continuing. "I introduced them! And it started out well, but when he got so secretive...I couldn't bear seeing him treat her like that.

The photo was older but me defacing the photo was recent...I didn't kill him! I swear!"

Several beats of silence.

Laura frowned. "Where and when were you thinking of meeting?"

"After you finish work. Come to my house on Brook Street—the blue Cape Cod with the copper weathervane. We'll be waiting." Ruby's tone softened. "I know what you must be thinking after that article, but it's not what it seems. None of it is."

Laura considered her options. Meeting alone with two women now connected to multiple suspicious deaths was risky, but this might be her only chance to get answers.

"I can be there around six thirty. But I'm not coming alone. I'll be bringing Evelyn and Jasmine."

A sound that might've been a humorless laugh came through the line. "Fine. Bring whoever you want. And Laura? Before you point fingers, just hear us out. That's all I'm asking."

The line clicked off.

She stared at her phone for a moment. Whatever awaited her at six thirty that night, one thing was certain: something was about to change.

⸻ ◦ ⸻

Late that night, after having talked to Ruby and Dulcie, Laura leaned forward in her chair in Evelyn's living room. "It's all here. Everything we need to solve this case."

Jasmine sat cross-legged on the couch, sorting through notes, while Evelyn maintained a thoughtful silence from her armchair. While Monty sat beside Jasmine, Oscar chose Laura's lap, purring as she stroked his fur.

"Three months ago," Laura continued, reaching for a card labeled 'Vernon's Timeline,' and holding it up, "everything changed. Look at this." She picked up a newspaper clipping. "Public perception versus private actions. The hammer was just misdirection. And Izzy was the perfect target."

The bung hammer. The rumors spread through town. The careful construction of suspicion aimed away from the killer.

"We need to call Detective Sergeant Ramirez."

Jasmine and Evelyn exchanged glances as Laura reached for her phone. Even Monty's ears perked forward.

"Laura?" Ramirez asked.

"We've figured out who killed Vernon Reed."

A long pause followed.

When Ramirez spoke, her voice carried a weariness Laura hadn't heard before. "I've spent the last two weeks interviewing, following forensic leads, and running background checks. Every time I think I have something solid, it falls apart under scrutiny. The fingerprints on the murder weapon belong to half of the farm's employees. The forensic timeline gives us a six-hour window with no witnesses. Our strongest suspect has an alibi that's unverifiable but not disprovable." She sucked in a breath. "So yes, I'm listening. But I need more than theories."

For the next fifteen minutes, Laura outlined what she'd pieced together.

"It fits," Ramirez said when Laura finished. "But we need more than circumstantial evidence."

"What if we could get a confession?" Laura asked.

"No." Ramirez's response was immediate. "I've been patient with your...involvement...but I won't allow civilians to confront a murder suspect."

Laura sighed. "Detective Sergeant, you just said your leads have stalled—"

"I understand what you're saying, but that doesn't mean I'm willing to put you in danger. Setting up confrontations with killers is how people get hurt. Or killed."

Evelyn spoke up. "What if it were conducted under your direct supervision?"

A long silence stretched.

At last, Ramirez spoke, for once hesitant. "Even if I were to consider such an unorthodox approach—and I'm not saying I am—it would require extensive safety protocols and backup plans."

Laura leaned forward, Oscar protesting as she dislodged him. "Malcolm Lancaster is handling Vernon's will."

"And this is related how?" Ramirez asked.

"Malcolm mentioned something interesting—Vernon changed his will shortly before his death," Laura said. "This could provide the perfect opportunity to draw out the killer."

"How?" Ramirez asked.

Laura exchanged glances with Evelyn and Jasmine before continuing. "Malcolm could host the will reading at his office. He could invite everyone connected to Vernon—Nicholas, Warren, Roy, Roxanne, Dulcie, Ruby, Izzy—all suspects in one room."

"Then?" Ramirez pressed.

"I'd lay out what we've discovered. When confronted with the evidence, especially the unexpected revelations in the will, the killer will reveal themselves."

A long pause followed. "This is unorthodox, Laura. Highly so."

"So is murder," Laura said, meeting Evelyn's approving gaze.

"If I sign off on this, and convince my chief of its efficacy," Ramirez said, "I need to be involved in every step of the planning. No surprises. No amateur heroics."

"Of course," Laura said.

Another silence ensued.

Ramirez sighed. "Let me speak with Malcolm Lancaster tonight. If he confirms what you've told me about the will and agrees to cooperate with law enforcement, I'll consider it. But this has to be done by the book."

"I understand," Laura said.

"I'll call Malcolm to discuss the logistics," Ramirez continued. "You need to understand, if we go through with this, it's a police operation. You three will be there only as witnesses. Is that clear?"

"Crystal clear," Laura said, glancing at her friends, who nodded in agreement.

"And you'll need to be careful. The person who killed Vernon won't hesitate to hurt someone else if they feel cornered."

After ending the call, Laura let out a long breath. "That's step one."

Evelyn's phone rang half an hour later. She grabbed it and glanced at the screen with a knowing nod. "It's the Lancaster & Porter business line. That must be Malcolm."

"Why do they have your number?" Laura asked.

"One of their real estate attorneys helped me with some permits a few year ago," Evelyn replied, then answered the call. "Malcolm? Yes, we're all here." She put him on speaker.

"Detective Sergeant Ramirez just called me," he said without preamble. "This is extraordinary, Laura."

"I know it's unusual," Laura admitted, "but it's our best chance to expose Vernon's killer."

"I agree," Malcolm said, surprising her. "Vernon was my client for fifteen years. He deserves justice." He paused. "The Detective Sergeant and I have worked out the preliminaries. My office at two pm tomorrow. She'll hav e officers positioned. I'll make the calls to ensure everyone attends—I'll cite 'urgent matters related to the estate' that require immediate attention."

"Thank you, Malcolm," Laura said.

After Evelyn hung up, Laura looked at the evidence spread before them, feeling the weight of what tomorrow would bring. "Do you think I'm missing something? Some detail that could unravel this theory or put someone in danger?"

Evelyn stood, moving to the teapot on the side table, pouring three cups of chamomile tea. "The pattern holds firm. The killer has been clever, but not enough to hide the truth."

Jasmine nodded, accepting a cup from Evelyn. "What if they don't confess?"

"The evidence speaks for itself," Laura said, sipping her tea. "People like this—they often can't help themselves. When cornered, when their carefully constructed reality crumbles, they lash out, to justify, to explain. That's when the truth emerges."

"We need to be prepared for anything," Evelyn cautioned. "The murderer will be desperate once they realize they've been caught."

Oscar stretched and moved to Evelyn's vacant chair, kneading the cushions.

"Tomorrow," Evelyn said, raising her teacup in a small toast, "Vernon Reed's murderer will face justice."

As they finished their tea and organized the evidence for tomorrow's confrontation, Laura couldn't help but think of everyone involved in the case. Each had secrets. Each had motives. Each had played a role in this tragedy.

But only one had committed murder.

# Chapter Twenty-Three

Four minutes until two o'clock. Laura's heart drummed against her ribs. The killer sat within arm's reach—breathing the same air, feigning the same confusion as everyone else. Three minutes now.

Soon, the careful web of lies she'd untangled would ensnare its creator.

She'd only been inside a law firm's office once before, and that was for confirming the details of her will, fifteen years ago. Never in her life had she thought she'd do something like this.

Jasmine, who sat next to her, gave her shoulder a gentle squeeze.

The meeting room spoke of authority—heavy oak shelving lined with leather-bound legal texts, diplomas adorning paneled walls, and, at its heart, the table where everyone sat.

Suspects, concerned parties...whatever role each had to play in this investigation would show itself. Steady now.

"Thank you all for coming," Malcolm said.

Words he'd said many times before, but in these circumstances? Perhaps not. She appreciated his willingness to take such a risk. Unusual situations called for unusual methods. He sat at the head of the table, shuffling papers. Among them lay one document at the center of the entire situation. The will.

"I'm Malcolm Lancaster, Vernon Reed's attorney for the past fifteen years."

Again, usual. Except the next words? Not at all.

"Before I proceed with reading Vernon's last will and testament, the circumstances of his death need clarification," He continued, gesturing toward Laura. "If you would?"

Izzy locked eyes with her from across the table, his fingers working at his Macramé—a different one to the plant holder she'd seen last. Same speed, same dexterity, but those hands shook. His gaze held the expression everyone else in the room did.

That fateful Sunday night. What had really happened?

Her conversation with Ramirez yesterday evening after visiting Dulcie's house had prepared her for this moment, but the weight of it still settled on her shoulders.

"I became involved in investigating Vernon's death because...the truth matters."

Izzy's eyes softened at this, though they were still distant. Uncertain.

"Darn right it does," Warren muttered, just loud enough for her to hear. He tugged at his collar.

"Evelyn, Jasmine, and I," Laura said, gesturing toward her friends, "have been gathering information. Three months before Vernon's passing, many people noticed significant changes in his behavior."

"Stopped coming to the Woodland Watch. Even withdrew his annual donation," Warren said, folding his arms across his chest. "I don't know what got into him."

Ruby raised an eyebrow. "Maybe your constant badgering put him off."

Warren sucked in a breath. "I would say the same could be said for the way you interacted with him, but we're in a lawyer's office, and I won't fight."

"How reasonable."

Dulcie placed a hand on her friend's arm. Enough, at least, to get her to fall silent.

Laura drew everyone's attention again. "He also lost weight, started seeing a massage therapist—"

"A what?" Ruby stared at her. "Vernon? Wanting to be touched?"

Laura shrugged. "It's like I said. Unusual. He also began making frequent trips to Burlington, for—"

Both Nicholas and Izzy spoke up at once.

"On business."

"Visiting his mother."

The two young men studied each other, brows furrowing.

Laura nodded. "He told different people conflicting stories."

Roy shook his head. Beside him, his wife Roxanne, surveyed the room with cool detachment.

"I don't understand why he thought that was necessary," Roy said. "He insisted on telling the staff it was for business, but he was visiting his estranged mother. Why, then of all times, to reconnect with her..."

"That wasn't the only reason," Laura said, as Dulcie's eyes filled with tears.

The room went still.

Laura's voice softened. "Vernon had been diagnosed with stage four pancreatic cancer. He had less than six months to live."

Dulcie hid her face with her hands, and Ruby wrapped an arm around her shoulders. Nicholas' eyes widened. Izzy, Warren, Roy, and Roxanne...didn't seem to know what facial expression to choose.

"Cancer?" The word came out strangled. Roy exchanged a horrified glance with Roxanne, whose perfect composure showed a crack—her eyes widening. "He never said...anything."

"Vernon kept his diagnosis private," Laura said. "From what we've learned, he told no one. This diagnosis prompted him to reconsider everything, including his will." Her gaze swept the room. "He was preparing for an end he knew was coming. What he couldn't have prepared for was someone would cut his remaining time short."

The silence that followed her words hung heavy, broken only by Dulcie's soft sniffles and the subtle creaking of chairs as people shifted. She'd laid the first cards on the table. Now she'd see how the others played their hands.

Malcolm nodded. "Thank you, Laura."

He lifted a sealed envelope. The rustling of the heavy paper as he extracted the letter was too loud, like the crackle of kindling just before a fire catches.

"Before I read the formal will," Malcolm said, "Vernon left this message." He cleared his throat. "If Malcolm is reading you this, the cancer won. And I'm...gone. It feels surreal saying that, but it's coming, isn't it? Regarding the will...I've made some choices you'll find surprising. I didn't make them without careful consideration. They reflect what I believe is right, not what's expected. I've lived my life following expectations for too long. At least now I'm choosing my path. And now," Malcolm said, setting aside Vernon's letter and picking up a thicker document, "the last will and testament of Vernon Reed, dated September tenth of this year."

Roy exchanged a quick glance with Roxanne. Warren raised his eyebrows and shot a look at Izzy, then Nicholas.

"To my partner of three years, Dulcie Sanderson," Malcolm read, "I leave my house at three-five-one Farmline Road, along with all its contents and my personal possessions, all personal financial accounts in my name only, except for specific items designated elsewhere in this document."

Dulcie closed her eyes while Ruby squeezed her hand.

"To the Woodland Watch organization of Silver Springs, I leave a bequest of twenty thousand dollars, to be used however they see fit."

Jasmine's eyes widened, her fingers moving to touch the organization's badge on her jacket.

"Any assets not mentioned shall be liquidated, and the proceeds donated to the Vermont Cancer Research Foundation." Malcolm paused. "And now, my fifty percent ownership share in Goldenleaf Apple Farm, along with a trust fund of one hundred and fifty thousand dollars. I leave this..."

The room gave a collective intake of breath.

"To Isaac 'Izzy' Lennox," Malcolm continued. "because of his unwavering dedication to our craft, his innovative spirit, passion, and integrity. He represents the future I envision for the business."

Izzy froze—the constant motion that defined him was absent. His hands flew to his mouth as he let out a strangled sound, halfway between a gasp and a sob. "I don't...I never expected..." Tears ran down his cheeks.

Ruby's eyes popped out of her head, while Dulcie let out an enormous sigh of...relief? Nicholas sat frozen, expression matching Roxanne's, Warren's, and Roy's. Evelyn and Jasmine exchanged knowing glances.

"I'm...free," Nicholas said.

A crack against the polished wooden table echoed through the office.

"This is outrageous!" Roy's voice boomed. He'd slammed his hand down. "This will is falsified. Vernon didn't get the time to change it before—" He froze, the words dying in his throat. His eyes darted around the ro om.

"Before what, Roy?" Malcolm asked.

"Before...his illness progressed," Roy said. "I only meant Vernon wasn't thinking clearly in his last weeks. The pain medication, the stress of his diagnosis..."

Laura lifted an eyebrow. "The timing is interesting, isn't it? He updated it after discovering...financial discrepancies."

Warren, Ruby, and Roy's faces drained of color. Izzy's eyes fell out of his head, and Dulcie gasped. Roxanne seemed shocked. Nicholas looked...guilty.

"Financial discrepancies?" Roy's voice cracked.

Laura nodded. "Vernon found out about the embezzlement."

"Embezzlement?" Roy sputtered. "Who could've—"

"The books don't lie," Laura said. "Neither do the fake invoices."

The office door swung open, and Ramirez strode in, her expression carved from stone. Littlefield and

Patterson flanked her, a half-step behind. Their presence compressed the air in the room, making it difficult to breathe. Chairs creaked. Several heads turned toward the window, calculating. Littlefield moved to stand in front of it, arms folded. Patterson positioned herself by the door.

Roy's face went ashen. "This is ridiculous. How on earth did this—"

"We have the evidence, Roy. All of it." Ramirez said.

Gasps filled the room.

Laura looked at Roy. "You were skimming from Goldenleaf for years. Starting small—inflated supply costs, fictitious vendors. But it added up."

"You don't know what you're talking about," Roy said.

"Vernon hired an independent accountant to review the books when he received his diagnosis," Ramirez said. "He wanted to make sure everything was in order before he died. The accountant found discrepancies in the supply chain payments. They all lead back to shell companies we traced to you."

"When Vernon confronted you about it, you realized everything was at stake. Your reputation, your standing, your son's future." Laura's voice remained calm.

A heavy silence fell over the room. Nicholas slumped back in his chair. Izzy stared at his hands, blinking. Warren facepalmed, shaking his head.

"You killed him," Nicholas said, staring at his father. "You killed Vernon."

"Nicky," Roy hissed. "Keep your mouth shut. This isn't—"

"I've had enough!" Nicholas shouted so loudly he made himself jump. He launched himself from his chair. "You know what? I'm disowning you. Both of you."

A vein popped through on Roy's neck. "You ungrateful little—why you—I was protecting your inheritance! Everything I've done has been for this family, for our legacy!"

Nicholas stared at his father. "A legacy? Is that what you call murder?"

"I protected what was ours!" Roy said. "I was preserving your birthright, your future!"

Something hardened in Nicholas' expression. "Music was all I ever wanted. You've always dismissed my passion as childish, impractical, unworthy of a Beckett. Don't talk to me about legacy. Don't tell me you know what's best for me. Twenty-four years, and did you ever once listen to me? No." He stared at his parents, fists clenched at his sides. "You know what? Never talk to me again."

Was Laura imagining it, or did Ramirez send Nicholas the quickest, subtlest nod of approval?

Ramirez resumed her ever-neutral expression, and turned to Roy. "Roy Beckett, you're under arrest for the murder of Vernon Reed." Then she turned to his wife. "And Roxanne Beckett, you're under investigation for obstruction of justice, accessory after the fact, and financial fraud. Please stand."

Roy's face contorted. "Outrageous!" He slammed his fist on the table, sending papers flying. He glared at Laura, trying to move toward her from around the table. "You! This is your fault!"

Littlefield moved with surprising speed, pinning Roy's arms behind his back while Patterson stepped between them, hand on her holster. Roy struggled against the senior patrol officer's grip.

"That's enough," Ramirez said.

Roxanne had gone pale, her eyes never leaving her husband.

As Littlefield read the husband and wife their rights, Roy's shoulders slumped, the fight draining from him. Around the table, the others watched in stunned silence as the police reduced the business owner and lawyer—both respected Silver Springs citizens—to handcuffed criminals.

"You spread the rumors about Izzy," Laura said, staring at Roxanne. It wasn't a question.

Roxanne lifted her chin. "We needed someone to blame."

"And when that employee got too close to the truth, you had Roy pressure Vernon to fire her," Ramirez said. "Convenient that her last job was at your law firm."

Roxanne's jaw tightened, but she said nothing.

"Then there was Dulcie," Laura continued. "You fed that story to Sharon Winters."

Dulcie gasped.

"There's still one question unanswered," Ramirez said, staring down her nose at the Becketts. "Where did you get the bracelet found at the crime scene?"

Roy scowled at her, staying silent.

Roxanne paused, then lifted her head. "I can tell you about that."

All eyes turned toward her, including Roy's. Where there might've once been fury, there was only...resignation.

"I had been at the Community Center the week before," Roxanne said, her voice taking on a clinical tone. "Organizing the legal aid clinic I run there monthly. While setting up, I noticed the display table where Izzy leaves his handcrafted jewelry for people to take." Her eyes flicked to Izzy. "I remembered thinking how distinctive they were—how everyone in town knew who made them."

She straightened—even in defeat, maintaining her poise. "When Roy called me, panicking, saying Vernon had confronted him about the money and things had...escalated, I knew we needed something to redirect suspicion. I still had the bracelet in my purse. Roy planted it where it was easy to find."

Izzy stared at her. "What did I ever do to you?"

"Nothing," Roxanne said. "That's why you were perfect. You were enthusiastic, visible, someone people could believe might act impulsively. And you had no power to fight back."

Littlefield and Patterson guided both Becketts toward the door. Roy cast one last seething look at his son, who'd turned away. The door closed behind them with a soft click, more final than a slam.

Warren stared at the space the Becketts had left. "I'll be...I never would've thought. Not in a hundred years." He directed his gaze to Laura. "So...what did the will say before all this mess?"

"The original will, unchanged for fifteen years, left Vernon's personal effects and liquid assets to Roy, and the business share plus a trust fund to Nicholas, just as Roy had always expected," Malcolm answered for her. "Dulcie wasn't mentioned. But two weeks before his death, Vernon changed everything. He added Dulcie, removed Roy entirely, gave the business to Izzy instead of Nicholas, and directed his remaining assets to cancer research."

Warren nodded, then shook his head, muttering to himself.

Izzy exhaled, long and low. "The trust fund. So that's why I didn't get the raise." The constant movement that characterized him—the fidgeting hands, the bouncing knee, the animated expressions—all vanished.

"Izzy?" Laura said.

When he spoke, his voice was quiet. "She offered me legal advice. She approached me after work one day and told me she'd help. 'Pro bono,' she said. All while knowing..." He drew in a shuddering breath. "She was right. About all of it. The enthusiastic theater kid. The impulsive one without power and with...a bad history."

Nicholas sat, his face a canvas of conflicting emotions, jaw working. "That's not who you are! That's who they wanted everyone to see." He leaned forward. "Do you know what I saw at the farm? Someone who showed up first and left last. Someone who took pride in their work when everyone else just collected a paycheck. Someone who knew every employee's name and birthday." His voice grew stronger with each word. "You're not just enthusiastic—you're passionate. You're not impulsive—you're decisive. And you're not powerless. Vernon saw your real power. That's why he left you his share."

Izzy stared at Nicholas, moisture gathering in his eyes again.

"Don't you dare believe what they said about you," Nicholas said. "Not for a second."

Warren cleared his throat, nodding. "The kid's right. We all saw the real you. Vernon most of all."

Izzy looked to Warren, then to Nicholas, and at last...to Laura, a complicated mix of gratitude and raw pain in his expression. "Thank you for believing me when no one else would."

Laura smiled at him. "That's what friends are for." Then she studied Nicholas' face. "You sensed something wasn't right. That's why you quit, isn't it?"

Nicholas looked up, meeting her gaze with eyes that seemed decades older than they had been just an hour earlier. "I couldn't put it into words until you explained everything just now. There was just this...feeling. I should've questioned more. He made me feel like I didn't understand business well enough to see the bigger picture."

"That's a classic tactic," Evelyn said. "Make you doubt your own perceptions so you stop trusting them."

"I don't know what to feel," Nicholas said, shaking his head. "My father is a murderer. My mother is his accomplice. The business I've spent my life trying to escape is now someone else's problem. And Vernon..." His voice caught. "Vernon was dying all along."

The remaining occupants of the room exchanged uncertain glances.

It was Izzy who broke the silence, eyes still glistening. "I'm sorry, Nicholas. For all of it."

Nicholas shook his head. "Don't apologize. Ever. Besides...you were the only one at the farm who called me what I wanted to be called." He managed a weak smile. "As terrible as this whole situation has been, I feel it's going to work out for both of us."

Warren nodded, and let out a deep sigh. "For everyone. I much prefer a manufactured rivalry to a real one."

Every head in the room turned toward him.

"Manufactured?" Jasmine asked, her brow furrowing.

Warren shrugged. "The rivalry between my farm and Vernon's. It was something we came up with when we were younger, just starting out. A marketing gimmick to drum up interest in both our businesses."

"But you seemed at odds," Laura said.

"As we got older, the play-acting became...I don't know, harder to separate from reality sometimes," Warren groaned. "The competition got too real over the years. Underneath it all, there was still respect. I never wanted..." He trailed off.

Warren and Izzy exchanged glances.

"You both knew, didn't you?" Laura asked. "About Vernon's illness."

Warren and Izzy stared at her, then at each other again.

Izzy sighed. "I...found him doubled over in pain in his workshop one evening about two months ago." His eyes dropped to his hands. "He swore me to secrecy. Said he needed time to get his affairs in order before people started treating him differently. I gave him my word."

"And after he was murdered?" Ramirez asked.

Izzy's fingers twisted together, the movement sharp and anxious. "I struggled. After people started suspecting me, looking at me like I was capable of..." He trailed off, swallowing hard. "I was afraid revealing what I knew would only make me look more guilty. And I'd promised him."

Warren cleared his throat. "Vernon let it slip during an argument we had. I'd confronted him about some strange behavior. He blurted out he had bigger things to worry about than our manufactured rivalry." Warren's face softened. "He regretted saying it, but once it was out, he admitted everything. Made me swear not to tell a soul."

"You didn't think this information might be relevant after he was murdered?" Ramirez asked, frowning.

"I didn't want to look even more shifty. We'd argued just days before. And...it has something to do with that day at the credit union." He looked at Laura. "I saw your face when you noticed me withdrawing all that cash."

Laura nodded. "It seemed unusual."

"It was for my therapy sessions," Warren said, his voice gruff. "Paid several months in advance. In cash. Didn't want it showing up on statements or checks that might circulate." His hands clenched into fists on the table. "A farmer my age, going to see a shrink? Once it gets out, people wonder if you're losing your grip, if you can be trusted with business decisions..." He exhaled. "If you're becoming one of those men who do things...without thi nking."

"That's why you canceled the industry conference the night Vernon died," Laura said, the pieces connecting.

Warren stared at her. "How did you know that?"

Laura gave a sheepish smile. "I saw it on your wall calendar. When you were signing the contracts."

He nodded. "When you have to choose between going to the New England Apple Producers Association's annual summit and your first therapy session..." He tilted his head, his expression sobering. "I've been living alone for too long. Start talking to myself. Arguing, really. Trying to drum up the courage to go to that first appointment. My neighbors probably thought I was having a breakdown on my porch that night."

"Why hide it?" Nicholas asked.

Warren's shoulders slumped. "I couldn't...admit when I needed help. Vernon was the only one who knew. He was the one who suggested it." His voice caught. "And he was right."

Izzy gave him a soft smile. "You're not alone anymore, Warren."

Nicholas uttered an affirmative sound.

After a few moments of silence, Dulcie spoke up.

"Ruby and I thought it might be cancer. I found the prescription bottles for painkillers after his death." She twisted her hands in her lap. "I told Ruby about it, and we researched the medication, and the doctor..."

Dulcie exchanged a glance with Ruby. "At first, we didn't want to look suspicious. Then, Ruby saw the article about my past in the Maplewood Memo..." She trailed off, blinking back tears.

"Why didn't you offer this information earlier?" Ramirez asked.

Ruby took over. "She convinced me we needed to tell someone."

"Two partners, both dead under questionable circumstances...how would it look if I produced evidence that Vernon was terminally ill? Like I was trying to create reasonable doubt, or worse, like I'd discovered his condition, manipulated a dying man into changing his will, and..." She broke off, shaking her head, eyes teary.

Laura looked at her. "Dulcie, I'm so sorry. For everything."

Dulcie lifted her head and gave the tiniest of nods.

Jasmine hesitated. "Since we're clearing things up...Nicholas, I wanted to apologize for calling you Nicky."

His eyebrows rose, and he shook his head. "Thanks, but it's on me. I should've said something." A slight smile appeared. "Speaking up for myself is something I'm working on now."

A contemplative silence settled over the room.

Malcolm let out a sigh, removing his glasses and polishing them with a handkerchief pulled from his breast pocket. "That was the most eventful will reading I've ever done. And I once had a client's parrot wreak havoc during the proceedings."

Dulcie managed a watery smile, and Nicholas' shoulders relaxed.

Even Laura had to smile. "Thank you for helping us, Malcolm. I'm so sorry for the intrusion and for disrupting your office."

Malcolm waved away her apology as he replaced his glasses. "It was no trouble, especially when it helped catch despicable people. I've known Roy Beckett for twenty years. Our firm handled his property transfers, business contracts, even his son's trust fund. I can't believe he would do something like this." He shook his head. "As for Roxanne...she worked in this town for years. I couldn't have expected that from her either."

"We often think we know people better than we do," Evelyn said. "Even in a small town like Silver Springs, where lives are so interconnected, there are still shadows where secrets grow."

Laura understood that sentiment. In her short time in Silver Springs, she'd discovered that truth, however painful, provided a foundation upon which healing could begin. Roy's deception had corroded the trust of everyone who believed in him—his son, his business partner, his community.

Still...as Nicholas pulled Izzy into a hug, as Ruby helped Dulcie to her feet, as Warren and Jasmine discussed ideas for future Woodland Watch projects...the first tender shoots of repair emerged. Silver Springs would heal from this, just as it had from other wounds in its long history.

Malcolm caught her eye across the room and gave her a small nod. Laura returned the gesture, grateful she'd helped bring justice, but even more grateful that tomorrow would bring a return to the rhythms of the café, the comfort of familiar routines, and the simple pleasure of belonging to a place worth protecting.

# Chapter Twenty-Four

A pre-dawn chill still swathed the September morning, fogging the windows of the General Store as Laura flipped on the lights one by one. It had been two and a half weeks since Roy and Roxanne's arrest, and Silver Springs was finding its rhythm again. Laura slipped into her usual opening routine—the motions were muscle memory by now.

A few minutes later, Eli rolled in after his early bike ride, offering her a quiet smile. No need for words. Outside, darkness still blanketed the town. Soon, the regulars would start drifting in, chasing warmth, caffeine, and maybe a little gossip.

The phone's ring sliced through the pre-opening quiet, startling them. Laura dried her hands on a dish towel and reached for the receiver.

"Silver Springs General Store, this is Laura."

"Hey, Laura!" Izzy's cheerful voice came through the line. "I'm outside with the Goldenleaf Apple Farm delivery. Mind opening the gate?"

"Sure," Laura said, unable to keep from smiling. "We'll meet you there." After hanging up, she turned to Eli. "Izzy's here with the delivery. Mind helping unload?"

Eli nodded, tying his apron strings.

At the back gate, Izzy waited beside his ancient pickup truck, the bed loaded with wooden crates. "Morning!" he called, bouncing on his toes. "Thanks for the help. Sales have picked up, so Maggie increased the usual order."

Laura unlocked the gate, swinging it wide. "I'm surprised to see you doing deliveries. Don't business owners usually delegate tasks like this?"

Izzy laughed, hoisting a crate from the truck bed. "Ordinary ones do. I'm still figuring out what owner I want to be. I know I'd rather be making cider or driving deliveries than sitting in Vernon's old office staring at spreadsheets."

"Fair enough," Laura said, accepting a crate.

"I'm pretty sure this is double what you usually bring," Eli said as they all trooped to the food storage cellar. "The sweet cider's a hit! Three customers were asking when we'd get more in stock just yesterday."

"It's the town's way of saying sorry for doubting you," Laura said.

Izzy ducked his head, grinning. "After everything, it feels good to be busy again. Almost...normal, you know?"

Laura nodded.

As they walked back to the truck for the second load, Laura gave Izzy a teasing glance. "And you're still using your old pickup. Doesn't the business have a delivery van?"

Izzy rolled his eyes. "Mock her all you want, but she's been on the road forty years without a single breakdown."

Laura had to grin.

They stacked the crates in the cellar, chatting about the cooler weather and how it was perfect for apple season.

When they finished, Izzy's expression brightened. "Before I forget! Warren and I are working on something new. A collaboration between Goldenleaf and Fisk Apple Works."

"Even with all that history?" Eli asked.

"Especially so," Izzy said, grinning. "We're developing a cider using a blend of our heritage apples. Calling it 'Reconciliation' seemed fitting. The first batch should be ready for tasting soon if you'd like to try it."

"I wouldn't miss it," Laura said, returning his smile.

Eli nodded, dusting off his hands. "That'd be great. I've got to get back to setting up before we open."

"Wait, both of you," Izzy said. "I've been meaning to ask you something."

Eli turned to face him, exchanging a glance with Laura.

Izzy rubbed the back of his neck. "Some friends and I are having a cookout at Meadowlark Point Park this Saturday at six. Nothing fancy, just good food and better company. I'd love it if you both could come."

"That sounds great," Laura said. "Thanks for the invitation."

"Yeah, count me in," Eli added with a smile. "Need us to bring anything?"

"Just yourselves," Izzy said, relaxing. "I've been so caught up in...everything...I haven't been the best at keeping up with friends or making new ones." He glanced at Eli. "And, hey, we've lived in the same town for ten years, and I've never really gotten to know you. That's on me, and I'd like to change that."

Eli's smile widened. "Yeah, I'd like that."

"I'll make sure we've got some vegetarian options," Izzy said. "How do halloumi and grilled veggie skewers sound?"

Eli ran a delicate tongue over his lips. "I can't believe you remembered. That sounds great."

"Of course!" Izzy said. "I'm a chatterbox, sure, but I listen too."

Eli grinned wider, if possible.

"My number's in the store contact list if you need something," Izzy said. "Besides, I still expect to see you both at our next play. Front row."

Laura tilted her head.

"Didn't I tell you?" Izzy's eyes sparkled. "The Players invited me back. Turns out Kenneth was friends with Roy. The whole thing with kicking me out? Roy convinced him to make a fuss. The theater group suggested Kenneth find another hobby."

"That's wonderful news!" Laura said.

Izzy nodded, grinning. "Speaking of the theater, the most amazing thing happened yesterday. We made our insurance deadline! Some anonymous donor sent exactly what we needed—two hundred and fifty dollars!"

"That's fantastic timing," Eli said.

"Right?" A low whistle escaped Izzy's lips. "Whoever it was, they saved our season. The postmark just said Boston."

A strange inkling of something piqued Laura's curiosity. She said nothing, though.

Izzy grinned. "First Saturday, then opening night of Wind In The Willows in three weeks. I'm holding you to both!"

Laura's curiosity got the better of her. "I was hoping to ask, did you ever hear about…Vernon's spiced cider mix? There were so many rumors…"

Izzy leaned against his pickup with a wry smile. "The infamous stolen recipe. After going through Vernon's notes and files, I discovered it was a collaboration."

"Between who?" Laura asked.

"Vernon and Warren," Izzy said. "They'd been working on it together for months, secretly meeting to develop something that would benefit both farms. Roy didn't know. He'd have seen it as a betrayal. Warren would publicly accuse Vernon of theft, Vernon would act indignant, and they'd both enjoy the buzz it created around the product."

"I knew it!" Eli said, grinning. "That lines up with what you mentioned about them pretending to compete, Laura."

"And now?" Laura asked.

Izzy smiled. "The spiced cider mix will be our second joint product with Fisk Apple Works." He winked. "Free samples for the employees at my favorite store in town, of course."

They all laughed.

"A pleasure seeing you both, as always! Alas, I must head back to work," Izzy said. "I've got a meeting with an accountant soon. I'm still trying to make sense of the financial records." He opened the truck door but turned back. "You'll both come Saturday? Promise?"

"We promise," Laura and Eli said almost in unison.

"Splendid!" Izzy's face lit up. "Bring your appetites. I'm making my aunt's slaw and her fried cornmeal dumplings. And bring anyone else from the store who wants to come."

The old truck rumbled to life, and Izzy waved as he pulled away. Eli and Laura returned the gesture until he rounded the corner and disappeared.

As they headed back inside, Eli glanced at Laura. "It's nice to see him doing better."

Laura nodded. "I think we're all finding our way forward after everything that happened."

Eli gave a thoughtful hum as they returned to their morning preparations, the familiar rhythm of the café beckoning.

———◆◇◆———

Laura slid coins into a mother's outstretched palm, her toddler clinging to a scuffed blue train, when the café door opened—and in walked the last two people she'd have expected.

Dulcie and Ruby.

She froze for a beat, trying not to stare as the mother coaxed her child toward a corner table. The last time she'd seen the two women was in Malcolm's office.

Today, something was different. Dulcie stood straighter, her shoulders relaxed, her light-brown complexion bearing a healthy glow Laura hadn't seen before. She wore a red scarf that brightened her usually subdued outfit, and she smiled, her hand resting on Ruby's arm. Something more hesitant replaced Ruby's assertive posture.

"Good morning. What can I get you today?" Laura asked the next person in line, an older man.

"A black coffee and a lemon cookie, please," the man said, sliding the exact change across the counter.

Laura rang up his order, her curiosity mounting as Dulcie and Ruby moved up in line.

"There you go," Laura said, handing the man his receipt. "It'll be ready in a few minutes."

He nodded his thanks and shuffled toward an empty table, leaving Ruby and Dulcie standing before Laura at the counter. Up close, the changes were even more apparent.

"Laura," Dulcie said. "I'm glad to see you."

"Likewise," Laura said. "May I take your order?"

Dulcie glanced at Ruby, who gave a small nod but remained silent.

"We'd like morning tea for two, please," Dulcie said. "With a pot of Earl Grey, if you have it. We'll be staying to drink it here." She gestured toward an empty table by the window.

"Of course," Laura nodded, punching the order into the register. "Anything to eat with that?"

Dulcie looked at Ruby again, raising her eyebrows.

"And two cinnamon rolls," Ruby said, her voice quiet. "Thank you."

"I'll bring it to your table in just a moment," Laura told them, accepting Dulcie's payment.

Laura took a steadying breath and lifted the tea tray, weaving through the café's familiar maze of tables. Dulcie and Ruby sat by the window. Their heads turned as she neared, the conversation halting.

"Here we are," she said, placing the tray between them—a neat arrangement of tea, milk, and pastries. "Enjoy! And if you'd like anything else, please let me know."

Ruby offered a polite smile. "Thank you, Laura."

She nodded, already turning to go when Dulcie's voice followed.

"Wait, Laura. Could we speak with you?"

She paused. The café had settled into its mid-morning lull. Jesse and Eli could cover.

"Of course."

Dulcie gestured to the empty chair. "Just for a moment."

Laura sat, aware of the tension thickening the air.

"We have something to say to you," Dulcie said, steam curling from the teapot as she poured. Her eyes met Ruby's across the table in silent encouragement.

Ruby straightened her shoulders. "I owe you an apology. The way I treated you and Evelyn was inexcusable." She twisted a napkin between her fingers. "I made terrible assumptions about your motives when you were only trying to help."

Laura watched her, maintaining silence.

"I was terrified," Ruby continued, her voice dropping to almost a whisper. "The thought of Dulcie being blamed because of her past..." She shook her head. "But that doesn't excuse my behavior. I hope someday you might see me as an ally rather than..." she trailed off. "An obstacle."

"I appreciate that, Ruby," Laura said.

"I need to apologize, too." Dulcie stirred sugar into her tea, the spoon clinking. "I should have trusted you with what I found among Vernon's things much sooner." The teacup trembled as she lifted it. "And I never properly thanked you—for solving the case and giving me closure about Vernon's illness."

"You were both caught in an impossible situation," Laura said. "I understand that."

"Still," Dulcie murmured, setting her cup down with deliberate care. "I could've handled it better. But I'm learning to trust myself again. To make my own decisions."

Ruby's expression softened with something between pride and chagrin.

"And how are you doing now?" Laura asked. "These weeks must've been difficult."

A smile transformed Dulcie's face—not the tentative half-smile Laura had seen before, but something radiant. "I'm doing much better than I expected. I've put Vernon's house on the market. The memories there were...complicated. Happy and sad in equal measure."

"She's staying with me for now," Ruby said. "Until she decides what she wants next."

"I've had enough romantic entanglements to last a lifetime," Dulcie said. "Vernon was a good man despite his secrets, but his death made me realize how much I've defined myself through my relationships with others." She straightened in her chair. "For now, I want to focus on my friendships, on building a life that's mine."

The sleeve of her blouse slipped back as she reached for her cinnamon roll, revealing a delicate silver bracelet. Catching Laura's gaze, Dulcie's fingers drifted to the jewelry.

"My brother Percival—Percy made this," she explained, tracing the intricate metalwork. "He's a jeweler in Hartford." A wistful expression crossed her face. "We lost touch after everything in Connecticut. The name change, moving here. When news of Vernon's death reached him, he drove all the way out to see me." She looked down at the bracelet. "After my husband and mother died, after all the whispers and suspicion...I built walls between different parts of my life." Her eyes found Ruby's. "I was wrong to shut out people who cared about me. I need to stop hiding."

"We're relearning what friendship means," Ruby said. "Without fear or control."

Laura nodded. "I'm glad for you both, and I accept your apologies. Thank you." She smiled at them. "Enjoy your tea."

"Wait," Dulcie said, her hand half-raised. "There's something else you should know. About what Sharon wrote in the Maplewood Memo."

Ruby leaned forward. "You don't have to—"

"I want to," Dulcie said. She met Laura's gaze. "Gregory was my husband. His death was an accident. He was changing a light fixture in our basement when he fell from the ladder. I wasn't home—I was at work with five colleagues who confirmed this. The medical examiner found alcohol in his system." Her voice softened. "He'd struggled with drinking for years."

She traced the rim of her teacup. "My mother had early-onset dementia. She sometimes forgot which medications she'd taken. The 'fatal allergic reaction' happened when she accidentally took a double dose, forgetting she'd already taken it earlier that day."

Laura sank back into her chair. "Dulcie...I'm so sorry."

"The insurance policies were nothing unusual," Ruby said. "Standard coverage. Gregory's was through his workplace, her mother's a modest policy maintained for decades."

"After the second death, the whispers started. I couldn't bear it." Dulcie shrugged. "So I changed my name back to my mother's maiden surname and came here for a fresh start."

"The investigations cleared her," Ruby said, her voice hardening. "Funny how the Memo omitted that."

Dulcie smiled sadly.

***

Later, when Laura was working at the counter, she turned to greet the next customer and forgot how to speak.

"Coffee, black, and a cranberry scone," Sharon Winters, the editor of The Maplewood Memo, said. "And...a moment of your time." She winced. "If you please."

Laura tried not to stare at her as she rang up the order. "Yes, of course. I'll deliver it to your table when it's ready."

Ten minutes elapsed, and she placed the mug and the plate with the baked treat on the table where Sharon sat. Laura remained standing.

Sharon looked up from her laptop, but didn't make eye contact. "I've been reviewing our coverage of recent events." She cleared her throat. "A generous patron over the years...were the Becketts."

"I see," Laura said, understanding beginning to dawn.

"The café manager who solved a murder. An outsider who thought she understood our town better than those of us who've been here for decades." Sharon grimaced. "My pride got in the way of my journalism."

A long silence stretched between them.

"Have you..." Laura began. How was it best to broach the subject?

"Apologized? To Lennox and…Sanderson?" Sharon's shoulders tensed. She broke off a piece of scone. "Yes. Just before I came in. It needed to be done. Face to face."

Laura nodded, trying to keep her expression neutral. What an admission to make.

"I'm writing a follow-up piece," Sharon continued, typing away. "Nothing flashy. Just the facts about the Becketts' arrest. No more baseless accusations."

"That's all anyone can ask for," Laura said.

Sharon took a sip of her coffee, her expression tight. "Twenty years running the Memo, and I've never had to eat crow like this." A rueful half-smile appeared. "Not tasty, I must say."

Laura's mouth twitched. "I imagine not."

"That's all I wanted to say," Sharon said, straightening her posture. "You can get back to your customers now."

Laura nodded. "Enjoy your scone." She turned back toward the counter, hiding a smile.

⊲◆▷

That afternoon brought a first for the General Store, and something close to a rebirth for the young man involved. The bell jingled, and Nicholas stepped inside, a guitar case in one hand, a folder of sheet music tucked under his arm. Several customers looked up as he walked toward the counter, the black case bumping against his leg.

"Nicholas!" Laura said, smiling, tucking her cleaning cloth into her apron pocket. "Right on time."

"Can't believe it," he said. "It's my first live performance for ages."

Laura nodded, noting the changes in his appearance since she'd last seen him. His springy curls had grown longer, cascading over his forehead, which he'd dyed an ombré aqua. He'd traded his usual flannel-and-canvas-pants combination for skinny jeans and a waistcoat over a deep blue button-up.

"Let me show you where we've set up for you," Laura said, coming out from behind the counter and gesturing for him to follow her toward a corner of the café. "Eli brought in a stool from home—said it's the perfect height for playing guitar. And we've positioned it so everyone can see."

Nicholas followed her gaze to the small performance area they'd created. A wooden stool sat on a modest platform, with a Silver Springs General Store mug repurposed as a tip jar on a small side table.

"This is perfect," Nicholas said. "Thank you."

"Maggie's been advertising your performance all week," Laura said. "We've had people calling to ask what time you'll be playing."

Nicholas' eyebrows shot up. "Really?"

Laura nodded. "Silver Springs is proud of its musicians. Especially those brave enough to follow their passion."

Nicholas gave a soft, sad smile.

"How's...the job search going?" Laura asked, changing the subject. "Are you...having any success?"

He exhaled, leaning in a little and lowering his voice. "I actually got lucky. Ryan Gallagher, a friend of mine...his dad runs Harmonic Supply. It's this record store, music school, and instrument shop all rolled into one." Nicholas scratched the back of his neck. "Amazingly, his dad trusted me enough to bring me on. Just trialling for inventory. I'm trying not to get my hopes up, but...it's been good so far."

A quiet smile flickered across his face.

"I'm glad," Laura said. "You deserve work that values your expertise." Her gaze fell on the guitar case he still clutched. "May I see what you'll be playing today?"

Nicholas set down the case and opened it, revealing a beautiful acoustic guitar with warm honey-colored wood and an intricate inlay.

"It's beautiful," Laura said. "Have you had it long?"

Nicholas's expression shifted, embarrassment crossing his features. "It was Warren's." He lifted the guitar from its case, fingers checking the tuning. "He mentioned buying it a while back, getting into music, but he gave up. It was just sitting in his cupboard gathering dust. I went to buy it from him...but I didn't want anyone to know. Making a secretive cash payment to Warren during an active murder investigation wasn't the smartest move."

Laura couldn't help but laugh. "Timing is everything."

Nicholas's shoulders relaxed. "I should set up."

"Break a leg," Laura said.

Nicholas set his guitar case down in the corner, absorbed in his task.

The doors to the back swung open, and Jasmine emerged, arms full of dish towels and napkins. She caught sight of Nicholas—and froze. The linens slipped from her fingers, landing with a soft thud.

"Whoops!" she said, dropping to her knees to gather them, stealing another glance at Nicholas, who was oblivious, his back to them as he adjusted his strings.

Laura hid a smile and knelt to help. "Everything okay?"

"Fine! Fine." Jasmine's voice rose an octave. "Is that...his hair...?"

"Blue," Laura said, grinning.

"Right. Blue." Jasmine busied herself putting the linens in their proper places. "He looks good."

Laura raised a single brow.

"Wait, no, I didn't notice anything. I just meant—" Jasmine trailed off as her gaze slid back to Nicholas.

Laura began plating up some afternoon tea orders, amusement bubbling just beneath the surface.

"The hair suits him," Jasmine murmured.

"I thought you hadn't noticed?"

Jasmine's eyes went wide. "I'm just...observant. Professional skill."

"Very professional," Laura said, grinning. "Don't worry. I won't say a word."

"You'd better not," Jasmine muttered, though there was no heat in it.

Laura nodded, still smiling.

A mere five minutes passed, then Judith entered the café, beaming when she spotted Laura.

"Good afternoon, Laura! I'm here for the live music," Judith said, approaching the counter.

"Hi Judith. He's just setting up now," Laura said. "What can I get for you?"

"A chai latte, please. Extra cinnamon." Judith leaned forward, lowering her voice. "I've been watching the bus stops like a hawk, you know."

Laura raised an eyebrow.

"The scarves," Judith said, her eyes twinkling. "All gone! Every single one we left. Not a trace remaining at any of the stops I checked."

The Warmth Where Needed project—making scarves to leave at bus stops around town for anyone who needed them as the weather turned colder—was a success.

"That's wonderful news," Laura said. "We've done well."

"Never a dull moment," Judith said, and gave Laura a knowing wink before heading off to a table with a good view of Nicholas' upcoming performance. She settled, and retrieved her Sudoku book to fill out while she waited.

—◆—

Lunch break was the one time of the day she had to herself. Until someone called her, of course. Laura's phone rang. Her mother's name flashed back at her.

She took a deep breath. She'd take the call, but this time...she'd try her best to stand up for herself.

"Hi, Mom," Laura said, tucking the phone between her shoulder and ear.

"Laura. I saw the news about the case being solved. The article mentioned you by name."

Laura paused. "It's been...an eventful few weeks."

"I imagine so."

A beat of silence stretched between them.

"Are you...safe? This business of getting involved in police matters—"

"I'm okay, Mom. Really." Laura set down her lunch, giving the conversation her full attention. "And I'm happy here."

The words hung in the air. Laura could hear her mother processing them.

"Happy," Bridget said, as if testing the word. "Even after everything that's happened?"

"Especially so." Laura's voice grew stronger. "I've found something here. Purpose. Community. People who value what I can contribute."

Another pause. When Bridget spoke again, her tone had shifted—still cautious, but softer. "The article mentioned you helped clear the name of that theater friend of yours. He'd been...wrongly accused? I hope he gets back on his feet soon. Doing that must've felt..." she trailed off, then tried again. "I may not understand your choices, Laura. This life you've built so far from everything familiar. But I can see they've led you to help good people."

Laura's throat tightened. "Thank you for saying that."

Bridget was silent for several moments. "Maybe next time you solve a murder, call your mother before the newspapers find out?"

Laura couldn't help it. She laughed. "I'll try to remember that. Love you, Mom."

"Love you too."

The line went quiet. Not an apology—but something better. Acknowledgement. A bridge built across the distance between them.

———◆———

As the day slid toward evening, the café still buzzed in the aftermath of Nicholas' unexpected popular performance. Christopher approached the counter, juggling several fabric shopping bags.

"Laura!" Christopher said, unbothered by his load. "I've earned myself a drink to go after the hard work of weekly shopping, wouldn't you say?"

Laura smiled. "You look like a man who's put in a full day's work. What'll it be today?"

Christopher set his bags down with an exaggerated sigh of relief. "Medium hazelnut latte, please. Nicholas was wonderful earlier, by the way. Had no idea that boy could sing like that. What a waste it would've been if Roy had gotten his way. Nothing worse than being forced down the wrong path."

Laura nodded and poured the steamed milk over the coffee, creating a simple leaf pattern in the foam. "Evelyn mentioned the Woodworkers were building something for the library's children's section. How's that going?"

Christopher's face lit up. "A storytelling chair! Should be ready next month. But that's not even the most interesting news. You'll never guess who joined the Woodworkers."

Laura raised an eyebrow, placing a lid on Christopher's latte. "Who?"

"Warren Fisk," Christopher said. "Showed up Tuesday evening and asked if we had room for a beginner."

"Warren?" Laura couldn't hide her surprise.

Christopher chuckled. "Never would've expected it, but maybe he's turned over a new leaf." He accepted the latte from Laura with a nod of thanks. "Either way, he's a pleasant fellow when you get him talking. Has a dry sense of humor I wouldn't have expected."

"I'm glad to hear it," Laura said. "Everyone deserves a fresh start."

"That they do," Christopher said, gathering his shopping bags. "That they do."

<hr>

The café had exhaled. With the last customers gone, the hush of before-closing routines took over—Jesse tallying the till, Eli sweeping neat arcs across the floor, Jasmine fussing with the chalkboard for tomorrow's specials.

Laura re-stacked shelves as Maggie emerged from her office and headed for the retail section. Her usual confident stride was diminished, replaced by a distracted shuffle.

So Laura approached. "Everything okay, Maggie?"

Maggie paused mid-reorganization of some pickle jars on a shelf. "Is it that obvious?" She sighed. "There are still almost three months to go, but planning for the Good Neighbor Guild Annual Potluck has already begun."

"What's that?" Laura asked, rearranging some handmade soaps.

"December event, the biggest community gathering of the winter festivities. Everyone contributes something representing their business or organization. The Guild board takes it seriously—especially Rina Sen, who coordinates everything."

Kathy appeared from the doorway leading to the offices upstairs. "Talking about the potluck already? Thought we had until at least November before the planning frenzy set in."

Maggie shot her wife a glance. "Rina's already firing off emails about 'elevating our communal culinary experience.'"

Kathy chuckled. "That woman! If it weren't for her, the Guild would've scheduled the annual general meeting for February thirty-first."

Laura had to hide a smile. "So...what does the General Store contribute?"

The conversation shifted to brainstorming. Laura listened, offering suggestions.

As they finished closing up, the sunset painted the sky with dramatic strokes of pink and orange beyond the windows. Laura smiled. Just months ago, she'd been a stranger in Silver Springs, and now she was discussing community traditions, anticipating social gatherings, and feeling the pull of belonging that came with shared experiences—both the dramatic ones, like solving a murder, and the mundane ones, like planning a potluck.

She filed out into the crisp September evening air.

Silver Springs didn't always make sense—but it had a way of working things out.

THE END

---

**Get your surprise reader bonuses here: cozycozies.com/pages/ss2thanks**

*Thanks for reading. I hope you enjoyed it.*

# THANKS FOR READING!

I hope you enjoyed reading! I have something extra for you if you're willing to leave a review...

You know how in your favorite cozies, neighbors help neighbors without expecting anything in return? I have a small favor to ask that won't cost you a penny, but could make all the difference to a fellow reader you've never met.

Here's another mystery that needs solving...

How can we help more readers discover cozy mysteries that bring them joy, comfort, and a relaxing escape from everyday worries?

I'll give you a few moments to think...

The solution? Your review!

Just like how the smallest clues matter most, your few words about this book could be the clue that leads another reader to their new favorite series.

Your review takes less than a minute but lasts forever.

- If you're reading this on your Kindle, just scroll to the bottom and tap "Rate and Review."

- If you're listening on Audible, tap those three dots in the top right corner and select "Rate & Review."

For all other places on the internet, I've put together a page of handy links! Visit **cozycozies.com/pages/ss2review**

Or, scan the QR code with your phone's camera below!

Once you're done, email me: <u>jodie@cozycozies.com</u> and tell me where you wrote it. I'll send your VIP bonuses!

If helping another book lover sounds like something you'd do, then you're exactly the kind of reader I write for. Welcome to our cozy community! I'm so grateful you took this journey with me, and I can't wait to share future books with you.

Your review, a true act of kindness, would mean the world to me and help so many others find their next favorite escape. From my writing nook, I'm sending you all the coziest reading vibes, and wishing you many delightful mysteries to unravel.

Have a wonderful day!

Cheers Jodie

P.S. If you'd like to receive exclusive short stories and bonuses, plus printable puzzles, discounts, and more...sign up for my newsletter at **cozycozies.com/pages/newsletter**.

P.P.S You can find all my books in all formats on your favorite online store. You can also get my books, special editions, and bundles directly from me at **cozycozies.com**.

# ACKNOWLEDGEMENTS

They say it takes a village, and writing cozy mysteries has shown me how true that is! My deepest gratitude goes to everyone who made this second book possible.

To Zach and Cam, for catching everything from timeline inconsistencies to character quirks that didn't ring true. Thank you for making this story so much stronger.

My family, who's been nothing but supportive. I appreciate you all!

And to my readers, who took a chance on my first book and asked for more. I can't thank you enough. This one's for you.

# Author's Note

Returning to Silver Springs for this second mystery, I wanted to further investigate what it means to be part of a close-knit community.

This book invites you back to a town grappling with a shocking crime. This time, the peaceful hum of harvest season is broken, not just by the usual rhythm of apple presses, but by the web of secrets Vernon Reed's death unravels.

Laura, with her keen observational skills and unwavering sense of justice, solidifies her place in Silver Springs. She embodies the curious spirit we all have when we notice something doesn't add up in our community.

As the investigation unfolds, we see how easily perceptions can be manipulated and how resilient the human spirit can be, even when faced with betrayal and false accusations.

Through characters like Izzy, who faces challenges and unjust suspicion, and Nicholas, who bravely seeks his own path despite his family's expectations, this book explores the impact of family legacies and what it takes to forge a fresh start.

Writing these mysteries has been my way of exploring how true belonging is found not just in shared joy, but in shared struggle and support.

The collective efforts of Laura's friends, from Evelyn's strategic thinking to Jasmine's observations and the skills of the Maplewood Crafters Club, highlight how community strength brings justice.

I hope your time in Silver Springs was filled with unexpected twists and satisfying moments, and this charming town has captured your heart.

I'm always eager to hear from my readers. Please share what you enjoyed in this story or tell me about the other cozy mysteries you love! You can find me at **cozycozies.com**

I really enjoy it when readers email me to say hello. The lovely folks who read my books are my kind of people!

I'm so lucky to have such a wonderful community. Which is why I'd like to introduce...It's The Cozy Life For Us!

It's a discussion group for people who love all things cozy (mysteries, puzzles, fiber arts, books, food) to share what we've been enjoying, reading, or making. There are also lots of member-only bonuses.

**Visit skool.com/cozy to join the cozy fun!**

# Character Compendium

- **Agnes**: Friend of Judith's who lives in Burlington.

- **Amelia**: The costume coordinator for the Silver Springs Players' production of *The Wind in the Willows*.

- **Anne Hughes**: A retired biology teacher who runs the Woodland Watch educational programs.

- **Anton Reynolds**: The General Store's chef.

- **Arlo**: Ruby's son, who's a junior in high school.

- **Benjamin 'Ben' Ashby**: Pete's son, who works at Ashby Hardware.

- **Beverly**: A member of the Maplewood Woolgatherers.

- **Bridget Evans**: Laura's mother. She's critical of Laura's move from Boston and worries about her.

- **Casey Jennings**: Acting Production Supervisor at Goldenleaf Apple Farm.

- **Charles Wu**: Evelyn Chan's late husband.

- **Charlie**: Dulcie Sanderson's English Springer Spaniel.

- **Cheryl**: The former accounts manager at Goldenleaf Apple Farm.

- **Christopher O'Reilly**: Retired carpenter, editor of *The Whittled Word*, and Maplewood Crafters Club member.

- **Clyde Hastings**: The owner of Timberline Tavern who helps with sets for the Silver Springs Players.

- **Connor Evans**: Laura's youngest brother who lives in California.

- **Cynthia Farnham**: Vernon's former partner.

- **Danny Evans**: Laura's middle brother, a program director in New York, and Callum's father.

- **Denise**: General Store customer.

- **Detective Sergeant Ramirez**: The second-in-command of Silver Springs Police department.

- **Dulcie Sanderson**: Vernon's partner, Ruby's best friend, and manager at Northern Necessities.

- **Edward Lee**: Judith's husband.

- **Eli Carter**: Laura's colleague and the General Store café's barista.

- **Elizabeth 'Liz' Andrews**: A retired drama teacher and committee member of the Silver Springs Players.

- **Evelyn Chan**: Laura's landlady and the leader of the Maplewood Crafters Club.

- **Francesca 'Fran' Palermo**: Works at Twilight Pines State Park. The Maplewood Crafters Club's resident birder.

- **Freya Romano**: The president of the Historical Society.

- **Ginny**: A member of the Maplewood Woolgatherers.

- **Gregory Castor**: Dulcie's late former husband.

- **Gus**: Fran's Bernese Mountain Dog.

- **Gwen Foster**: A neighbor to Goldenleaf Apple Farm.

- **Hazel Thornton**: Writes the 'Local Lowdown' column for *The Maplewood Memo*.

- **Isaac 'Izzy' Lennox**: Goldenleaf Apple Farm employee and theater enthusiast.

- **Iris**: General Store customer.

- **Janet Collins**: Administrative Assistant at Goldenleaf Apple Farm.

- **Jasmine Williams**: Laura's colleague. She's a member of Woodland Watch and the Maplewood Crafters Club.

- **Jay Wilson**: Co-owner of Mountainside Books, Trenton's husband, and an amateur photographer.

- **Jesse O'Connor**: Laura's colleague, and an arts school graduate.

- **Josephine Kirby**: Friend of Judith's and mother of Mia.

- **Joyce Adler**: The Adult Circulation Librarian at the Silver Springs Public Library.

- **Judith Yoon**: Evelyn's friend, a Maplewood Crafters Club member, retired editor, and keen puzzle solver.

- **Katie Fowler**: Village Skein employee, and a regular at the General Store café.

- **Kathleen 'Kathy' Quinn**: Co-owner of the General Store and Maggie Brook's wife. A former architect.

- **Kenneth Fraser**: The director of *The Wind in the Willows*.

- **Kirsten**: A costume department volunteer for *The Wind in the Willows*.

- **Laura Evans**: General Store café manager and amateur sleuth.

- **Lavinia Reed**: Vernon Reed's estranged mother. She lives at Lakeside Pines Assisted Living in Burlington.

- **Layla Ahmed**: The owner of Red Trillium Bakery. She supplies the General Store café's baked goods and pastries.

- **Leo Nash**: Jasmine's friend and a board member of Woodland Watch.

- **Maisie Watkins**: Local resident of Silver Springs and friend of Sharon.

- **Maggie Brook**: General Store co-owner and Kathy's wife.

- **Malcolm Lancaster**: A probate attorney at Lancaster & Porter and Vernon's lawyer.

- **Malik Rivers**: A seasonal worker at Goldenleaf Apple Farm.

- **Marcela Torres**: The Town Clerk and a member of the Maplewood Crafters Club.

- **Martha Henderson**: Evelyn's friend, Historical Society Vice president, Good Neighbor Guild president, and a member of the Maplewood Crafters Club.

- **Melinda Winrow**: The committee chair of the Woodland Watch.

- **Meredith Perkins**: The co-owner of Silver Springs Mobile Home Park.

- **Mia**: Josephine's daughter. She works as a cleaner.

- **Monty**: Evelyn's light bluish-gray Burmese cat.

- **Noah**: A Goldenleaf Apple Farm employee.

- **Nicholas 'Nicky' Beckett**: Roy and Roxanne Beckett's son and employee at Goldenleaf Apple Farm.

- **Officer Littlefield**: A senior patrol officer for the Silver Springs Police Department.

- **Officer Patterson**: A patrol officer for the Silver Springs Police Department.

- **Oscar**: Evelyn Chan's dark-brown Burmese cat.

- **Percival 'Percy' Wetherington**: Dulcie's brother, a jeweler in Hartford.

- **Peter 'Pete' Ashby**: Ben's father and owner of Ashby Hardware.

- **Poppy**: A costume department volunteer.

- **Rina Sen**: Coordinates the Good Neighbor Guild Annual Potluck.

- **Romy**: A costume department volunteer for the Silver Springs Players.

- **Roy Beckett**: Co-owner of Goldenleaf Apple Farm.

- **Roxanne Beckett**: Roy's wife, a lawyer and the owner of Hearthstone Street Legal Services.

- **Ruby Callahan**: Dulcie's best friend. Part-time employee at The Village Skein and Goldenleaf Apple Farm.

- **Sadie Evers**: Toby's wife. She lives across from Warren Fisk.

- **Samuel 'Sam' Walker**: The owner of Goldenrod Roasters.

- **Sharon Winters**: The editor of *The Maplewood Memo*.

- **Silvia Evans**: Laura's grandmother.

- **Stewart Perkins**: The co-owner of Silver Springs Mobile Home Park. Meredith's husband.

- **Terri**: The actress who plays Toad in the Silver Springs Players' production of *The Wind in the Willows*.

- **Toby Evers**: Sadie's husband, a vegetable farmer.

- **Trenton Burke**: Jay's husband, co-owner of Mountainside Stories.

- **Valeria 'Val' Del Solar**: Historical Society volunteer.

- **Vernon Reed**: The co-owner of Goldenleaf Apple Farm.

- **Warren Fisk**: The owner of Fisk Apple Works.

- **Yanni Petros**: An Australian transplant who runs Wanderer Pantry and a member of the Maplewood Crafters Club.

# ABOUT THE AUTHOR

Jodie Morgan is an author of cozy mysteries, short stories, puzzle books, joke books, and riddle books. Her novels welcome readers to the charming town of Silver Springs, in Maplewood County, Vermont. Jodie's books are filled with intriguing puzzles, memorable characters, and the satisfying solutions cozy mystery readers love.

When she's not plotting her next book, you'll find her reading, savoring a coffee (with cream, always!) or working on her latest knitting or crochet project. She loves to travel as this sparks ideas for her writing. Her most satisfying creative moments come from quiet evenings at home with her supportive family.

**Find out more about Jodie at <u>cozycozies.com</u>.**

*Author photo taken by Tal at the Granny Square in Sydney, Australia.*

# ALSO BY JODIE MORGAN

*For a complete bibliography of all Jodie's books, visit cozycozies.com/pages/catalog.*

**Silver Springs Mysteries**

1. Murder At The Summer Cheese Festival

2. Murder At Goldenleaf Apple Farm

**Official Bingo Packs**

1. Bingo In The Green Mountains

2. Bingo In The Kitchen

**Official Joke Books**

1. Laughter In The Green Mountains

2. Laughter In The Kitchen

**Official Puzzle Books**

1. Puzzles In The Green Mountains

2. Puzzles In The Kitchen

**Official Riddle Books**

1. Riddling In The Green Mountains

2. Riddling In The Kitchen

## Official Short Stories
- Exclusives

    a. Hope Has Whiskers

    b. Lost Becomes Found

    c. Keeping It Hidden

- Widely Available

    a. Recipe For Revenge

    b. Cataloged Under Deception

    c. Puzzles She Packed

www.ingramcontent.com/pod-product-compliance
Lightning Source LLC
Chambersburg PA
CBHW030536190726
48283CB00006B/1943